SUMMER IN YOUR EYES

An utterly heart-warming romance about second chances

CHRIS PENHALL

Choc Lit

A JOFFE BOOKS COMPANY

Choc Lit
A Joffe Books company
www.choc-lit.com

This edition first published in Great Britain in 2023

Cover art by Jarmila Takač

ISBN: 978-1-78189-538-2

To Sarah and Hannah,
Gareth, Ann, Kevin, Barrie and Sam
and Isabella

ACKNOWLEDGEMENTS

I count myself as very lucky to have extremely supportive people in my life. And they are all also very interesting people who are useful sources of all sorts of information.

So, to my intrepid friends — my uni chicks and their chaps — Jill, Sandi, Sue, Loui, Mark and Mike — thanks for all the tips and going on very interesting holidays.

The more I write, the more people I meet who also love to write, and quite frankly, this helps me to write. Lizzie Chantree is a great friend, fabulous author and business-woman, and last year we set up a regular free buddy-writing meet-up in a local café. It's a great place to talk about plots and writing, and drink coffee, of course. I also wrote a lot of this book at those sessions — so hello to all our writing buddies and thanks for the motivation! Also, thank you to Deborah Stephenson for our coffee-fuelled writing and chats in various venues across the city.

And thanks for Laura and all of those at Fête Grays Yard in Chelmsford for being so accommodating and hosting our buddy-writing group.

Thanks to my publishers, Choc Lit and Joffe Books, for making this happen, my editor, and Lyn Vernham, who founded Choc Lit and made my childhood dream to be a published author come true. I hope you enjoy your new adventures!

And, of course, thank you to the members of the Tasting Panel who read the manuscript and said 'yes': Julie Lilly, Cheryl Woodbridge, Deborah Warren, Emily Smeby, Fran Stevens, Gill Leivers, Lisa Vasil, Lorna Baker, Lynda Adcock and Michele Rollins.

PROLOGUE

Marrakech glowed pink in the sunset, the rooftops warm, dusky and mysterious. Holly wrapped a yellow blanket around her shoulders and sank back into the hammock on the sun deck of the *riad*, trying to conjure up the right words in her head to capture the magic. But she couldn't find them — they felt beyond her reach, hovering in the air, not ready to be written.

'It's too beautiful,' she said to Ed, who was sitting on a chair next to her, editing photographs on his laptop.

'Nothing's too beautiful,' he laughed.

'I mean, I can't describe it. I don't know if I can write anything that does any of this justice.'

'What — the city, or the time we've spent here?' He closed his computer and stood up, holding out his hand towards her. 'Do you want to come down from there?'

Holly wiggled herself towards the floor, then gave up. 'This seemed like a good idea when I climbed in.' She giggled as he put his arms around her and guided her feet down. Walking to the far end of the roof garden, they stood for a while in silence. 'There are thousands and thousands of people down there,' murmured Holly eventually. 'But up here, there is only us, the sunset and the stars.'

1

'You old romantic.' Ed cupped her face in his hands. 'So, what film are we in now, Holly Merriweather?'

'Oooh. For once, I can't think. Didn't they film *Sex and the City 2* here? Yes, I think they did. One of the *Mission: Impossible* films? But . . .'

'But what?'

'No one's made a film about *this* — to show how this feels now, with you.'

Ed moved over to the table and opened his laptop again. 'I have — look.' He pressed start on a series of short films. 'Here's the *riad*, here's the square — Jemaa el-Fnaa — at night, Jardin Majorelle . . .'

'Those are absolutely amazing.' Holly kissed him lightly. 'I suppose it's because you've been working here for three months and have more of a proper feel for it. I've just swooped in for a week, so I'm seeing it differently. I want to add something to my blog about the whole experience, but can't seem to get it together.'

'You've been writing it in your head again, though, haven't you?' He touched her cheek gently. 'I've seen you with that faraway look in your eyes — writing a sentence, deleting it, then gazing into the distance for more inspiration.'

'Is it that obvious?' Holly watched the city lights begin to flicker around her.

'Only to me. And it is one of the many reasons I love you.' He squeezed her hand. 'I've been thinking.' He sat down on a deep scarlet velvet sofa and patted the space next to him. Holly joined him, laying her head on his shoulder and closing her eyes. 'Maybe we should settle for a bit? We've been travelling for years, Holly. Going off in our own directions — you with all your bar and restaurant work, and your writing as well, and me and the hotel stuff. Just catching up for a week here or a month there together. It's been great, but . . .'

'What are you trying to say?' Holly looked up at him.

'I want to settle. Don't you?'

Holly's heart began to flutter excitedly. 'Yes, I do,' she murmured.

He squeezed her hand tightly. 'I've found this business selling artisan cheese at events, and to shops — it's up for sale.' He stood, picked up his laptop and clicked on a website he'd bookmarked. 'And look, there's a cottage on the North Yorkshire Moors we can rent. It's got outbuildings and the right amount of space.' His voice was suddenly animated. 'We can develop the business, and you can still write. In fact, you can write about how we're doing. It'll be great for marketing. I've got my savings — I don't spend money when I'm travelling as the company pays for everything — and you've got your grandparents' inheritance. Imagine us in an old farmhouse! You can grow tomatoes, we can get a dog. We can just settle down.' He kissed her hand.

'That sounds rather romantic.' Holly sensed herself being swept along by his enthusiasm, muting the little voice in the back of her mind whispering, *Another random idea? Like the wholesale craft beer and the salami truck that never actually happened?*

Someone began to strum a guitar, the music drifting over the rooftops as the light began to illuminate windows one by one in the growing darkness. Holly's heart started to race and she felt heady with excitement. 'It *has* been twelve years since the school disco.'

He laughed. 'Twelve years since our first kiss. Twelve years together. We spent all of university apart, and I feel we've just never quite got ourselves in the same place for long enough, Hol. I want to try. It's the next step. It's what we're supposed to do.'

For a moment, Holly felt like she was floating in the sky above the city, among the stars and the gossamer wisps of clouds, looking down at Ed holding her hand and gazing into her eyes.

'I do, too,' she whispered to him. 'Are you asking what I think you're asking?'

Ed got down on one knee. 'Holly Merriweather, will you move to a cottage in the countryside and sell cheese with me?'

She laughed. 'I will, Ed. I will.'

CHAPTER ONE

Even now, when I close my eyes and try to remember, all I can see is pink, gold and amber. Deep red rose petals. Cool marble tiles. Hidden spiral staircases. Secret alcoves strewn with luscious, bright cushions. Palm trees in the courtyards. Cool blue pools. Tranquillity, silence, safety, sleep . . . that weekend in Marrakech visiting my dreams, always and for ever.

Holly closed her laptop slowly.

'That's the last of the past then,' she sighed. 'The end of all of that. The thing I couldn't write because it was too special. Ha ha ha.' She looked over at Isabella. The cat yawned, stretched, then firmly closed her eyes.

'Should I start a new page with "The New Beginning" typed at the top, Isabella? No. Well, you wouldn't have an opinion on that anyway, as you are a cat. But!' She reopened her laptop and clicked on the link for her website. *Holly Merriweather — Have Laptop, Will Travel.*

'No,' she said decisively, closing it again. 'My Marrakech write-up is finally done. But no one will read it as I haven't written anything for two years, for goodness' sake!' Putting the computer in its case, she looked out of the window at her old car, already packed with her suitcases and books.

'I'm sick of living in an old farmhouse in the middle of a field. It was fun for a while, but it's time to move on. Whatever happens next is bound to be better than sitting here on my own.' Holly shook her head. 'It really couldn't be any worse.'

Isabella sighed loudly.

'Are you excited about the move?' She stood, put her shoes on, picked up the cat and carried her speedily to the pet carrier, which she had hidden in the bathroom. 'The element of surprise always works best,' she whispered, clipping it shut as Isabella hissed. 'Yes, and I love you, too. Right.'

Holly shrugged on her jacket, put the rucksack on her back, picked up the laptop, grabbed the cat carrier, then struggled out of the front door, pulling it firmly shut behind her with her free hand.

Then she climbed into her car, turned on the engine and drove away.

'Don't look back,' she muttered. 'Don't look back. The future is bright and the past is sad. Onwards and upwards. Or forwards, at least.'

Just before Holly left Ardleigh Farm for good, she paused at the junction at the end of the lane next to the sign telling everyone it was one and half miles to the village. She switched on some music and pulled out on to the main road accompanied by the Clash's "London Calling".

'I'm not nesting like all my friends, Isabella,' she shouted above the music. 'I'm un-nesting. Taking a leap. Having a new adventure. And you're coming with me.' The cat responded with a long, plaintive meow. 'Yes, I know you've had no say in the matter. But we're in it together.'

The song changed to "Midnight Train to Georgia".

'I must have been a strange mood when I put this play-list together,' she said to herself. 'As I'm in a car, and it's half past nine in the morning, and I'm going to London.' She glanced at the cat again. 'I'm being a bit overexcited, aren't I? Don't worry. It's nerves. I'll start crying soon, and once that's done, I'll be okay.'

Isabella chirped.

'Absolutely,' responded Holly, as she drove up the slip road to join the motorway. 'I'll be quiet now. Speak later.'

* * *

Holly manoeuvred the car into the cobbled mews. The pavements were dusted with cherry blossom, resting gently like translucent pink snow, and purple wisteria clung to the walls of the pretty houses either side of the road. Checking the address in her diary, she got out of the car and eagerly fished the front door keys out from her handbag.

'I'm in a Richard Curtis film,' she whispered to the cat carrier. 'Hugh Grant is going to appear at any moment, isn't he?' She scanned the street to check she was on her own, then jumped up and down, squealing quietly. 'Result! *Result*!'

Taking the carrier out of the front seat, she opened the door of her new house and walked in — then tripped up. The carrier skidded along the floor until it hit the wall underneath the bay window with a muffled thud. A loud and very long meow echoed around the room as Holly lay sprawled in the hallway. 'Ow,' she muttered, awkwardly clambering on to all fours, then pulling herself up using the door handle.

'Sorry, Isabella,' she wheezed. 'That step caught me by surprise. I'll be with you in a minute.' Waddling stiffly over to her pet, she kneeled down and opened the top of the carrier. The cat climbed out, began to purr immediately, chirped briefly, then walked into the kitchen.

'Glad you're all right then.' Holly watched Isabella's long, fluffy tail disappear. 'It's not the best start to our brand-new life in my dream home in my dream location — well, rental property *close* to my dream location — us both sliding face down along the floor!'

Another loud and very long meow echoed around the room.

'I haven't unpacked your bowls yet!' This time, Holly was greeted with a short, angry wail. 'Oh, all right,' she muttered, standing up again and closing the kitchen door so the cat couldn't escape. She went back outside and began unpacking the car, carefully stacking her boxes in the hallway and living room. Then she rummaged through her rucksack and pulled out a tin of very expensive cat food bought with the sole purpose of bribing her rescue cat. '*Et voilà*! I thought of almost all eventualities.' She opened the tin and put it down. 'Right — back in a sec.'

Opening the blinds as she moved through the rooms, the light flooded through the house as if she'd turned on a switch. The high ceilings made the space feel bigger than it was, and it looked as though an interior decorator had done their best to give it the feel of a Moroccan *riad*, with brightly coloured floor tiles in the kitchen and bathroom, plump, patterned cushions scattered over the beds and a lush red velvet sofa in the living room. Bronze filigree light fittings hung from the ceilings, and the walls were pink, yellow and green, so it all felt fresh, bright and alive, which had been the thing that had drawn her to the house when she'd first been sent the photos. Most importantly, it was also very cheap as it belonged to her best friend's cousin, who, for reasons Holly didn't want to think about, wanted to rent it out for a very small amount of money indeed.

Most of Holly's money had disappeared into the sadly failed artisan cheese business begun so hopefully by herself and Ed, so she felt like having the house almost handed to her was a kind of gift from the universe to help her recover from all the wasted effort of the previous few years.

Walking to the kitchen, she unlocked the back door and edged out, pulling it shut behind her. 'So, here I am,' she sighed, sitting down on the decking. 'Must add "clean up that old garden furniture" to my to-do list.' The lawn was neat and littered with daisies, the borders bursting with unruly purple, pink and white flowers. 'Add "find lawnmower" to the list.' She smiled to herself. The sound of traffic and voices carried in the air. *People . . . life . . . energy*, she thought. *Thank God.*

Someone began strumming a guitar close by, the chords drifting around her. Her mind clicked back to the rooftop in Marrakech, when she and Ed were bursting with love and dreams for their new life together, but she shook her head to push the memories away, then forced a smile and looked up as if she could see the notes and follow them to their source. 'Perfect,' she murmured, closing her eyes, already writing words in her head.

I finally sat on that first nervous day in the tiny, overgrown garden, the whole world opening up in front of me once again after a countryside pause that had come to the end of its usefulness. And here I was, not on a plane, or a train or a ship, but in London, following a childhood dream to live slap bang in the city at last. Among people and life and vibrancy, and not on a farm in a field near a hamlet next to a village. Which was lovely. It was all lovely — the people, the place, the sense of community. But that step into the unknown was the beginning of the end to something. And now I'm starting again . . .

She remembered reading the advert for the job just as Ed was packing up, both sad but resigned to the end of them: the end of the business, the end of their dreams of a life together. Determined to make a new future for herself, but panicking about how she would do it, she'd been immediately curious when a job alert had popped into her emails.

Experienced travel researcher required for exciting new project based in London. Twelve-month contract. Could be extended.

For the first time in about a year, Holly began to experience a small bubble of excitement. 'That's me,' she said to herself, reading the rest of the advert. 'Looks *really* exciting, actually.' Then she'd noticed the words at the bottom of the alert: *Fambridge Books*. 'Fambridge Books? Oh, my goodness!' she'd almost shrieked, then looked up at the shelf next to the television and the row of guidebooks displayed on it.

'*London: How I See It* by Seth Fambridge,' she shouted to the cat. 'Only my favourite travel book!'

'Are you all right?' Ed was standing at the door, a pair of wellington boots in his hand.

'Yes. I've just seen an advert for a job at Fambridge Books.'

His eyes widened. 'Wow! The books that got you into travel writing.'

'My childhood inspiration.' She stood up. 'Along with all the films, of course.'

'Ah yes, *Three Coins in the Fountain, Roman Holiday* . . .'

'Must go back to Rome sometime.' Holly looked at him and realized as she said it that they would probably never go anywhere together again.

'Well,' he said quietly. 'I'm putting the last of my things in the suitcases. Are you sure you'll be okay here on your own for the next few weeks?'

'I've got all my films to keep me company. And Mum and Dad are going to be driving up every so often, so I'll be fine. Isabella and I will be off, too. Somewhere or other. Actually, I may have found a place. I mentioned to Melissa that all . . . this . . . was finishing.' She turned back to her laptop, unable to say what she really meant. *We're finishing.* "This" made it feel slightly easier to say, somehow. 'So!' She tried to sound upbeat. 'I'll just get applying for this job and keep my fingers crossed.'

* * *

The memory faded slowly, and she was back in her new home in London again. She stood up and walked back inside. Taking a notebook from her rucksack and opening it on the first page, Holly read the list she had made when she'd found out the job was hers.

1. *Start Dream Job with Fambridge Books.*
2. *Start writing my travel blog again, with more social media posts, possibly a podcast, but this time about London — do alongside full-time job.*
3. *Approach publications who used to commission my work to see if I can do anything for them again — also do alongside full-time job.*

4. *Get back on track with money and writing to replenish my lost savings.*

She found a pen and added:

5. *Proper job with well-known publication equals better CV, equals more opportunities, equals, in twelve months' time, the world being your oyster, Holly Merriweather.*
6. *Move on. I always move on. When I stayed in one place for four years, look what happened.*

She read it again, added an exclamation mark, then walked upstairs and put the notepad next to her bed. At the same time, a window banged shut outside and the music stopped.

Closing her eyes, Holly tried to remember the words she had formulated in her head in the garden so she could write them down. 'Today is the first day of my London adventure, tomorrow is the first day of the job that has got me here,' she said firmly to Isabella, who was now sitting on the window-sill. 'I need to get on and write.' Then she went on to the landing and looked down at the floor in the hall. 'Oh — so many boxes to unpack,' she muttered, looking longingly at her laptop case propped up against the wall behind them. *Be like Tom Cruise in* Mission: Impossible *— just leap down stairs and over them to get to the computer,* she thought, *so you can start writing instead of doing the sensible thing and unpacking.*

She did the sensible thing and walked down to the hall, then opened a box. The first things she saw were some offi-cial-looking letters addressed to Ed, which had arrived at the cottage after he'd left. Taking them out, she put them on the table and irritably composed a text message.

Hi. Wondering if you've read my last couple of texts? I've got some letters for you and I need your address. You must have one by now? They look official. H.

She stared at the message for a moment, trying to work out why it looked unfinished. Then realized it was because she hadn't added a kiss at the end. All those little letter Xs sent in thousands of messages. *No longer required.* But she still felt confusingly sad as she pressed send.

'Replace a sad memory with a good memory,' she shouted to Isabella and began to compose another message to her friend.

Hey, Melissa. This house is wonderful. Thank you for telling me about it. I'm so grateful to your cousin . . . even if he's only letting it out for such a tiny amount because of tax purposes. It's like someone has given me a present! I feel like I'm in a film!

She pressed send and walked back into the living room. Her phone buzzed with a new message. *Which one? M x*

Eat, Pray, Love. Holly

No, no, no — Julia Roberts in Rome does not count. Melissa

Under the Tuscan Sun? Holly

Again, wrong country. What about Beetlejuice? Melissa

Wrong country, too, and completely the wrong genre, frankly. Holly

I'm about to go into a meeting — leave it with me — I'll come up with a good one. Melissa X

No, I'll come up with a better one. Holly Xxxx

Holly put her phone down and began to unpack.

'Cheap rent or not, it's only cheap for Primrose Hill. I've got to make this job work,' she whispered to Isabella, who was now sitting on the sofa fastidiously cleaning her tail.

CHAPTER TWO

Emerging from the Tube station at Tower Hill, Holly stood for a moment, then turned around with arms outstretched.

Drama queen, muttered her inner voice. *It's not like you haven't been here before.*

Holly shrugged it off happily. 'Visiting is different to living here,' she said quietly, nearly knocking over a woman who was hurrying past her. 'Sorry, sorry,' she shouted. 'Just excited.'

The morning sun shone over the Tower, the sky a perfect clear blue, the steady stream of traffic in front of her a vibrant, moving soundtrack to the start of the day. The odd angry beep of a horn and shouts of "get out of the way" added dramatic beats as she crossed the road.

Taking her phone out, she filmed herself walking over the bridge, weaving past people moving determinedly in the opposite direction, then she stopped and turned west. The Thames glowed silver as it flowed under London Bridge, the top of the dome of St Paul's Cathedral visible over the rooftops to the north, and the Shard almost shimmering in the morning light.

Holly felt herself jump up and down excitedly inside. Why, when she had travelled to so many distant lands, was she so captivated by a city almost on her doorstep? She'd been swept along by the buzz of Bangkok, marvelled at the city lights of New York, sighed constantly as she'd been enraptured by the beauty of Lisbon — and she'd written about all of them and many more.

It's all those films. There was her inner voice again. *All the ones that made London look romantic and lovely and not like real life at all.*

Speaking of which, thought Holly. *I'm going to Bridget Jones's land.* She paused and googled "Bridget Jones's flat near Borough Market", deciding to take a look at it after work. Then she began to walk again while composing a blog post in her head.

It all began on the first of May of a year I won't mention in case I don't finish this till next year, I said to myself, as I walked to my brand-new job in the centre of London — my first proper one after years of travelling and working in bars and as a local guide in all sorts of places, writing about it all for newspapers and magazines and my own blog and so on and so forth.

But today is the beginning of my first proper adventure after Ed decided that an old farmhouse in the middle of nowhere on the North Yorkshire Moors wasn't remote enough and left for the Isle of Skye to follow a dream to live in a croft that I never knew he had — the dream, I mean. I don't mean I never knew he had a croft.

'Must word that differently,' she muttered to herself.

So, my mid-year resolution number one — will be incredibly successful in my exciting new career. Resolution number two — when a man does appear, make sure he doesn't want to live in a self-sufficient fashion without easy access to electricity — if he wants to do that, we can build him a shed. And, what did Bridget Jones say? I will not form any romantic attachments to any of the following . . . oh . . . well . . . no clue. So, maybe no romantic attachments for a while, as I am a modern woman and I—

Her thoughts were abruptly interrupted as a man fell up on to the pavement from the steps under the bridge into a crumpled heap, landing in the middle of a group of tourists in front of her.

Holly paused for a moment, listening to a lot of noisy chatter among the group as they seemed to try to check he was all right, which died down as he pulled himself up to his full height.

It sounded like they all emitted a collective audible sigh as he did.

Holly felt the world had switched to slow motion while the man leaned over and brushed the dirt from his trousers, then looked down at the coffee stain on his shirt. 'Accidentally threw it all over myself on my plummet to the floor,' he announced to the tourists, who appeared to be gazing at him in a kind of awestruck silence. 'I'm not used to shoes. I've been living in flip-flops in Costa Rica for years.' Then he ran a hand through his black, curly hair, scratched the stubble on his chin and smiled. 'Very embarrassing. But thank you for your help.' He then turned and began to briskly walk away as everyone watched him go.

The sound of a train chugging noisily over a nearby bridge seemed to bring an end to the scene, and the world felt like the pause button had been switched off, as real life suddenly resumed. The group in front of her began to talk again, and Holly's feet started to move towards London Bridge station, pushing thoughts of the rather beautiful man to the back of her mind. 'I have a new job to do and a new life to lead,' she announced to herself, checking the next part of her route to work on Google Maps.

* * *

Standing outside her new office building, she took a long, deep, positive breath, having lost the mobile phone signal a few times, meaning the directions had annoyingly disappeared from the screen. She'd wondered whether she should do a few circuit walks of the immediate location — which could be a "good thing", as it would allow her to see bits of the area she wouldn't have known were there, but also could very much be a "bad thing", as there was a possibility it would make her late for the first day at her brand-new job. So, managing to control her usual instincts to gaze and pause and take photos, Holly had focused on actually getting to her destination. Eventually, down a narrow, cobbled street — which she had walked past at least three times in the past ten minutes — she had found a sturdy wooden door with several buzzers on it that seemed to be the correct address.

During the job interview, which had been done via Zoom from the cottage — on the audio-only setting as the internet was playing up and the video wouldn't work — she'd pictured a room full of travel writers busily creating their copy, the low tap, tap, tap of fingers on keyboards filling the air, while in a side office, very glamorous people sat around a long table having a meeting about the wonderful travel writing they should be publishing next.

And today was the day she would be part of the team, too. Putting on her glasses, Holly ran her fingers down the list of names beside the door until she found Fambridge Books, then she rang the bell and waited.

'Hello?' A confused-sounding female voice answered.

'Hello. I'm Holly Merriweather. I'm starting work for you today.'

'Oh, yes,' the voice said. 'Of course. Do come in.'

Holly waited for the door to click.

'Just . . . wait . . . um . . . sorry. Godfrey's left . . . He's the office manager — was — and does — did — all the techy stuff, like opening the door. Oh, for f—'

The door clicked, and Holly pushed it open quickly in case it locked itself again.

'Honestly!' She heard the voice sigh. 'You're in. First floor, door on the left.'

The interior of the office block reminded Holly of a scene from Hogwarts in the *Harry Potter* films, with a carved oak staircase creaking almost musically as she walked up it, a large stained-glass window to the front casting green, red and blue light on to the walls, and the eyes from the portraits of clearly very important people from many centuries ago watching her as she ascended. She mentally filed it away so she could write it down later, then paused outside a door, which had a sign that announced *Fambridge Books Ltd*. She felt a wave of excitement surge through her body. Checking her long, blonde hair was still tied neatly back, she ran her tongue across her teeth to check there was no cabbage or spinach stuck there, even though she'd had a pain au raisin for breakfast, then touched her waist to make sure her skirt wasn't tucked in her knickers again, even though she was wearing some very brightly patterned trousers. Then she took another deep breath, smiled and pushed the door gently open.

'Oh.' She searched in vain for all the busy people hard at work on their important assignments. All she saw were empty desks. It was as if someone had pulled the needle from a record. Like they did in films.

'Hello, hello, hello!' The owner of the voice on the intercom was sitting at the far end of the room, repeatedly prodding a keyboard and peering irritably at the computer screen. 'Where are you?' She leaned back in her chair and sighed. 'Where have you gone now?' Looking up, she smiled faintly at the sight of Holly. 'It's all gone a bit pear-shaped today.' She stood up and walked towards her, pushing long, curly, black hair behind her ears. 'Everyone who's supposed to make the place run smoothly is not here anymore, and my heart's not in the admin side really. Still, I will learn. You take that one.' She pointed towards an armchair next to a coffee table and pulled a seat up herself as Holly sat down, her nerves finally getting the better of her.

'You have lovely trousers.' She waved at the woman's yellow-and-orange floral pair. 'I do love a nice pair of colourful trousers. Sets the tone for the day. I'm Holly, by the way. Holly Merriweather. But you know that as I told you at the door. It was you, wasn't it?' She told herself to stop . . . think . . . smile, then took a breath and tried to re-set both the volume and speed at which she was talking. 'Sorry about that. I'm a little bit nervous. This is a wonderful opportunity for me, and I'm thrilled to be here.'

The woman beamed at her. 'I loved your clothes as soon as you walked in the door. You lit up the room with them. You really are a breath of fresh air.'

Holly felt herself blush. 'Oh . . . thank you!'

'I'm Claudette Fambridge.' She waved her arms, gesturing around the room. 'And this is sort of all mine. And my son's. He's helping out.' She leaned forward. 'And we need your help, Holly. We need a kick-start.'

'Well, I'm very enthusiastic as you can probably tell.' Holly glanced at her own pink-, green-and-yellow trousers, with a splash of red, which she had chosen to put on that morning precisely because she believed they almost screamed enthusiasm.

'And I love your red shoes!' Claudette put her foot on a chair and pointed at her feet. 'I decided on my black Dr Martens today with the red flowers on them — we match nicely.'

'Oh, I love them.' Holly looked at the design closely. She put her right foot on the chair next to Claudette's. 'We're almost shoe twins.'

Claudette laughed and put her foot back on the floor. 'My son, Jack, was very impressed with your writing style — both your blogs and your freelance work. And your social media presence, as well. I don't really read guidebooks or travel literature, you see.' Claudette stood up and walked over to a fridge. 'I really need some water. You?'

Holly stared at her. 'But you own a travel book company,' she blurted out. And then she wished she hadn't.

'Ah!' Claudette laughed again, carrying a bottle and a couple of glasses back over to the table. 'That was all my late husband. He was the writer, devoured other people's travel writing, built this company up into what it is today.' She sat down and poured the drinks. 'Which is a company that isn't what it was.'

'Oh dear.' Holly felt a knot begin to form in her stomach. Was this dream job not going to last very long at all?

'My eldest son has given up his rather exciting role in Central America to help me bring the whole thing back to life,' she said, smiling.

To Holly, she looked rather sad for somebody who was smiling. She picked up her glass and took a sip of water.

'We found all these old proof copies of some updates to the guidebooks in the storeroom, you see. They were Seth's last guidebook project, but he hadn't told anyone he was writing it — and then he died . . . that was eight years ago. We had just about got to the stage of deciding to wind the company up, then I found them completely by chance.' Claudette stood up. 'Jack will tell you all about that bit. It's all a bit raw for me. I mean, my husband passed away quite a long time ago, but it seemed like a sign. Unfinished business, if you see what I mean.'

Holly stood too, remembering how upset she'd been when she'd heard about Seth's death. 'I'm so sorry. It must be difficult for you.'

'I'm sure it will be worth it in the end.' She waved her hand around cheerfully. 'And rather exciting in its own way.'

Holly looked around the room. 'I'm very honoured to be part of this project. Alongside my colleagues. Do they do a lot of hybrid working?'

Claudette appeared not to hear and walked over to a grey cupboard in the corner of the room, opened it, then took a handful of books out and put them on a desk. 'Here they are.' She stepped back. 'We've divided the work up into north, south, east and west London. You've got north. But it's a bit vague.'

Holly picked up one of the books and ran her hand along the front cover. It was white with black lettering, and had a sepia photo of a man and a woman walking away, their backs to the camera. The woman was wearing a red beret, the man a blue blazer. They were holding hands. '*London: How I See It Now*,' she said quietly, then looked up at Claudette. 'I read all the originals as a child. And then Seth's travel books. They are one of the things that inspired me to write about travel myself. I took his first book with me everywhere. It's a bit worn now . . . but it'll take pride of place in my house when I've unpacked properly.'

Claudette beamed. 'Seth loved his work. He'd be thrilled to know that.' She opened the front cover of one subtitled *South West: All Leafy and Grand*. 'These are slightly different.

He looked at how things had changed since the first set he wrote in the eighties and nineties. But then more things have changed, haven't they? So, we need to update them again before we release them into the wild. They will be a record of London that can be used as a reference for future generations.' Then she closed the book and gazed at the cover. 'That's me and Seth, taken so many years ago.'

'And used on the covers of all the *London* books,' cut in Holly. 'I thought they were models!'

'Oh, no! We couldn't afford models when we published the first one,' Claudette ran her fingers over the image. 'And we rather adored the photo so kept it for all of them.' She looked around the room. 'Now, why don't we get you set up on a computer so you can get to know how the office works, and we'll brief you properly tomorrow?'

'Sounds good to me.' Holly followed her to a desk.

'Have this one. I'm not much use, although I'll get you connected to our website and internal communications.' She sighed. 'Oh, I miss Godfrey.'

'Oh dear . . .' Holly sat down, not sure how to respond.

'He was Seth's right-hand man for years, but he decided to retire six months ago when we were taking the final steps to winding up. He's having a wonderful time back in Barbados. He hasn't messaged for days — said he'd eaten something that upset his stomach. But he really should stop his friends tagging him on social media on their nights out.'

Holly switched on the computer.

'He thinks because I'm the same age as him I don't check Instagram, and *I* think because he's the same age as me, going out partying most nights of the week could be detrimental to his health. We couldn't have managed this place without him, though.'

'Are you getting anyone to replace him?' Holly watched the screen flicker into life as Claudette pushed a folder towards her.

'Ah, no. Jack says we have to manage it all ourselves currently — he has absolutely no idea as he's new to all this.'

She shrugged. 'Men! Anyway, all the log-in details are in here. Just see today as a kind of low-key induction.'

'Righty-ho.' The word slipped out of Holly's mouth before she could stop herself. *Right or okay*, hissed her inner voice. *What on earth is righty-ho?*

* * *

Claudette had decided to close the office at three, and told Holly to take the rest of the day off, as 'I am in charge and have an art exhibition to go to across town.' So, Holly had taken one of the guidebook proofs in order to do some research when she got home — right after she'd found the local supermarket and fed Isabella, of course.

The remnants of a light spring shower lit the pavements with an incandescent, shimmering glow. Holly studied droplets of rain hanging on to the white petals of a trailing magnolia climbing the walls of a café, then took some photographs with her phone. 'I'll write something later,' she mumbled to herself as the bus came to a halt in front of her. 'And, hopefully, this is the right route this time.'

Deliberately getting off at the stop before the one she needed, Holly walked towards some traffic lights as a group of tourists, following a guide brandishing a very large umbrella above his head, headed straight for her. She tried to avoid them by moving to the edge of the pavement, but they seemed to spread out, so she found herself walking against what felt like a tide of people. Weaving around them to get out the other side, she wasn't even sure if she was walking in the same direction she'd been heading in before she'd been sucked into the crowd.

'Mabel! Mabel!' A small, curly-haired dog raced past her while she was still getting her bearings as a tall man wearing a lime-green-and-yellow baseball cap rushed after it with obvious irritation. 'I need you back on the lead, Mabel!' He disappeared around the sharp bend in the road, and she followed him absentmindedly, because she needed to walk somewhere and didn't really want to follow the guided tour.

Taking out her phone again to check where she was so she could find her way to the supermarket, Holly held it above her head and waved it around in an unsuccessful attempt to get a signal. But as she carried on walking, she tripped over the dog, which had darted across the pavement just as her owner had tried grabbing her, and Holly tumbled to the ground.

'God, I'm so sorry. Are you okay?' She found herself face to face with the man, whose vibrant hat was remarkably still on his head. That's all she could make out, apart from the grey, close-cut beard and sunglasses.

The dog was gazing innocently at her. 'Hello, Mabel,' she muttered. Mabel's tail began to wag at the sound of her name. 'You are a lovely.'

'She's a lovely something or other. A cross between all sorts of things. I call her a Labrapugalsatian.' The man stood up and held out his hand to Holly. 'She is essentially unknowable.' Mabel barked as Holly picked up her bag. 'Are you all right? I'm so very, very sorry.'

'No, it's okay.' Holly looked up at him. 'I'm having a strange day where I keep walking round in ever-decreasing circles in an effort to navigate my way to actual specific places.'

'Well, it sounds like you need to find another way to navigate that's a bit more straightforward. Or maybe there's something in the air today.' Mabel barked again and began to pull on the lead. 'Let's get you to a café and check you're not injured.' He held his hand out again and Holly took it, allowing him to drag her to her feet.

'I've got an unknowable rescue cat called Isabella.' Holly patted Mabel on the head. 'So, I understand.'

'Still, you could have been hurt, so . . .' He looked at the dog and tried to sound stern. 'You have behaved very badly.' Mabel licked his hand. He sighed. 'There was a time I had some authority.'

Holly looked at the tree-lined street ahead, which opened into a small square, with the road snaking around a narrow green space to the other end. On the corner was a small café with some tables outside. The whole place had an air of being left behind, she decided, as she glanced at the row of shops on either side.

The man smiled at her. 'Just let me get you coffee or tea or water or something, so I know you're not too shaken up before you go.'

She looked down at her, now slightly grubby, trousers and began to follow him. 'Okay, thank you. That's probably sensible.'

When they reached the café, the man pulled a chair out for her and waved at someone inside. 'The usual,' he shouted, then looked at Holly.

'Chai latte, please,' she said as she sat down.

'And a chai latte here. Don't look at me like that. I know you want to close, but Mabel has caused another little accident and I want to make sure this lady is okay.' He sat down and sighed. 'Once again, I can only apologize for my dog's behaviour. She slipped the lead somehow and wanted to come over and see her friends.' Mabel had abandoned them and was sitting in the doorway of the dry-cleaner's, where a blonde woman was patting her head. 'She's not actually my dog. I inherited her from the guy who used to run the convenience store.'

Two large mugs were placed on the table in front of them by a young, kind-looking man. 'Are you all right?' he asked. 'What kind of accident? Do you want me to call an ambulance?'

'No, thank you. I'm fine.' Holly smiled up at him. 'Just a bit . . . how you'd normally feel if you fell over, I suppose.'

'Accident?' A deep voice burst out from inside the café. 'Did you say accident?' A large man with a bushy, black beard strode out towards them.

'She's okay, Viktor,' said the other man. 'No need to fuss.'

'Are you sure you're all right, my dear?' He sat down next to her. 'Paulo here always says things are all right and they aren't always.'

22

'And you like to dramatize things.' Paulo sat down too and pulled his chair closer to Holly.

'It was all Mabel's fault,' Mabel's owner said. 'And look at her now. Not a care in the world. Butter wouldn't melt.'

The dog turned and trotted over, as if she knew she was being talked about.

'What has she been up to this time?' said the blonde woman as she followed Mabel.

'She tripped this lady up,' boomed Viktor.

'Honestly, it's fine.' Holly waved her leg in the air. 'Look — everything is as it should be.' She picked up her drink and took a long sip. 'This is lovely.'

'They do the best coffee here,' said the woman, patting Mabel on the head again.

'And you do the best dry-cleaning, Marialena.' Viktor touched her arm fondly.

'This is becoming far too sentimental for me.' Mabel's owner picked up his drink and finished it.

'He's an old softy, really,' Marialena laughed. 'I mean, what would have happened to Mabel here if it wasn't for you?'

Holly settled back in her chair with her latte. She was enjoying being around people again. Living in a farmhouse in the middle of a field in the middle of the country hadn't been good for her at all. She'd spent most of the time in the village café and at the pub.

'Her owner lived in the flat above the shop.' He put the empty mug on the table. 'He was taken into hospital one day. Asked me to look after her.' He tweaked the dog's ear and pulled out a treat from his pocket. 'He never came home, sadly. And I didn't have the heart to do anything other than let her stay. Although,' he leaned towards Holly and began to whisper, 'I don't actually like dogs. Or cats. Or animals. But don't tell the old girl. It may hurt her feelings.'

'Big softy,' Marialena repeated, before she walked back towards the shop as she noticed a customer lingering by the door. 'If it wasn't for Mabel, you would have stayed in your own shop and never talked to us,' she called back. 'She made you come outside and mix. Mabel rescued you!'

The man grunted.

Holly picked up her drink and inhaled the steam again before taking another sip. 'Oh, that's *really* good.' Then she tweaked Mabel's ear, too. 'Funny how sugary drinks make you feel better. Even though they are very bad for you.'

'One of life's conundrums.' The man leaned forward 'Are you feeling okay? I have to go and do a few jobs in the shop now, you see.'

'Yes. I'm fine, thank you.'

'I'm glad you are feeling okay,' shouted Viktor, standing up. 'We've got to close up soon.' He smiled kindly at Holly. 'Come and see us again.'

'Yes, yes, come and see us,' echoed Paulo, following him inside.

'They all seem very nice.' Holly stood up.

'Mmmmm,' muttered the man.

'Now, I've just got to work out where I am so I can get to the supermarket.'

'Oh, that's easy.' The man put some coins on the table before standing up too. 'Just carry on up past the hardware store, walk around the planters, then turn right into the lane and you'll find yourself on the main road. Then it's straight ahead.'

'Thank you.' Holly picked up her bag as he walked over to a shop with a sign half obscured by some out-of-control ivy that almost covered one of the walls. All she could see were the letters *CAL* and a display of record covers in the window.

'Have a good rest of your day. I didn't ask your name when you were sitting on the floor. So?'

'Holly.'

'Holly.' He pushed the door to the shop open.

'And yours? Given you've just bought me a sort-of-rescue coffee.'

He turned round. 'Oh, don't worry about that. You'll remember Mabel's name — mine is immaterial.' Then he walked inside, followed by the dog, and closed the door firmly behind him.

'Interesting name — Immaterial,' Holly muttered, briefly wiggling her feet to make sure they still worked. A clock struck six in the distance. 'God, is that the time? Isabella needs her food. And I need something easy and preferably microwavable so I've got time to do more unpacking.' She hurried out through the lane on to the main road as instructed and spotted the big orange supermarket sign in the distance. *Don't forget to write this little adventure down when you get home, too*, she thought, crossing the road and joining the throngs of people moving along the street. *And don't forget to come back. What a lovely place.*

* * *

Letting herself into the house a bit later, she glanced around, expecting a welcoming wailing meow or even a little chirp or purr from the cat. But it didn't come.

'Isabella?' she called, unpacking the contents of her shopping bag on to the kitchen counter. 'I'm home! Food!'

There was still no sign of her pet, so she walked into the living room and began to move the unpacked boxes. 'Oh God, there isn't a way out, is there? She hasn't somehow got into the garden, has she?' Holly checked the patio doors and all the windows, then kneeled down to look under the bed.

A pair of wide, green eyes stared at her, unblinking.

'Oh no! You haven't been there all day, have you?' she asked softly, reaching her hand out. Isabella edged backwards. Holly lay down and rolled under the bed, too. 'Has it been a bit weird here on your own?' A car horn beeped outside. 'I suppose it's very different to living in the countryside. In a farmhouse. In a large field.' She stroked the cat's head. 'You'll get used to it — remember how you got used to me and Ed when you strayed into our garden on our first day in Yorkshire? Plus, I've got some really expensive cat food to bribe you with.' She eased herself along the wooden floor and clambered to her feet, using the bed to help her.

'It's here!' she shouted, heading back to the kitchen and waiting for the sound of feet pitter-pattering after her. But nothing happened, so taking a fork out of the, as yet unpacked, box of kitchenware, she opened a tin of cat food and scraped it out into the bowl, making as much noise as possible, then placed it on to the floor next to the water bowl. Isabella appeared immediately, almost skidding around the corner into the room.

'Hungry?' Holly laughed, placing ready-made macaroni cheese into the microwave and switching it on. 'I will get myself organized enough to cook. But not today. Today, I have to get on with unpacking. And I've got to write something for the blog.'

Isabella purred contentedly as Holly tried to remember where she'd left her laptop. The microwave pinged and she pulled out the meal, suddenly feeling very tired. 'I'll just have to do it later, once I've worked out where everything is,' she mumbled, sitting on the sofa and beginning to eat.

What shall I write? she wondered. *I'll begin with: Today I started my new job. My dream job, searching for hidden treasures in London so I can help bring some classic, influential and iconic guidebooks up to date. The office block reminded me of Hogwarts.*

I'll have to add a bit there, she decided.

I met one of my new bosses — lovely trousers.

Also add a bit there, she thought.

On my way home, I got stuck in the middle of a crowd, and found myself on the other side before tripping over a dog called Mabel. A man called Immaterial—

No, that's no good. Where was it? What was the name of that square? Lots of tripping up today with that gorgeous man doing it, too, on Tower Bridge . . .

Isabella jumped up next to her and tried to put her face in the macaroni cheese. Holly nudged her gently away. 'I'll check what that square is called on the way home from work tomorrow,' she said decisively. 'And write it all down then. Now, I need to finish unpacking so I can wear clean underwear tomorrow.' She sighed.

Standing up, she went to the kitchen and opened the window slightly, and over the sound of the traffic, the strumming of a guitar seemed to glide in the air, just like it had the day before. Closing her eyes for a moment, she pictured the notes floating gently into the kitchen and dancing around the room. 'Who is that?' she whispered, just as the music stopped.

Her phone illuminated briefly, flagging up some memories from three years ago. There she was, standing in the cottage garden, behind her a riot of pansies, geraniums, climbing roses and fuchsias, with the sun shining high in the cloud-dappled sky. She was laughing, of course. Ed was probably pulling faces at her behind his camera.

Flicking the screen to the next picture, she stared at a photo of Ed eating a slice of cheese. Their cheese. The first batch of cheese they had made themselves to sell alongside the goods they'd buy in. She could feel their excitement and anxiety almost leaping out of the picture, because they had put everything they had into this venture, and under all the romantic ideas of living a simple life, where they could spend all their time together rather than arranging a week here, three months there, was the reality: they had to make it work. They had to make money.

Holly felt a lump in her throat and had a sudden urge to cry. But she wasn't sure whether it was because they didn't make any money or that it turned out that, in the end, spending all their time together really hadn't been such a good thing at all. And, on top of that, she'd discovered that she didn't like cheese that much either.

CHAPTER THREE

The following day, Holly pressed the buzzer on the office door as a van sped through a puddle next to the pavement, spraying water as it went.

'I can see you. I've worked it out!' Claudette's voice crackled through the intercom. 'Do come in.'

Holly hurried in to escape the rain. It seemed to have appeared from nowhere, soaking her trousers, which now clung wetly around her ankles.

'Oh dear,' said Claudette as she walked into the office.

'Surprise rain.' Holly tried to sound bright. 'I woke up to lovely blue skies in Camden. A cloud has appeared south of the river.'

'Just one cloud?' Claudette waved a packet of chocolate digestives in front of her. 'Medicinal biscuit?'

'I only saw one.' Holly took a biscuit and sat down. 'Thank you. Ordinarily, I'm trying to be sugar-free.' She rolled the bottom of her trousers up to help dry her legs. 'But it may help with the general yucky ankle-dampness.'

'Ah yes.' Claudette pointed at the notes on the side of the packet. 'It says that here. Suitable for general yucky ankle-dampness. You're in luck.'

'Gosh, there's something for every condition these days.' Holly laughed just as something dropped loudly to the floor in another room.

'Oh. For. God's. Sake!' shouted a male voice irritably. 'Why is everything just falling to pieces in this place!'

'Jack!' sang Claudette. 'Our newest member of the team is out here now . . . so . . .'

A man tumbled into the room and a small wicker basket also rolled out next to him. 'Who put that bloody basket there?' he grumbled.

'Jaaack!' sang Claudette again. 'This is Holly.'

'Sorry,' he muttered, holding on to a nearby desk, and as he began to stand, Holly watched him pull himself up to his full height in what felt like slow motion. It was the same man who had tripped up on Tower Bridge. She wondered if he was moving in slow motion all the time, or whether that was just the effect he was having on her. Or whether watching Keanu Reeves in *The Matrix* and then *The Matrix Reloaded* the previous evening was really the problem.

'Hello,' she heard someone say in the distance as he began to move towards her, pulling at his collar as if it were strangling him. 'Are you all right?'

'What?' she said eventually, as the world gradually began to move at the correct speed again. 'Oh — this? Just got caught in the rain.' She put her left leg in the air, allowing her trouser to drip on to the floor. Quickly realizing this could look a bit strange, Holly lowered her leg to the ground and sidled out from behind her desk, holding her hand out to shake his. 'I'm Holly, but you know that now, of course.'

He took her hand and smiled, looking directly into her eyes. 'I got attacked by several old files and a bin. I normally enter rooms with a little bit more finesse. I'm just not used to proper shoes. It's a long story.'

'Oh dear. Ha ha ha!' Holly's fourteen-year-old self took control briefly. 'That's funny . . . ha ha ha!' *Stop it, stop it, you're going to snort . . . Too late.* She stepped back slightly, stood behind her chair and picked up her chocolate digestive. 'Medicinal,' she said quietly.

'Has Mum shown you all the computer stuff and everything?' He loosened his tie and seemed to sigh with relief. 'This is my second shirt of the morning. I ruined the first one. I did the same yesterday. I usually wear T-shirts.'

'Jack's been out meeting our new investors. A power breakfast, I think?' Claudette poured herself a cup of coffee from the machine in the corner of the room. 'Very 1980s.'

'Ahh.' Holly was deliberately trying not to say anything while looking out of the window in order not to stare at Jack. A tiny dust cloud of crumbs fell on to her top. Brushing them off, she sat down and turned to her computer, pressing a couple of keys purposefully.

'Holly and I share a love of vibrant trousers,' Claudette continued.

'That's good.' He picked up his phone and appeared to scroll through some messages, then looked up again and smiled. 'Right, shall we have a quick chat, Holly? I've got to head on out again for another meeting in half an hour.'

'Of course.' Holly got to her feet, ready to follow him into an office.

'Oh, we'll do it here — it's fine.' He pulled up a chair and sat down, so Holly did, too. 'Right . . .' He looked at her expectantly.

'I'm very happy to be working here,' Holly said eventually. 'I'm looking forward to getting out and about.'

'Excellent!' Jack's phone buzzed, and he glanced at it before scowling briefly, then turned his attention back to Holly. 'So, Mum says she's shown you the old guidebooks.'

'Yes, I'm thrilled. I really am.'

His phone buzzed again and he nudged it away, his smile tightening. 'So, the brief is that we want to bring our old guidebooks up to date and release them as combined *Then and Now* editions — both in print and as eBooks. We'll also do some social media stuff — Instagram reels, TikTok, that sort of thing — using all your expertise, of course. We've got a small team going out to the places featured by my father in the original books and finding what's still there, and if it's not there, what's replaced it. London's full of hidden gems.'

'Absolutely. Who else is in the team?'

Jack's phone began to buzz intermittently. He sighed. 'I'm sorry. I've got to sort this out. So, we'd like you to spend as much time as you like out of the office exploring, as long as you come in at least three times a week for a few hours just so we can all collaborate. Okay? When Mum has worked out how to use the diary on the computer, we'll start scheduling the office days in. Great.' He stood up, picked up the phone and walked quickly outside, almost slamming the door shut behind him. Then he opened it. 'We particularly love the way you wrote about the places you visited as if you were in a film. My father liked to highlight film locations in the books. And also, music venues. Plus, we loved those posts you did with your partner—'

'Ex-partner,' interrupted Holly quickly.

'Ah, right . . . ex-partner. Well, they were very engaging.' Then he walked back into the corridor and let the door bang shut behind him once again.

Claudette poured herself another cup of coffee. 'He used to run an outdoor pursuits centre in Costa Rica until last month. So, not everything over there is quite sorted out.'

'Ah.' Holly hadn't realized her heart had been racing until it was back beating at its regular speed. *I can't have this*, she thought. *I can't already have a crush on him. I'm an adult. I must not mix business with pleasure.* 'Look what a mess that made of everything last time,' she said out loud.

'What mess?' Claudette gave her a bright but puzzled smile.

'Oh.' Holly brushed the rest of the crumbs from her top. 'I made a right mess of the biscuit.'

'Easily done. Now, day one of exploration. Where are you thinking of going as your first assignment?'

Holly took the guidebook out of her bag and opened it at a random page.

Claudette pulled it over so she could see it. '*Primrose Hill. A pastel-coloured dream that everyone should have at least once in their lives*,' she read.

'This would be a nice, easy one to start off with.' Holly couldn't keep the delight out of her voice. 'And I live very close, so it would help me get to know the area.'

'Ah, we used to live in Primrose Hill.' Claudette's face lit up. 'It was in a tiny one-bedroomed flat on the top floor of an old Victorian building. We'd go out exploring every weekend and Seth would make notes when we came home. I think he'd had the idea for the guidebooks already but kept it to himself.' She stopped talking suddenly and gazed out of the window, then looked back at Holly, smiling again. 'We used to go swimming in the mixed pond on Hampstead Heath and . . .' Her voice trailed off, and she sat down, clearly attempting to look business-like. 'Now. Can you take pictures of everything relevant, and we can decide where we want to send our photographer when we come to editing?'

'I'll video some of it, too.' Holly put the guidebook in her rucksack and picked it up. 'For social media.'

'Of course. I forget about that. I've got you down as working from home and out and about tomorrow. Can I reschedule a proper meeting with my son for the day after? You need more of a steer than simply "go outside and see what's there!"' She laughed kindly.

'That would be useful.' Holly made a mental note to prepare herself for her next encounter with Jack that would not involve her talking rubbish, blushing or giggling inanely. *Good luck with that*, whispered her inner voice.

'Oh, and Seth loved music.' Claudette's face was animated again. 'One of his passions was recording as many music venues as he could. So many have gone now. If you could keep a separate record of what's standing instead of them, that would be very useful.'

'Right . . . so, I'll get going now then.'

'Absolutely.' Claudette looked outside. 'The rain has stopped. And no time like the present.' She held out the packet of biscuits. 'One for the road?'

Holly took one. 'Thank you,' she said, waving goodbye to Claudette as she left the office.

'Off to walk around a bit — and it's my job!' she squealed quietly at a painting of a smiling man with close-cropped black hair on the stairwell, then she strode out into the street as jauntily as she could.

* * *

Holly left Chalk Farm Tube station and crossed the street, heading over the railway bridge towards Regent's Park Road. As the road curved, she stopped, enjoying the pinks and purples and yellows of the houses. Taking out her phone, she recorded the words, '*Like I'm in a film*,' to add to her blog and took a photo to use for that and for the guidebook job. *I'm on my way!* she thought, then pressed record again. '*Actually, it really is like I'm in a film — they used a nearby road as a location. I am a* Paddington *nerd, after all.*'

Setting off, she took photos of some of the little cafés and independent shops she noticed, stopping to buy a coffee from a busy delicatessen next door to a grocer's shop with exotic, colourful fruit and vegetables on sale outside. She took another photo standing by a red-brick building with a green sign on top — *Chalk Farm Garage, Proprietor, The Flight Petroleum Co Ltd*, it read. She made a mental note to look up its history, then ambled on. When she got to the entrance to the park, she paused to make notes against the entries in Seth's guidebook to check how much had changed. The street was full of chatter and laughter, thronged by a lively stream of people strolling slowly, walking purposefully or hurrying somewhere that was possibly very important. The trees lining the pavement seemed to shine such a deep, lush green, she felt she was walking through a richly coloured chalk painting.

'It definitely feels like I'm in a film,' she said, but this time to a post box, as if she was a character in a movie talking to inanimate objects. *After all*, she thought, *Shirley Valentine talks to a wall.* A shaft of sunlight burst through a crack in the clouds and she found herself laughing.

Walking into the park, she wandered up to the top of Primrose Hill past a man standing with his arm outstretched next to the path. A large yellow-and-blue parrot swooped out of a nearby tree and landed on his hand. Holly stood and watched, ready to break into an excited round of applause. No one else took any notice. 'London,' she muttered happily, filing it away as another incident to write about.

She imagined a sweeping shot, the camera flying high above the city, gradually gliding down over the rooftops until it paused in the park to linger on the cityscape in the distance. *Would I have dramatic, wistful or romantic music over that?* she wondered. Digging out her phone, she took a series of photographs. 'How many of those buildings weren't there when Seth wrote the book?' she asked herself, scrolling through the pictures.

Two dogs began to bark at each other as their owners pulled them back apologetically, and a group of teenagers jumped around after a frisbee. A line of people was standing on the ridge of the hill taking photographs just as she had done, so she sat on the grass for a while, listening to the chatter and the laughter, and enjoying the warmth of the late spring sunshine on her back.

Cutting down through the park back to Regent's Park Road a bit later, she stopped on a bridge to take another photograph of Regent's Canal, lined with pretty, colourful boats, then paused outside Cecil Sharp House, checking Seth's guidebook. 'Ah, still here.' She listened as music drifted out from the main door, carried in the air and across the road, while the sound of feet began to tap rhythmically to it. Holly walked up the steps and glanced inside, watching the class for a moment. *What's that film?* she wondered — *not* A Chorus Line — *that other one* — Shall We Dance? *I must look it up.* Then she headed back towards where she'd come from, deciding to check out Chalcot Crescent to see if there were any other blue plaques put up there since Seth's day.

She noticed a man wearing striped baseball cap, leather jacket and a pair of sunglasses dart out of a tiny backstreet, pulling a reluctant dog on a lead behind him.

That's Mabel! she realized. *And that man — Immaterial. Ask him the name of the square so you can actually start writing your blog again instead of constantly finding other things to do.*

'Oh!' Holly waved. 'Hello, Mabel, and . . .' She stopped, deciding shouting "Immaterial" at someone would sound rude at the very least. So, she crossed the road, breaking into a trot to try to catch him up. He turned a corner and she followed him, but he disappeared among swathes of pedestrians, so all she could see was the dog's tail wagging happily. Holly swerved around, trying to catch his attention by waving at his back, but had to stop at a junction to let several cars pass, following him with her eyes as he turned right into another street. But, by the time she got there, he was nowhere to be seen. The sound of a coffee machine steaming inside a nearby café suddenly made her feel thirsty, so she gave up the chase, bought a sandwich and a drink and took them to the park. She decided to try to find the square again on her way home after she'd topped up on provisions from the supermarket.

Once in the shop, she scanned an onion, carrot, tin of tuna and some tomatoes and pasta, as well as some more cat treats, then put them in a bag before beginning her quest to find the square again. As she searched, her phone vibrated in her bag.

'Hi, Melissa! I wondered when you'd call to check in on me.' She carried on walking as she spoke. 'Yes, I know I should have lived in London when you did instead of waiting till you'd moved out to Surrey, but you know it wasn't deliberate.' Holly felt she was being swept along by a sea of people. 'I'm just trying to find somewhere — sorry if I sound distracted. Yes, I'd love to catch up. Tonight? Great! See you at seven at Coal Drops Yard.' Putting the phone back in her bag, she stopped walking and retraced her steps.

'I could have sworn it was here,' she muttered, as commuters swarmed around her. She spun around slowly, hoping to find a clue, walking to the next set of traffic lights, then back again. A clock on an old warehouse wall chimed six. 'Oh well.' She sighed. 'I'll just have to try again tomorrow.' Then she made her way home to drop off her shopping and do a quick change before meeting her friend.

The pile of letters addressed to Ed was the first thing she noticed as she opened the door, and it was as if she were in the cottage in Yorkshire again. She was sitting on the sofa as he opened an envelope and read through the letter inside. She remembered his shoulders hunching as he did.

'Everything okay?' she'd asked.

'What?' He'd looked up, smiling a bit tightly. 'Fine. Of course. Just a marketing letter.'

She'd turned back to her laptop.

'Have you managed to actually write something for your website about the business?' His tone was uncharacteristically sharp. 'Instead of staring into the distance and composing the words in your head? You don't actually seem to blog anymore. You just think about it.'

'I haven't had time to write anything. We've been too busy. And you said we need to concentrate on the day-to-day running of it all rather than writing about it, anyway.'

His face almost crumpled before he managed to rear-range it back into a smile. 'Yes, of course. I'm just very tired, Hol. I'm going to have a bath and get an early night.'

A car horn beeped loudly close by, bringing Holly back to the present. 'Honestly, me and my films, making a drama out of a few envelopes,' she muttered, hanging her bag on the door and walking upstairs to the bathroom.

* * *

'I love this place,' shouted Melissa, trying almost successfully to make herself heard above the music. 'Do you remember this bit of King's Cross before the redevelopment?'

'Vaguely,' yelled Holly. 'But whenever I was back in the UK, I was working relentlessly in bars and cafés to save up for my next adventure, so I'm discovering London again as if it's all new.'

Melissa passed her a cocktail. 'I've got you a pina colada. To remind us of illicit drinking at school. And it's an eighties night, so two-for-one till eight.'

Holly took a small sip. 'I've got a long day tomorrow, so I really must be sensible.'

'Oh, when did you become so grown up?' Melissa winced. 'I haven't actually seen you in four whole years what with one thing or another. Can we rewind to that and you can be grown up next time? Although I *do* have to leave by nine.'

'So, wild partying till then?'

'Till the clock strikes nine. Yes.'

'Like a very sedate Cinderella.' Holly looked down at her friend's shoes. 'They *are* quite sparkly.'

'If I lose one of them when I run to catch the train, I'll be very annoyed. They cost quite a lot.'

'Which Cinderella are you, though? Disney cartoon? Lily James Cinderella? *The Slipper and the Rose*? What about *Ever After*?' Holly stirred the cocktail stick in her glass thoughtfully.

'There weren't that many when we did our Cinderella film-watching marathon when we were eight.'

'We're a lot older than that now.' Holly took a larger sip of her drink. And then another. And another. 'So, how is the world of PR?'

'It's okay.' Melissa put her glass down on the bar. 'Actually, I'm thinking of training as a teacher, to be honest. Now we've moved out to Surbiton, I'm craving a change. I never thought I'd say this, but I need a rest from glamorous events. How's the new job?'

'I think it's going to be fun. And I really want it to work. But, you know, I expected there to be more people working in the office. It's a bit quiet. But early days, I suppose.' Holly finished her drink. 'Shall we have another now we've started?'

'Ooh, listen.' Melissa spun round. 'Karaoke! It's kara-oke.' She almost jumped up and down with excitement. 'I'm putting our name down. Yes, get me another.'

'I'm not sure I—' Holly realized she was now talking to her friend's back — 'want to sing in public on this occasion,' she trailed off as she watched Melissa hurrying to speak to the man in charge of the karaoke machine. Two more pina coladas were placed in front of her. 'Psychic bar staff!'

'Not really.' The woman behind the bar laughed. 'The two-for-one deal means you've already paid for two cocktails each.'

'Ah!' Holly laughed, too. 'Psychic bar staff sounds much more fun, though.' She looked around the room. 'People, people, people,' she said to herself. 'I really *did* miss people.'

'Right.' Melissa appeared by her side carrying two more drinks. 'Oh dear, we appear to have over-ordered.'

'I'll just eat the fruit off the stick on that one,' said Holly firmly. 'New job. Can't afford a hangover tomorrow.' She took a sip of her drink. 'Although, this is very nice . . .'

They sat with their cocktails a little while longer, but then Melissa got up and pulled Holly towards the karaoke machine. 'It's our turn in a minute!'

'Where did all these human beings come from?' mumbled Holly. 'I'm not sure I want them to hear me sing. What are we singing, anyway?'

'Bananarama, "Robert De Niro's Waiting". Remember? Our go-to song at parties. Thanks to your dad and his obsession with eighties music. I still remember the lyrics!' She handed Holly a microphone. 'I hope you still do, too. Even though the lyrics are over there on that screen in gigantic letters.'

The mic squealed with feedback and Holly tapped it. 'Helloo, hellooo?'

Melissa grabbed her arm. 'Welcome, ladies and gentlemen. We are *not* Bananarama with our rendition of one of their popular eighties hits.'

A group sitting nearby whooped with encouragement.

The music began to play and the friends started to sing. Holly swayed in time to the song. 'Everybody do this!' she shouted, waving her arms around her head, while trying to hold the microphone artfully. 'And now this,' she yelled, spinning around, then knocking into a table behind her. Melissa pulled her back, and as she faced the bar again, she noticed a man staring at her. He looked familiar, but Holly couldn't work out how she knew him so carried on singing, spinning around again a couple of times. But as she did, she suddenly realized who the man was. Her heart sank and landed with a thud.

Jack Fambridge. My new boss's son. The man I'm supposed to be having probably quite an important work meeting with tomorrow. Oh no!

Their eyes locked for a moment, just as Melissa shouted, 'It's five past nine,' a third of the way through the final chorus. She put her microphone down with a bang that reverberated around the room.

'Don't you mean "9 to 5"?' shouted someone from the front. 'Great song.'

Melissa picked up her bag and hurried from the stage, followed by Holly. 'Sorry, sorry,' she shouted to everyone. 'Emergency! She doesn't want to lose a shoe or anything.' Then, realizing it didn't make sense, added, 'We had a conversation earlier about Cinderella — you had to be there.' She handed her microphone to one of the bar staff and kept her eyes focused on her friend's back, mainly so she wouldn't look into the eyes of her new colleague as she stumbled out into the night.

CHAPTER FOUR

The alarm screamed repeatedly until Holly shouted, 'Alexa, stop!' Then she rolled over and opened her eyes. Isabella was staring at her. The cat licked her nose and then jumped on to the floor.

'I'm not sure the smell of cat food is something I need at the moment. Can you wait a bit?' Holly muttered, stretching her legs and wiggling her toes. Climbing out of bed, she walked around the clothes she had thrown on the floor the previous evening and headed for the kitchen, where she poured herself a large glass of water, drank it very, very quickly, then had a flashback that made her face flush red.

'Ohhhh,' she sighed to Isabella. 'There's nothing like accidentally staring into the eyes of your new boss's son who, incidentally, is also your colleague, across a crowded room when you're . . .' A flash of embarrassment almost overwhelmed her. 'Still, could have been worse. I could have drunk more than two cocktails and attempted "Let It Go" from *Frozen* again. It *was* just two, wasn't it? Or did we stop for another on the way home?'

The cat jumped up on to the counter and stuck her head in the glass. 'No. Nope. Don't do that.' Holly picked her up. 'Okay, I'll get your breakfast now.' Opening a tin, she glanced at her laptop. 'I'm sorry I haven't started my blog yet. I'll do it later. I promise,' she muttered. 'And now I'm talking to my computer.' She rolled her eyes at the cat.

Taking a long, hot shower, she opened her wardrobe and scanned it for a suitably sensible outfit, settling on a long, plain, red dress. Isabella was now sitting on the bed, watching Holly panic. 'It's plain! I can't do any better than that.' Holly got changed, put her make-up on and rushed out of the door.

* * *

Jack waved at her from his office just as she walked in.

'I know we had our meeting pencilled in for twelve thirty, but I've got to rush home and wait for the washing machine repair man to come this afternoon.'

'Of course.' Holly plastered a buoyant smile on her face, trying not to stare longingly at his tousled hair and unshaven face. She glanced around the office so she could focus on Claudette and say something witty or interesting, or anything that would stop her gazing at Jack. 'Claudette not in today?' she asked eventually.

'She's having her hair done, then doing some guide-book-related research, I believe.'

'Oh, I didn't realize she was one of the writing team.'

'We all are. All hands on deck. Me, you, Mum, her friend Lillian, my second cousin Jordan . . . and Uncle Francis . . . I think.' Jack sat down in an armchair in the corner of the room. 'Let's have the chat here.'

'I assumed there was a bigger team of writers than that.' Holly sank down into her chair and tried to look serene, despite a rising concern that this wasn't quite the successful and growing company she'd assumed it was.

'There will be.' He smiled reassuringly. 'We were about to finally wind the company up until we found the guidebooks in the store room.' His mobile phone began to ring, but he pressed something and it stopped immediately. 'Sorry about that. We felt we had to finish what my father had started. And had to make a decision to do that quickly for various reasons. So, we're all out and about but still growing as a team.'

'Ah, right. Very good.'

'That's why you saw me in Coal Drops Yard last night.' He smiled again, but this time Holly thought there was a glint in his eye.

Holly bit her lip. 'Oh, it *was* you. How embarrassing.' She sank down even further into her seat.

'It was very entertaining. Quite tuneful. Excellent exit.' He looked like he was going to laugh.

'Melissa had a train to catch and forgot the time.' Holly began to relax. 'We hadn't seen each other for a while and regressed to our childhood selves.'

'How are you feeling this morning?' Holly didn't think she'd imagined that he'd raised an eyebrow.

'Absolutely and surprisingly fine. I think it's because I ate all the fruit in the cocktails.'

'Of course.'

'And had a kebab on the way home,' she laughed. 'What were you researching in Coal Drops Yard?'

'A huge amount, to be honest. None of it was there when my father wrote the books. It was just a twinkle in a property developer's eye.' He picked up a book that was on the coffee table in front of them, leafed through it until he came to a particular page then showed it to Holly. 'I think my mother mentioned that my father loved music. He loved London and almost everything about it, but old music venues were his passion. So many of them are gone now. But he took lots of photographs, and there are a few good ones of a place called the Cross, which used to be near where we were last night and, of course, Bagley's, as you can see here.' He put the book down and leaned forward. 'How have your first couple of days been, Holly?'

'I got a lot done yesterday.' She took out her notebook and phone. 'I was in Primrose Hill, which is both lovely and very convenient for my new house.' Bringing up the photograph she had taken from the top of the hill, she put it on the table in front of him. 'This is very different to the one in the book.'

'Wonderful — we also have an idea to talk to some of the people who live and work in the buildings that are still there, and some that have moved on if we can find them. We'll do that via our updated website and social media to drive people to buy the books.'

'Fantastic idea.' Holly felt a surge of enthusiasm. *This will really look good for me*, she thought.

'But that will take a while. We've rather hit the ground running, so all of that has to take a back seat till we've got some content. And a confirmed publication date, of course.' Jack's phone began to ring again. His face clouded as he looked at it. 'I'm sorry. I have to take this. Keep up the good work.' He stood up and hurried back into his office, slamming the door shut. Then he opened it again. 'Where are you off to today?'

'I'm going to write up my notes, upload my photographs, and then I plan on visiting the area around Camden Market. Is that okay?' She heard his phone ring yet again.

'Perfect.' The door was shut slightly more aggressively this time, and so Holly got up, logged on to the computer and began to work, trying to push Jack and his very attractive stubble to the back of her mind.

* * *

Buying herself a burrito from a food stall in Camden Market, Holly decided to pop home to eat it so she could enjoy the late spring sunshine in the garden.

Beaming, she ambled down the tree-lined road of white, pink and blue Victorian villas. 'This is just so lovely,' she said out loud.

'It absolutely is!' A man walking a Great Dane on the other side of the street waved at her.

She waved back, then turned into the tiny cobbled mews and opened the door to her new home cautiously to make sure the cat wouldn't hurl herself outside.

'Isabella!' she shouted. 'Isabella. Fancy a cat treat?' Holly walked into the kitchen and took out a box of cat food, shaking it loudly. 'Helloo? Where are you hiding?'

Putting the food down, Holly searched the rooms, looking under her bed, rifling through her wardrobes and checking the few still-yet-to-be unpacked boxes while an uncomfortable knot began to form in her stomach. 'Oh God. You haven't got out, have you?'

She pushed at the cat flap. It opened. 'Oh! I thought it was locked when we arrived.'

She was starting to panic as she opened the back door. 'Isabella. Isabella?' she tried to sound calm, but the thought of her beloved tiny cat stuck outside in unfamiliar surroundings made her feel physically sick. Hurrying back inside, she grabbed the box of dry cat food and began to shake it again, heading back to the garden as she did. 'Isabella? Isabella?' Holly began to search the foliage, pushing back overgrown bushes and looking up into the cherry tree to see if she could spot the cat's small frame on one of the branches. 'I remember you climbing up the trees in the orchard next to the cottage,' she shouted. 'It wasn't good then and it won't be good now.'

The memory of Isabella swaying fearlessly on a branch as the winter wind blew fiercely across the distant fields ran through her mind, like a little film. Holly standing underneath waving at her. The cat looking down, appearing to enjoy the ride.

Holly sank to the floor. That had been the same day that Ed had driven off into the distance to start a new life living on a remote part of the Isle of Skye. She also remembered watching his Volkswagen van get smaller and smaller until it became almost a pinprick before it disappeared.

The sound of a car horn blasted her back to the present. 'Oh, Isabella,' she shouted, frustrated. 'At least you were easy to spot in the orchard. No one else lived within three miles of it. It's not the same here!'

A wailing meow rang out from another garden and Holly immediately stood up. 'Isabella?'

There was another meow, drawing Holly towards a fence on the left. 'You've jumped next door, haven't you?' she muttered, pulling a large, empty plant pot towards her, turning it upside down and climbing on it so she could see over the other side. Isabella was sitting in the middle of the lawn staring back at her.

'I've got to go out to do more work,' Holly hissed. 'You're not supposed to be allowed out till we've been here for six weeks. Come back now!'

A tiny, pink cherry blossom drifted down from a nearby tree. Isabella chased it briefly and then sat on the grass again.

Holly got down from the top of the plant pot, retrieved the box of cat food she had bought into the garden and began to shake it again, then hauled herself on to the pot and waved it over the fence just as a dog barked and ran out from the house. It stopped in front of Isabella, who just looked at it with indifference. The dog's tail began to wag and it barked again.

'Mabel?' Holly peered over the fence.

'Mabel!' shouted a male voice in the distance. 'Come back. I need to go out and you need to come with me.'

'Immaterial?' Holly muttered as he hurried over to the dog and tried to put a lead on her.

'Oh, and another animal in the garden. I don't like dogs, I don't like cats, and yet here we are.' Mabel started to run around in circles, barking happily.

'Hello!' shouted Holly, still shaking the box of food.

Immaterial looked up at her. 'Are you trying to lure me into your garden with tasty treats?'

'No! I'm trying to lure my cat back.'

'Ah, she's Mabel's new friend, it seems. Good luck with that.'

'I have to go out, too.' Holly stared at Isabella, who seemed to be quite happy where she was.

'Well, new neighbour,' he said. 'Sorry I can't remember your name — I'm very bad with names — you didn't seem that tall when Mabel knocked you over.'

'It's Holly. And I'm standing on a large pot.'

'Well, Holly, I will, if you don't mind, chase your cat towards you — for her own good, you understand — hopefully she will jump over the fence back to her home and Mabel will, as a result, do as she's told.'

The dog barked at the sound of her name, then dodged away from her owner's next attempt to get her on the lead. 'But you always like walking,' he muttered, then strode over to Isabella, who didn't move until he attempted to pick her up. She padded away, then sat down again, repeating the exercise every time Immaterial got close to her.

Holly continued waving the box of food as Mabel's owner gradually and very slowly herded the cat over to the fence, then managed to pick her up just as she was distracted by another stray pink blossom that had floated on to the grass.

'Here you are,' he said, holding Isabella up so Holly could grab her.

'Thank you!' Holly clutched the cat. 'I still don't know your name. You didn't tell me when we first met.'

'It's Caleb.'

'Thank you for my cat.'

'You're very welcome. I hope she doesn't come back. No offence. Mabel's difficult enough as it is. God knows what she'd be like with a friend.' Then he turned and began to walk back into the house.

'Oh, and what's the name of the square where your shop is? I've been looking for it and it feels like it's disappeared — although, obviously it hasn't.'

'It's the Brigadoon of Primrose Hill — can only be found once every hundred years. And every year.' He seemed to be smiling. 'And every other day of the year. So, it's not like Brigadoon at all, actually.' Mabel began to run around him again. 'I've got to get on, sorry. It's called Farthing Street. It's not really a square. It just looks like that because they sealed off the end with planters to stop cars using it as a rat run.'

'Oh good! Now I can write about it.'

46

He stopped and turned around. 'Write about it?' His smile had faded, and she noticed that he'd pulled his hat down further over his head.

'I'm a travel writer and I need to start writing for my own blog again. And I thought how I found it — by accident — was rather interesting.'

'How many people read your blog?' he asked slowly.

'I used to have a lot of subscribers, but there's been a long gap, so who knows? I'm not mentioning you or Mabel, by the way. I'm just saying I found it by a happy accident.' For some reason, Holly felt like she had to reassure him.

'Right.'

'I'm also writing about moving into London when all the people I know of my age are moving out.'

'Ah . . . well, good luck with it,' he said quickly, then strode back into the house, followed by Mabel, the door shutting loudly behind them.

Isabella began to wriggle, so Holly got gingerly off the plant pot and hurried back into her house, wondering why her neighbour had reacted so strangely. *Maybe that's just how he is*, said her inner voice, which sounded a lot like her mother on this occasion. *Don't overthink it. Just accept it.*

* * *

Holly taped the cat flap shut, dragged a large suitcase over to cover it, put some books on top of that, then went back out to finish her day's work. Pausing at the top of the road under a hawthorn tree bursting with bright white flowers, she took out the guidebook proof and turned the pages. A wisp of puffball from a dandelion floated over and landed on top of a photograph of a Victorian building with impressive stone steps leading up to an arched doorway. The sign above it said *The Bollington*. Next to the picture, Seth had written:

> *One of those musical gems you find in the most unlikely places.*
> *Once a Victorian school, these magnificent high-ceilinged rooms*

have echoed with the music of bands such as the Rolling Stones, the Beatles and U2 in their early days, and I must mention some particular favourites of mine — Aswad, the Specials and Eddie and the Hot Rods. Iconic eighties band the Lights made their debut here in 1981 and recorded their only UK live album in front of a home crowd at that infamous gig on 15 August 1988, where internal fighting spilled over into a full-scale brawl involving both the band and the audience. However, the building now seems to be sadly unused. My fingers are crossed that it doesn't get knocked down or redeveloped. Maybe someone will bring it back to the life it should have again. And, as a regular visitor, it was some life, let me tell you.

Holly looked at the map. 'Farthing Street. Well, I never,' she said out loud, looking upwards as if somehow there'd be an arrow to get her there. 'I should have followed Caleb when I had the chance.'

Taking out her phone, she typed the address into Google Maps and began to walk, turning left at the end of the road, feeling excited to be able to visit the street again but also about the idea of being able to show Claudette and Jack some information on one of Seth's beloved music venues. Striding forward purposefully, the sound of drilling that had seemed far in the distance began to move closer until she reached a *Road Closed* sign.

'Oh.' The signal on her phone disappeared at the same time. 'Why is this street so difficult to find!' she said out loud. 'I need an umbrella and a high wind to blow me above the rooftops and set me down like Mary Poppins.'

'Can I help you, dear?' A tall man touched her arm. 'You look a bit lost.'

'I am and I'm not.' Holly looked up and smiled, then did a double take. His face was smeared with what looked like splodges of black paint.

'Happens a lot round here,' he said. 'They keep changing the road layouts, so if you're not a local, following that Goggle Maps thing is no help.'

'Can you point me in the right direction of Farthing Street?' She looked at him hopefully. 'I keep missing the turning.'

'Ah, the one with that funny old record shop that's hardly ever open?'

'I know there's a record shop there.'

'Well, you're very, very close.' He turned her around gently so she was facing the way she had just walked. 'Just turn right here.'

'Oh, and then where?'

'That's it.'

'How did I miss that?' Holly glanced around to try to work out how she'd walked past it.

'People are always missing it these days. That's why the place is not doing so well. You used to be able to drive through it and out the other side, till the council put those planters in to calm the traffic. Calmed everything else, too.' He sighed. 'Pity. Well, I've got to get on.' He opened the door of his van and took out a long brush. 'These chimneys won't sweep themselves. Toodle pip!'

Closing the door behind him, he walked into the large Victorian house behind them.

'Toodle pip,' murmured Holly, turning into Farthing Street. 'Hope I can find my way out again.'

The narrow road opened into a wider street, lined with cherry trees shedding the last of their blossom on to the pavements below. A couple of customers were sitting outside the café as Holly walked past, and she glanced in to see if she could wave hello to Viktor and Paulo, but they were weaving in and out of tables, focusing on their work.

The record shop had an *Open* sign on the door, and there was someone chatting to Marialena in the dry-cleaner's. Holly looked around properly this time and saw an old-fashioned hardware store tucked into the corner, next to the newsagents and an empty shop. Next to that was *Lulu's Gorgeous Emporium of Delectable Frocks*, a twenty-four-hour convenience store, a shop selling kitchenware and a hairdresser's. In between them was the old Victorian building she was

49

looking for. 'Bingo,' she almost shouted, hurrying over to it and trying to open the door, picturing the expressions on Jack and Claudette's faces when she arrived in the office with her first "Musical venue, then and now" photo.

It was firmly shut. She took a few steps backwards and looked up — the thick, red wooden doors appeared newly painted and the arch of a stained-glass window above them seemed to be freshly cleaned.

'You'll have no luck there,' shouted a voice from within the clothes shop. Holly assumed it was Lulu and walked inside. A woman with bright red hair locked into a high, tight bun on the top of her head was on the top of a ladder. She laughed. 'I saw you on the CCTV. I have no magical powers. Well, not many.'

'Ah . . . are you Lulu?' Holly smiled at her.

'No, no!' The woman coughed. 'God, this dust is everywhere. Lulu is my sister. She's cleared off to India to an *ashram* for—' she looked above her as if searching for a number — 'about seven years so far. I'm Bev.' She slowly descended the ladder, dropping her duster on the floor ahead of her. 'It's like painting the Forth Bridge trying to keep this place clean,' she muttered.

'I'm Holly.' Holly felt a rising excitement. I'm a travel writer and I'm doing some research on the Bollington.'

Bev began to move the ladder to the back of the shop. 'Where's that?'

'Next door. I was trying to get inside.' Holly took the guidebook out of her bag and opened it, waving it at Bev hopefully.

'That old place? That's been empty for years. I've never seen anyone go in. Just people doing up the outside sometimes.'

'You don't know who owns it, do you?' Holly's excitement was slowly ebbing away as she tried to manage her own expectations. Jack and Claudette might be slightly impressed by her discovery. Even though she wasn't really discovering anything — just an old building that used to be something. Just like a lot of old buildings.

'No idea.' Bev picked up a lime-green sundress and held it up next to Holly. 'This suits you. Do you want to try it on? It says you all over. Your name — I reckon it's got a sort of gardening vibe.'

'Holly.'

'I was right.' Bev beamed. 'Holly, green dress. It's as if I knew.'

Holly decided it was easier not to mention she'd already introduced herself. She also liked the dress and was almost tempted to stretch her hand out to feel the fabric. *You are working!* her inner voice said sternly.

'Maybe another time.' Holly fished around in her rucksack for a pen. 'Do you know anyone who may have an idea of who owns the building?'

Bev hung the dress back up. 'You could try old Mr Mysterious at the record shop that never opens,' she suggested. 'He's been here for years.'

'Mr Mysterious?' Holly assumed she was talking about Caleb.

Bev rolled her eyes and shook her head. 'There's a story there, but I've got no idea what it is. I'm a big-picture person, not really good at the minutiae — or facts, I suppose.'

Holly nodded, thinking about his response when she'd talked about the blog. 'I'll ask him when I see him. He's my neighbour, actually.'

'Ah! Do keep an eye on his comings and goings. We all reckon he's a spy or something!' Bev laughed just as her phone began to ring. 'Must get this, but do come back. That lime-green dress really *does* have your name on it. Not literally. But you know what I mean.'

Holly put the pen back in her bag, deciding that making a note of *Ask Mr Mysterious, AKA Immaterial, about The Bollington. Could be a spy* sounded like a cut-price James Bond film. And James Bond wouldn't make notes anyway, would he? She walked back into the street, took a few photographs of the Bollington, thought about popping into the café for a coffee and to ask a few questions, but decided to return another day. Instead, she found her way back to the main road, then back up to Camden High Street to continue the easier and less mysterious part of her day's research.

CHAPTER FIVE

'I think I may have found something quite exciting.' Holly moved her computer so Jack and Claudette could see her photos. She pointed at the Bollington. 'There you are. That old music venue was featured in Seth's very first guidebook — it had quite a story even then. If we could just get inside, that would be a really good hook to help get people interested in the books.' She smiled expectantly at them. 'It was a school, then used by the local church as a community hall, and then, in the 1950s, it became a club.' She looked up at them, trying to read their faces. 'A lot of famous bands played there, including the Lights, who did their first gig and their last gig there just before it closed. My dad is a bit of an enthusiast about music — especially the eighties — so it's really caught my interest.'

'Well done, Holly.' Claudette clapped her hands. 'Where is it exactly?'

'It's in a road not far from where I live. Actually, that could do with a boost, too. It's a bit run-down and forgotten about, which is a pity.'

'We need to come up with a strategy for these finds.' Jack sat down. 'I'm sure we'll all come across some significant ones that could help with publicity.'

'If I can get inside, I can take some photographs and start posting.'

'We need a proper plan for that.' He looked serious. 'I don't know what as I've never done it, but I don't think we should just start flinging stuff up on social media straight away.'

Holly glanced around the empty office. *That road is not the only place that needs some help*, she thought. *This business could do with some, too*. 'Have you a specialist who can do that? I can do the posts, but a PR person could help us formulate a campaign.'

'Not currently,' Jack said.

Claudette squeezed his hand. 'You've taken on a lot very quickly, Jack. It will all come together.'

'I've got a friend in PR,' Holly interrupted. 'She may be able to help give a bit of advice.'

'That would be lovely.' Claudette nodded encouragingly at her. 'Until we are in a position to actually expand our workforce, that would make a big difference.'

Jack got up and nodded, unsmiling. Holly felt a flutter again. Even when he was in an apparently bad mood, she had to stop herself edging closer to him. She cleared her throat and tried to focus. *This is your job, and you have to make it work*, she thought. *You've already lost almost all your savings on cheese. Ramp up the enthusiasm*.

'I'll give her a call and see if she can help.' Holly watched Jack as he checked his phone.

'Thank you.' Claudette leaned forward. 'As you seem to be doing all this much more quickly than us, can I send you off to Battersea Power Station? Jack was supposed to go today but he has some issues still outstanding in Costa Rica that are demanding his attention.' They both watched as he walked silently into his office and closed the door. 'And, so we don't get behind with our schedules too much, it would help.' She walked over to the cupboard and took out the relevant guidebook, then placed it on Holly's desk.

'Of course.' Holly picked up her bag. 'I'll get going. I was going to start with Hampstead today, but I can catch up easily. The days are getting longer now so the light will be fine for exploring.'

Claudette touched her hand. 'This is all a bit more complicated than it appears on the surface, I'm afraid. But we are moving in the right direction. With your help, of course.'

'Of course.' Holly nodded. 'I was reading Seth's section about swimming on Hampstead Heath. You mentioned it the other day, didn't you?'

'Ah yes.' Claudette looked at the floor briefly then smiled up at Holly again.

'It was so lovely, I thought I'd give it a go myself. When it's warm, obviously.'

'I haven't done that for so long.' Claudette got up and put the kettle on.

'You could come with me.'

'Oh, I'm not sure.' Claudette had her back to her. 'Although.' It looked as if she were taking a long, deep breath and making herself taller somehow. She turned to Holly. 'But maybe I will. Perhaps it's time.'

'Shall we try for in a couple of weeks then?' Holly opened the door to leave. 'I'll keep an eye on the weather forecast to make sure it's not going to be too cold.'

* * *

Walking towards London Bridge, the light breeze that caught her hair made Holly feel slightly restless as she replayed the conversation with Claudette and Jack. Then it became a film of Jack's face, then Jack walking into his office, then Jack closing the door behind him. All in slow motion. Glancing towards Borough Market, she almost crossed the road, fighting the urge to lose herself in the crowds in search of artisan bread or speciality tea for later. Or a doughnut.

And then it came.

'We can't carry on like this, Ed.' Holly began to walk faster, trying to get away from the memory that seemed to be chasing her down the road. *'Our outgoings are more than what we're bringing in, and it seems to be getting worse.'*

'Dreams take time, Hol.' He grabbed her hand and pulled her towards him. *'We just need a bit more time.'* She remembered how his arms had felt around her — reassuring and strong and constant. *'We're in this together, and we will make it work.'*

'Yes,' she said, *breathing in his familiar scent of sandalwood and coffee and fresh air, trying very hard to believe him.*

She stopped on the pavement and stared at the sky, unfocused and still, as passers-by weaved around her like a stream flowing past a stone.

'Right.' She shook her arms slightly as if the memory would fall out of her fingers. 'Right.' A London bus drove past and her mind clicked to the present. 'God. How do I get to Battersea?' She opened her Citymapper app, saw *boat* and decided travelling on the river would be fun, then quickly found her way to the embarkation point and hopped on. *I can write about the journey for my blog*, she thought, beginning to take photographs. *Kill two birds with one stone.*

Sitting by the window, Holly watched London pass by — Tower Bridge, the Tower of London, St Paul's, the South Bank — as if she were in an old film that somehow took its characters to all the main city landmarks just to prove they were there. The low thrum of the engine comforted and calmed her, and she closed her eyes for a moment. Just for a moment.

'The next stop will be Embankment.' Holly opened her eyes in a panic as a man sitting next to her moved his shoulder, on which she had been dozing, slowly and very politely away.

'Oh goodness. I'm so sorry.' She checked her mouth to make sure she hadn't dribbled either, then felt herself smile a little too wildly. 'It's the boat. It's like a pram, isn't it? Rocking you to sleep. Well, to me, anyway.'

The man nodded and looked back at his book.

Holly sat upright and took the guidebook out, deciding to do a bit of research before she arrived, given that she'd almost run out of the office before even checking what she was supposed to be looking at.

BATTERSEA POWER STATION
Comprised of two recently decommissioned power stations
— Battersea A and Battersea B — the iconic four-chimney
structure still stands tall against the London skyline. Built
by the London Power Company, designer Leonard Pearce
and architects J. Theo Halliday and Giles Gilbert Scott gave
us the gift of both industry and beauty within what was one
of the world's largest brick buildings with original Art Deco
interior fittings and décor. So, of course, it has been rightly
granted Grade II-listed status.

One day, I hope it will be brought back to life again:
repurposed, recycled and loved once more.

'That's just so lovely. I really must start writing my new stuff,' she muttered to herself as the boat began to pull in to dock at Battersea. 'Instead of just saying I'm going to.' Standing up, she joined the queue to get off and made a voice note on her phone. '*The two iconic chimneys still standing, a symbol of regeneration and progress, of an old industrial beauty reimagined and treasured,*' she said quietly so no one else could hear. 'Now where are the shops?'

She took several photographs and made a short 360-degree film of the river and the development, before sitting on a bench and opening the guidebook again, wondering how to make the "then" and "now" more interesting. Because then it was all industry, and now it was something else entirely — just as Seth had hoped. Deciding to see if she could get into the Lift 109 experience, she brought the website up on her phone and booked a slot for 11 a.m., meaning she wouldn't have to rush to get there in time. She barely noticed the architecture she was supposed to be describing as she made the booking.

As soon as Holly got into the experience itself, she found herself falling back into her comfort zone, learning about the area's history and how it had changed. By the time she got in the glass lift to make the ascent, the niggles she had brought with her from the office had almost disappeared. She took her phone out and prepared to take some photographs, just as someone hurried in and stood in front of her. Holly looked up. Jack looked down. 'Hello,' they both said at the same time. 'What are you doing here?'

A child standing behind her tripped over, nudging her almost a breath away from Jack's neck, which smelled of patchouli and cinnamon and was vaguely intoxicating. Trying not to breathe in again she edged back, attempting to gather her thoughts so she could compose a coherent sentence. 'What a coincidence,' she said eventually, briefly gazing into his dark-brown eyes. 'I've been taking photographs.' She waved her phone at him, unable to stop herself from smiling a bit too enthusiastically.

'I thought you were going to Hampstead today.' He frowned. Holly tried not to be mesmerized by the surprisingly attractive lines on his forehead. 'That's what was on the schedule when I looked.'

'Your mother asked me to come here instead, to help out . . .'

'Oh. She didn't mention it. Sorry if I seem rude. I don't mean to be. Stuff to sort out on top of the business stuff. Decided to come and do some actual guidebook work to take my mind off it.'

'Yes, I forgot about all my worries for a while when I was looking round the exhibition.' She didn't say, *worries partly triggered by you, unfortunately somehow sending my mind back to Ed*, but the thought sent her edging back again so she inadvertently nudged the child who had tripped up, who then toppled into someone else.

'Oh, sorry, sorry.' Holly turned around and stepped on somebody's toes. 'Oh, sorry again. I'll just move over here.'

Jack took her hand, and Holly felt a surprisingly pleasurable shiver trickle from her fingers up along her arm. 'Shall we move a bit further to this side?' He guided her towards another window.

'Yes, I'm a bit dangerous in this bit. I reckon it's tilted.' She tried to laugh.

'So, Holly, you have worries, too?' He looked at her with interest.

'No more than anyone else.'

'Wow, look at that! You can see Canary Wharf!' another passenger exclaimed from the other side of the lift.

God, I'm so busy trying not to stare at Jack, I've forgotten to look at the view, thought Holly, spinning around and gazing outside. 'I'll just take some photos as a guide . . . or do you want to?'

'Your phone's out, so why don't you?' Jack checked his phone and read a message. 'Never stops,' he mumbled.

Holly stared out of the window and tried to concentrate on what she could see. But she couldn't really see it. She was having an argument with herself, so the glow of the river, the iconic London skyline and the aircraft seemingly floating in the air above the rooftops as it made its descent to Heathrow were reduced to things she pointed her camera at.

He's a colleague. You can't fancy a colleague. Yes, you can. You just can't do anything about it. I don't want to find him attractive. I found Ed attractive and look where that got me. Don't do that — you were in a long-term relationship with him for nearly sixteen years. And you only worked together for the last four . . . three . . . three and a half . . . two and a third. I hate cheese. No, you don't. Yes, well, I hate what it did to our relationship.

She sighed and steeled herself. She knew what was coming next.

It wasn't just the business though, was it, Holly? When it came down to it, you weren't enough for each other. It only worked when you were both jetting off around the world in different directions.

'Goat's cheese was just the catalyst,' she sighed.

'Cheese?' Jack looked up from his phone.

'Did I say that out loud?'

'Something about goat's cheese?'

'Nothing else?'

'No. Was there something else?'

'No . . .' She trailed off, unsure what to say next. 'Well, this is a very nice glass-lift trip,' she said eventually.

Jack leaned towards her. 'I have a confession to make. I've been on my phone going through old messages and torturing myself.' His voice was quiet.

'Oh . . . ?'

'About things I should have said, things I shouldn't have said, things I should have done, things I shouldn't have done.'

'Oh dear.' A row of questions formed on the tip of her tongue.

'That's another thing I shouldn't have said.'

'What was?'

'That.'

Holly wondered if the lift was actually a time machine and she'd been catapulted about ten minutes into the future so she'd missed an important part of the conversation.

'You have a very expressive face.' Jack touched her arm. 'And I think what it's expressing at the moment is confusion. Am I right?'

'Um, yeesss,' said Holly slowly.

'I shouldn't have told you about the reading of the messages and all that.'

'Ahh.'

'Which is what I meant when I said that's another thing I shouldn't have said.'

The lift finished its descent and the doors opened.

'There's more to it than goat's cheese.' Holly couldn't stop the words coming out of her mouth.

'I'm sure there is,' Jack nodded seriously.

Holly looked at him and fought off the urge to ask if he wanted a coffee, so they could discuss the cheese and his messages, and she could gaze into his eyes and wrap her arms around him.

'Well, I'd best be off to Hampstead then as you've got Battersea under control.' She waved at him and almost ran out of the lift, wondering if she should write a manual entitled *How Not to Talk to a Man*, *How Not to Impress Your Boss's Son*, or maybe *How to Conduct a Bottom-Squeakingly Embarrassing*

Conversation with Someone You Want to Impress in Less Than Ten Steps.

* * *

'I wish you could see me,' Melissa managed to say in between the laughing. 'I am literally lying on my back with my arms and legs in the air waving them around with such baby-like glee, as I haven't heard anything as funny as that in a very, very long time.'

'You aren't literally lying on your back.' Holly was sitting in a café at Trafalgar Square. She'd had to disembark the Tube due to the fact her sporadic giggling was causing a bit of a stir among some of the passengers.

'I would if I could. I wanted to paint a picture for you of how I actually feel rather than look.'

Holly snorted with laughter and took a sip of her iced tea in order to stop herself. 'I'm embarrassed. So embarrassed.'

'You're not used to being out in the wild around men other than Ed, though.'

'I'm not going to be like this for ever, am I?' Holly bit her lip. The giggling was beginning to subside a little. 'I used to be able to talk normally to all sorts of attractive men when I was in a relationship.'

'You'll get used to it. It's only been a few months since you both actually officially . . .'

'Consciously uncoupled.' Holly tried to sound upbeat. 'Although, apart from the business, we weren't really together for about a year before.'

'That's right.' Melissa sounded doubtful. 'No one left. You left each other.'

A wave of sadness swept into Holly's stomach. She dealt with it by changing the subject. 'Anyway, can you advise on this publicity plan for Fambridge?'

'Oh, yes. I temporarily forgot why you really rang. You shouldn't have distracted me with tales of your strange adventures.'

'I need to stay focused. This is my new career and my new life, and I can see that Claudette and Jack are a bit all over the place. And that won't do at all. Not for them and not for me.'

'Oh, welcome back! The adventurous Holly Merriweather in one of her go-for-it moods.'

Holly grinned. 'It's nice to feel I've got something to aim for again. Something that's mine. Talking of which, I'd better get back to work and head to Hampstead. I'll send you some info about what we're trying to achieve.'

'All right — and if you're going to try to impress any-one, I'd write down some lines to use in advance. Don't try to be spontaneous.' Melissa practically guffawed and was still spluttering with laughter when Holly ended the call.

Throwing herself into her work, Holly regained her focus by walking from Hampstead station along Haverstock Hill, then across through the grand, well-kept Victorian ter-races, past Keats House, and then on to the Heath. Once there, she sat on a bench and marked her notes to correspond with the places that Seth had written about. She looked up. The trees in the distance were a deep, rich green, the last buds of colourful spring blossom waving in the breeze. A barking dog ran after a ball thrown by a laughing child, while a group of women pushing prams ambled past, filling the air with chatter. The mixed pond glistened like glass in the distance. Holly turned the page of the book and began to read Seth's words quietly under her breath.

> *It's funny how the simple fact that in the middle of the city is a stretch of water I can swim in with the love of my life, sealed my own love affair with London. The walks back to our little flat, our hair damp, our skin glowing in the sun, the rain, the wind and the fog were some of the happiest times of my life. And I will never, ever forget them. I hold them in my heart wherever I go.*

Holly's stomach filled with butterflies — the same excitement she'd felt when she'd sat in the corner of the library, having picked the book out randomly from the shelves when she was ten. She'd only noticed it because of the shiny cover with the two figures walking towards what she imagined to be more exciting adventures. The pictures and maps somehow drew her into their world, and she found herself entranced by the author and his joyful view of London. To her, a shy little girl who lost herself in movies, he made it feel like a giant film set, full of history and glamour and fun.

Holly looked up again as a couple walked along the path to the lake. Seth's books had shown her that everything was worth celebrating — the simple and the complicated, the beautiful and the seemingly mundane.

Maybe when I have a swim in the pond, I'll find some of that lyrical Seth Fambridge magic myself, she thought. *It's worth a go, anyway.*

On her way home, Holly decided to have another look at the Bollington, hoping Caleb would not only be in his shop, but that it would be open too so she could ask some questions. Seth's new guidebook deserved a good story, and something told her that the Bollington could be it. Although she couldn't work out exactly why she felt that.

Edging the door of the shop slowly open into a guitar-fuelled wave of Echo and the Bunnymen's "Seven Seas", Holly scanned the empty room for Caleb. It smelled musty and somehow neglected, despite its pristine rows of vinyl, all illustrated with bookshop-like notes about the songs or the artists.

'Hello?' she called as the track finished, trying to make herself heard as the music suddenly jumped to "My Kingdom" and Mabel barked from a room behind the counter.

'Mabel!' she shouted as the dog bounded towards her, and she bent down to stroke her head.

Caleb ambled out from the back of the shop. 'Hello, neighbour.' He smiled. 'Are you a fan of vinyl?'

Holly looked up. 'Me? I love music, but my father is the expert. Echo and the Bunnymen were one of the soundtracks to my childhood, though.'

'What very good taste your father has. So, how can I help? Are you looking for a present for him?'

'That's a good idea, but not the reason for my visit. I'm interested in the Bollington and I'm told that you may know something about it.'

'Told by who?' he asked after a pause.

'The lady in the clothes shop — Bev, I think her name is.'

'Is that what she said?' He turned around and walked back behind the counter. 'Well, she's wrong. She probably knows more than I do.'

'Oh, I assumed as it was a very well-known music venue, you'd have some information.'

'Well, I don't.' He opened his laptop. 'It's just an old club that closed. Like so many. Nothing special.'

He's not actually telling the truth, Holly thought as he began to scroll through something. *There's something . . .*

'Why do you want to know about it?' He was still looking at the screen.

'It's partly to do with my job for a guidebook company. They're doing a *London Then and Now* series based on the old *London: How I See It* series by Seth Fambridge.'

Caleb looked up. 'Seth Fambridge? Now that rings a bell.'

'He loved music venues so included a lot in his books.' Holly walked over to the counter, followed by Mabel. 'I just thought the Bollington might have an interesting story. Plus, I can write something about it for my own travel blog. When I actually start writing it again . . .' She trailed off.

Caleb turned his attention back to his work. 'I doubt there's a story. Like I said, places close down all the time.'

'Well, if you remember anything, can you let me know?' Holly smiled hopefully.

'I won't, but I will if I do. I've got to get some online orders out now, so if you'll excuse me.'

'Of course. Well, as we're neighbours, I'm easy to find.'

He grunted as she opened the door.

'Bye then,' she sang, despite her disappointment. But as she walked out into the street and glanced over at the abandoned old building, she decided she was not going to leave it there. There was definitely something to find out. 'And when I find that thing out, it's going to help us all,' she said to herself determinedly. 'Hopefully. I think. Well, maybe. No, definitely.'

* * *

Sitting in her garden once she got home, Holly typed her notes up on to the laptop, then opened another file in the hope that the words in her head that she had planned for her blog would somehow fly out on to the screen. But her hands just hovered over the keyboard, poised, with nowhere to go.

'Why can't I just start writing?' she asked Isabella, who was lying down next to her and cleaning her paws. 'It's part of the plan. Guidebook writing for actual money and experience, and me writing to get myself out there again.'

Typing in the address of her blog, she scrolled through a list of pieces she had written, counting how many she'd done over the years and how many magazines had commissioned her to write for them. 'I know I can do it,' she said. Isabella got up and wandered over to a magnolia tree, then plopped herself underneath it.

Holly looked at the computer again. 'Venice. Ah, I remember. That was one of my first.' Clicking on the link, she studied the screen. There she was, standing on the Bridge of Sighs.

The first time I visited Venice was after a storm.

We had stayed on a campsite in Mestre, which is on the mainland on the other side of the Liberty Bridge. There had been torrential rain overnight with powerful bangs of thunder and lightning, and when we finally climbed out of our tents, the morning was dark and murky.

The bus taking us across the causeway was full and we were the last people to get on. At the time, I was not best pleased that I had to stand at the front, but as the driver began to take us over the bridge towards Venice, the clouds slowly began to clear and the rooftops of the city gradually, almost magically, came into sight. I watched, mesmerized, as we drew closer. Gossamer-thin wisps of cloud draped themselves around the buildings then billowed out again, the breeze trying to pull them away as if they were silver curtains being drawn open to welcome the day. The sea on either side of us was dark and flat, but as the minutes ticked by the greyness dissipated, illuminating the dome of St Mark's in the distance, the sky now a silky and bright blue. And by the time we disembarked, it was as if the rain had never happened.

Oh, I thought, I feel like I'm in the first shot of an epic film with the camera swooping across the bay. But I wasn't. I was on a bus after a rainstorm, and I don't believe Venice could ever have looked as beautiful as that.

Closing the laptop, she picked it up and walked back into the living room, just as her phone began to play the introduction to Adam Ant's "Prince Charming". 'Dad!' she said in delight as she answered it.

'Hello, hello, hello! How's my favourite daughter?'

'I'm all okay, thanks. How was your holiday?'

'Just wonderful, my dear. I spent so much time dressed as Adam Ant. I'm having trouble shifting the make-up, though.'

'The heat made him sweat so much he kept having to reapply it,' Holly heard her mother shouting.

'I may go as one of Duran Duran or Spandau Ballet to the next one,' her father said. 'I quite liked dipping my toe in the water of the New Romantics. Never did it when it was current. Or maybe I could go as Boy George?'

'Who did Mum go as?' Holly asked, just for fun. She already knew the answer.

'No one,' sighed her dad. 'She just goes as herself. But one day . . . ?'

'Nope. I'm there for the music, darling. I'm just an older version of how I looked in 1983, so I go as myself.' Her mother's voice began to sound more distant until the noise of a hoover began to overwhelm the conversation.

'Not going to another eighties convention in Thailand again,' shouted her father. 'The humidity didn't really help.'

'Well, I enjoyed myself. Dressed in a swimming costume and flip-flops the whole time.' Her mother had turned off the hoover, probably to make sure she could be heard. 'Because *I* am not an idiot!'

'Yes, yes.' Her father sighed again. She heard a door slam, then the vacuum cleaner was switched on again in the distance. 'So, how are you settling into your new home?' It sounded like he'd moved to another room as the hoovering noise was fainter.

'It's lovely.' Holly glanced around her. 'Almost unpacked — it's been a busy few days.'

'Good, good. Your mother and I can't wait to come and visit.'

'Anytime you want, Dad.'

'Maybe we could fit in a few gigs after we've said hello. The drive back out here to St Albans has been revolutionized by my new satnav. Well worth the investment. A lot of cross-country routes and occasional farmland though . . . think I need to tweak the settings. Took us to a working barn last time. Your mum was furious . . .' He seemed to move closer to the sound of the hoovering. 'Weren't you, Julie — that barn?'

The hoover was promptly switched off. 'It stank, Gary. It wasn't funny. You drove through all that pig—'

Holly heard the door slam shut as the hoover began to hum again.

'Anyway,' said her dad. 'I saw there was a Brad L. Finnegan retrospective on at the Diddee Club in Waterloo.'

'The Diddee Club. Are you sure?'

'And the Unfurled are doing a comeback gig at the Kitchen Tap in Barnes, or near Barnes at least.'

She heard a string of muffled words accompanied by vacuuming coming from her mother in the background, this time closer.

'Your mother says what shall we do with all those DVDs and videos? We're downsizing.'

'I'll collect them and bring them down. Anyway, you've been planning on downsizing since I left home!'

'Your mother says she doesn't think your place is big enough for all your films, and why don't you let us dispose of them humanely?'

Holly felt herself bristle. 'I've managed to fit all my guide-books in here.'

'How much space have they taken up?' Her father chuckled.

Holly looked at the stack of books piled in the corner of the living room. 'Horizontally or vertically?'

'Our point exactly.'

'But it's part of my childhood, Dad.' Holly felt her voice rise to an almost wail at the end, just as the sound of guitar music began to float in from outside again. 'Who is that?' she mumbled.

'What?'

'Muttering to myself. Actually. Have you ever heard of the Bollington? It's a music venue near where I live.'

'Oh, the Bollington. Oh yes. Happy days.' The sound of the hoover overwhelmed the conversation. 'Oh, she's here again . . . nowhere to hide this time. We'll call next week to arrange a date.'

The phone went dead and Holly smiled, trying to picture her father dressed as Adam Ant.

You won't have to imagine it. It'll be all over Instagram soon, she thought.

'True enough,' she said, standing up, making a mental note to call him again soon to talk about the Bollington, then looking back over at her laptop. 'I must start to actually write this new stuff!' she almost shouted, then sat down again and turned on the television.

CHAPTER SIX

'Here it is.' Holly turned the corner into Farthing Street followed by Melissa, who had finished work early so she could talk about, as her text said, *Strategy, plans, branding and all the useful things I can help you with using my expertise and all that. So put a word in for me with the Fambridges in case I can add them to my client list. Ta. Luv ya xx*

'Well, well, well.' Melissa paused at the end of the road. 'This is absolutely lovely. Who'd have thought this would be just off the main road? And so peaceful.'

'I thought we could catch up over a coffee at the café?'

'I'd like to meet your cat, too, though, Holly. Your house isn't far, is it?'

Holly found a table and pulled out a chair. 'It is and it isn't. I have to walk around a few streets to get here, but it doesn't feel right and I don't know why.' She lowered her voice. 'I mean, I used to navigate my way around the world, but since I've arrived here, I can't seem to find my way properly. I keep getting lost and tripping over and . . . that sounds a bit mad, doesn't it?'

'No comment.' Melissa sat down opposite her and took a purple notebook with daisies on it out of her handbag, followed by a gold-plated pen.

'Always a sense of style.' Holly waved at Paulo as he walked out of the café. 'Can I have an oat milk latte, please — and a . . . ?' She glanced at Melissa.

'The same. Thank you.' She opened her notepad and leaned back in her chair. 'What an absolutely gorgeous day.'

'It's so green and lovely here, isn't it?' Holly sighed. Over the past couple of weeks, she had got into the habit of popping into the café for a morning coffee when she was on her out-and-about days, or a refreshing cup of tea on her way home.

Viktor bounded up to them. 'Hello, my dear. How are you today?' he bellowed. 'And you have a friend with you. Welcome.'

'I'm good, thanks, Viktor. This is my best friend from school — Melissa. She's a PR and marketing whiz-kid who's helping come up with some ideas to publicize the company I work for.'

'We could do with some help ourselves,' Viktor sighed, and sat down. 'Two years ago, we were rushed off our feet. Now they've changed the layout, it's only regulars and people who are lost and in a hurry to get to where they are lost from. No passing trade that wants to linger for a while.'

'I'm happy to come up with a few ideas.' Melissa took a sip from the drink Paulo had just placed in front of her. 'I'm thinking of starting out on my own.'

'I thought you were thinking of becoming a teacher?' Holly took a sip, too.

'I am. And I'm not. I'm dabbling in ideas.'

'The dress is still waiting for you, Holly!' Bev waved at her as she locked up the shop.

'Maybe after payday!' Holly called back over.

'I was just saying how things have changed recently,' Viktor said to her. 'Your usual?'

'Yes, please.' Bev walked over and sat at the next table. 'I was talking to Kwan, who owns the hardware shop over there. He said that his rent had been put up again and he may have to move somewhere else or just close down because people can't be bothered to seek him out anymore. I think he said it was his rent. Did he?' She took off her jacket and put it over the chair. 'Anyway, it's not good.'

'The hairdresser's closed last week.' Viktor wiped his hands on his apron. 'One day it was there, and the next day there was a *Closed Down* sign in the window.'

Paulo put an iced tea on the table. 'We need to do some events, Viktor. It's early summer now. We have a licence to trade in the evenings. We need to make the most of our surroundings.'

'But it costs money to do that,' Viktor boomed sadly. 'And we have to advertise. Which also costs money.'

'Leave it with me and I'll scribble a few ideas down over the next few days.' Melissa took another sip of her drink. 'This is really rather lovely coffee.'

'What's that noise?' Holly looked up as the sound of rustling wings began to fill the air around the trees that lined the road.

'It's beautiful,' sighed Viktor. 'We call it their evening party — the birds. I just love watching and listening to them.'

'I can't hear the traffic or the planes or the sirens.' Bev was looking up, too. 'I just hear them, fluttering and chatting to one another. Can you hear it?'

And they all sat and watched and listened as the sun began to lose its warmth, still glowing over the rooftops as the birds gathered above them.

'What a special place,' said Melissa, when they finally began their walk back to Holly's house.

'Yes, it is,' Holly murmured. 'And I haven't even told you about the Bollington yet.'

'The what?'

'It's an old music venue next to the dress shop. It's all closed up and unused, but the outside is being looked after. If I can find a story about that, it would be great for my employers, for Farthing Street and for me.'

'Disused music venues are ten a penny, I'm afraid, Hol,' Melissa put her arm around her. 'What are you thinking? Opening it up and putting on a show like Judy Garland and Mickey Rooney?'

'Ha ha. Well, you may mock, but you never know.' They turned the corner into the mews. 'I'm looking forward to seeing what you've come up with now we're not distracted.' She unlocked the front door of her house and led the way inside.

'And I'm looking forward to meeting Isabella.'

* * *

Travelling to the office on the bus the following day, Holly went over her speech in her head. *Melissa is a very experienced PR and marketing executive, and I think her ideas are easy to implement, not costly, and in some instances completely free, and I really believe we need to start telling the world about what Fambridge Books has planned.* She pictured Jack and Claudette listening to her, clearly admiring her vision and sense of purpose. Claudette was nodding, smiling, and Jack was standing up and walking over to her, then taking her hand and shaking it, staring into her eyes and getting closer and closer.

Someone pressed the bell and Holly was back on the bus. *Thank God.* Her inner voice was clearly relieved. *What you need is to get on to the dating apps pronto, so you have other men to think about — who you do* not *work with!*

Gazing out of the window at the people and the traffic, she sat back in her seat. The heat and light of the last few days had been replaced by the patter of summer rain on the window as the bus approached the stop. Standing up, Holly sighed. *Don't look directly into his eyes, and think about dating apps,* she thought, stepping out on to the pavement. *But mainly don't look directly into his eyes.*

Waiting in the queue to grab a coffee, she checked the messages on her phone.

Hey ho, Hol. It was her father. *We're heading down to the big city tomorrow. Last-minute decision. There's a gig in Richmond we want to see so we'll stay near Heathrow. But as it's Saturday, can we take you out for lunch?'*

She smiled. *Yes please,* she typed.

Richmond station 1 p.m. Be there or be square. Ha ha!

Her phone buzzed again.

We have no idea where to eat, so if you've heard of somewhere great in the area, let us know.

Walking up the stairs to the office, Holly tried to psyche herself up. *I am a strong, motivated woman like Sigourney Weaver in* Alien — *oh no, wrong genre. Thelma and Louise? Ah no. Wonder Woman? Wrong clothes.* Reaching the landing, she paused before murmuring, 'Anything with Katharine Hepburn in it.' She continued to shuffle randomly through the films filed in her mind until, by the time she'd pushed the door open, Holly was full Julie Andrews as Maria walking into the von Trapp family residence for the first time.

'Goodness me, that's quite an entrance.' Claudette looked vaguely surprised. 'You look like a woman on a mission.'

'Really?' Holly felt thrilled that her motivating tactics had worked. 'I am, actually.' She put her bag on the desk. 'Is Jack here?'

'There's a leak in the kitchen again,' he shouted. 'The mat on the floor is absolutely sodden.'

'I'll phone the landlord.' Claudette sighed. 'It's not exactly glamorous, is it?'

Jack walked into the room, and Holly diverted her attention to her bag. 'I've got some notes from my friend, Melissa. Have you all read the email I sent last night?'

'Last night?' Claudette looked confused. 'I was at an art exhibition till late. I've only just logged on myself.'

'Very impressively keen.' Jack sat down opposite her. 'I've read through it and there are some good ideas.'

'Excellent.'

'Maybe not quite ready for them yet.'

Holly bit her lip and took a breath. 'But you need to let people know what you're doing. There'll be such an appetite. You've gone from published books, to a magazine, then to only a virtual presence on the website. Now you're back to books again — and they're iconic. I think you need to get the word out sooner rather than later.'

'He's not confident enough in it.' Claudette stood up and put her hands on her hips. 'I know you're not, Jack. But you have got to do *something*! I mean, it was your idea to do this.'

'It was yours, too,' he said, almost petulantly.

They stared at each other wordlessly for a moment.

'Does anyone know any good places to eat in Richmond upon Thames?' blurted out Holly to break the silence.

They both stared at her as if they'd only just realized she was there.

'I live there. Well, near Kew Gardens, actually,' Claudette said. 'There are so many places. What do you like to eat?'

'I'm meeting my parents. My mother is a carnivore. My father is vegan. I eat anything.'

'No problem.' Claudette sat down and opened her emails. 'I'll send you a very long list and you can choose.'

'I'm at Mum's to help go through some of Dad's stuff tomorrow — I haven't been in the country long enough since he died to help till now — and then I'm paddleboarding on the river.' Jack picked up his briefcase. 'Come and wave if you happen to amble by.'

'I will. Yes.' Holly addressed her answer to his left ear, which was as close to his eyes as she dared get.

'And. Look. Mum's right. I am a bit slow to get this going. So, I'll give a couple of my contacts a call — you know the ones who are now living or working in some of the buildings my father wrote about? Maybe you could interview them and we'll get our website people — that's cousin Layla — to add another blog section to it . . . soon. Not yet. But soon.'

'Fabulous.' Holly beamed. 'Something to force me to write at last.'

* * *

The following day, Holly hurried up the steps to the street from Richmond station and scanned the groups of people gathered outside, searching for her parents. Taking her phone out of her bag, she checked the time and then shuffled over to a shady spot where she could be easily seen.

I'm outside the coffee shop next to the station, she typed, then sent them both the text.

We're over the other side of the road. Outside the pub. Mum. Holly looked over, and as a red London bus pulled away, she saw her father taking photographs while her mother waved at her. *It was a very famous old music venue. Your dad's ecstatic. As you can imagine.*

Holly laughed, then crossed the road and hugged her mum.

'How's my girl?' her mother asked, stepping back and holding her hands.

'All fine.' Holly waited for her father to notice she was there.

'Give him a minute.' Her mother rolled her eyes. 'Now, where are we going to eat? I'm famished. We thought we'd go to Kew Gardens afterwards. Passed Kew on the train.'

'Sounds good.' Holly tapped her father on the shoulder. 'Dad? Holly to Dad, Holly to Dad. Are you reading me?'

He jumped, then began to chuckle, waving his phone at her. 'This is a very well-known site and I got carried away with myself.' He kissed her on the cheek. 'As usual.'

'That's interesting, Dad, because that may be useful to me.'

His eyes lit up.

'You know what you've started, don't you?' Her mother began to walk towards the river. 'I need to get you both away from here, so I can enjoy this lovely, sunny day and not listen to your father go on and on and on and on.'

'It's called being an enthusiast, Julie.' He fell into step with her and Holly began to follow.

'Let's walk and talk then,' said Holly.

'It was the Railway Hotel years ago. Hosted Crawdaddy Club. The Rolling Stones kicked off their career here.' He stopped for a moment and showed her a photograph of a blue plaque. 'See — the twenty-fourth of February

1963. And it says that the Beatles first met them here on Sunday the fourteenth of April 1963. It's a sign.'

'A sign?'

'Your father was born on 14 April 1963.'

'Yes, I know that. But a sign about what?'

'He doesn't know. You don't know, do you, Gary?' Her mother carried on walking, then turned right suddenly into a narrow, cobbled lane. 'I'm heading for the green.'

'I'm trying to find people connected to some of the places featured in the old guidebooks, Dad.' Holly touched his arm. 'Especially old music venues. Don't suppose you know anyone, do you?'

'I knew it was a sign, Julie,' he shouted at his wife's back. 'You heard that, didn't you? Holly wants my help.'

'Look — there's a cricket match on the green!' Her mother turned back to them. 'We'll be inside tonight, Gary. Let's enjoy outside.'

They stood for a while, watching the game. 'It's like a postcard, isn't it?' Holly whispered to her mother. 'A quintessentially English scene.'

'Are you thinking of how to describe it on your blog?' Her mother took out some peppermints and offered one to her.

'I can't seem to get started with it.' Holly took the sweet and put it in her mouth.

'The muse is not visiting?' her dad asked. 'Oh, and look how far he's hit that ball. Is it a four?' He began to clap.

'No,' sighed Holly, 'the muse is giving me a wide berth at the moment. Anyway. If you know anyone who knows anyone who has an interesting story about an old London music venue, let me know.'

'I'm all for signs,' he whispered. 'I was right. Don't tell your mother I said that.'

'I *can* hear you.' She gave him a withering look. 'Shall we walk along the river? Where are we eating?'

'I've booked us in at a boat — we've got half an hour to get there, so we can have a lovely amble.'

'And what a gorgeous day for it. Love your red dress, by the way. It's all flouncy and fun.' Her mother touched the fabric. 'But your hair needs a cut — it's a bit untidy.'

'Left here,' muttered Holly, pushing her fingers through her hair self-consciously.

'Oh, and given what I've just said, leave it alone!'

'Sorry, Mum.' They walked past little, white houses, their gardens bursting with the pinks, reds, yellows and oranges of summer blooms.

Gorgeous. Just gorgeous, thought Holly trying to construct a descriptive sentence in her head so she could write it down later. 'Gorgeous,' she sighed. 'That's all I've got.'

* * *

Sitting down at the table on the open deck of the boat next to the bridge, Holly leaned her head back, looked at the sky and breathed in the warmth.

'What a beautiful day.' She put her rucksack down on the floor. 'And what a lovely place. Claudette, who owns Fambridge Books, suggested it.'

'She clearly has excellent taste.' Her mother was taking her glasses out of her handbag.

'Why don't you just get bifocals — varifocals — those, you know, multipurpose glasses, whatever they're called?' Holly's father got his phone out of his pocket and began to take some photos of the river and the people walking past on the bank.

'Because I do not want them, Gary.' She put her glasses on and began to study the menu, then put them on her head as if they were sunglasses and looked at Holly. 'So, when are you collecting all your DVDs and videos and things? Did your dad mention it?'

'You see, if you had those other types of glasses, you could seamlessly read the menu, then move your head up and speak to your daughter without the need for all that fuss.'

'There is no fuss. I like my glasses.' She held the menu up and pointed at it. 'I think you need to order some food quickly as you're clearly beginning to get hangry.'

'I'm not,' he muttered, taking it from her. 'I never get hangry.'

'I do miss you both,' Holly smiled. 'Despite all the grumpiness.'

'I'm not grumpy,' her parents chimed in unison, then they all began to giggle.

They ordered their food and chatted about Thailand and the festival, then today's gig and where it was, before moving on to Holly's new life.

'I can't wait to see your house, Hol.' Her mother took a sip of her water. 'It sounds lovely.'

Holly leaned forward. 'It is. Who'd have thought I'd get a place like that for what I can afford?'

'It's all about who you know.' Her father tapped the side of his nose conspiratorially. 'Ask no questions and you'll be told no lies.'

'I think it's just to do with tax, Dad.'

'Have you met anyone new? A new man? To replace Ed?' her mother cut in, her face momentarily creased into a frown as she mentioned his name.

'It's a bit soon, Mum.' Holly dug her thumbnail into the palm of her hand to stop herself sounding like a teenager.

'It's never too soon. You deserve to be happy.'

'I am happy. I'm concentrating on getting my career back on track.'

'You working for Fambridge.' Her father beamed proudly. 'When you told us about the job, we were so proud of you.'

Holly felt a flutter of pride. 'Well, I'm enjoying it.' She decided not to talk about the fact the office was falling apart or that she seemed to be the only full-time employee.

'Look, there are people paddleboarding.' Holly's mother pointed towards the river, where a group of eight appeared to be effortlessly gliding along the water. 'Oh, look — one of them is waving.' She began to wave back. 'That's very clever, isn't it? Paddling and steering and then waving at the same time.'

Holly glanced over briefly, then looked again, as she realized that the waving paddleboarder was Jack. The world switched to slow motion once more. Holly shook her head gently, trying to get it back up to regular speed, then accidentally knocked her cutlery on the floor.

'Is he shouting something?' Holly's father asked, which seemed to do the trick. The soft, cinematic, sepia glow around Jack, currently affecting Holly's vision, dissipated immediately. 'At us? Is he looking at us?'

Jack was turning his board so he could get closer.

Holly wanted to watch him sail towards them at the same time as wanting to not watch him and to go somewhere else. Because she knew what was coming.

'Who's that? Do you know him?' Her mother turned towards her, eyebrows raised knowingly.

'I'm not sure.'

'Not sure? He's heading right this way. Have you anything to tell me, Julie, before this handsome young man parks by the boat?'

'Don't be ridiculous, Gary,' her mother giggled. 'I wish! Paddleboards don't park anyway, do they?'

'You've still got it, darling. So, you shouldn't be surprised if I get a teeny bit jealous.'

'Oh, Gary.' She beamed then looked at her daughter again. 'You *do* know him. Who is he?'

'I work with him,' Holly admitted, just as Jack lost his balance and fell in.

'I think he's trying to impress you.'

'No, Mum! No, he's not,' Holly felt her face turn red. 'He's my boss's son. We work together. So, no. Just no!'

'Pity. He's a very handsome man.' They watched as he clambered back on to his board and sat on it, then he managed to move closer so they could hear him.

'Embarrassing!' he laughed, his skin glistening as the sun illuminated the drops of water on his body.

Holly bit her lip, then smiled in what she thought was a professional yet friendly way. 'No. I can't paddleboard.

You can't either, can you, Mum? Or you, Dad? So don't be embarrassed.' Then she heard herself laugh in what sounded like a high-pitched squeal.

Her mother raised her eyebrow at her again.

'This is Jack, who I work with,' Holly managed to say eventually. 'And these are my parents. But you probably worked that out.'

'Well, it's very nice to meet you, Jack,' said her father. 'Fairly unusual circumstances, but memorable.'

'I haven't done this since I moved back from Costa Rica. I'm rather out of practice. I seem to be falling over a lot, tripping over, toppling into water.' He smiled, his eyes crinkling attractively. 'I blame the weather. It's not the weather. Obviously.'

'Costa Rica, you say?' Holly's father picked his phone up again. 'There's an eighties music festival over there next May.' He began trying to search for something online. 'No, can't find it. Thought you could tell us about the venue.'

'I'd be happy to. Just let Holly know where it is and I'll get back to you.'

'Do you live here, Jack?' asked her mother.

'My mother does. I grew up here. I live in Rotherhithe at the moment. I decided to get on the river today as the weather's so glorious.'

'It is.' Holly nodded. 'Anyway.'

'Anyway.' Jack smiled. 'I'd best get back to the group. Enjoy the rest of your visit.' He began to paddle towards the middle of the river, then waved. 'Bye.'

'Bye,' they all shouted.

'He seems very, very nice,' said her mother eventually.

'He is. And we work together.' Holly watched as the waitress walked over to their table. 'Ah, good. Time to order food. I'm hungry.'

She began to compose a sentence in her mind for her blog as her parents placed their orders.

The light was stretching the days, illuminating the houses in Primrose Hill so they glowed warmly as the sun got lower, the trees heavy with leaves. Window boxes decorated the buildings so . . .

Try to remember that for when I get home and actually have a computer keyboard in front of me, she told herself.

* * *

Holly looked out of the window as the train pulled away from Kew Gardens, having said a noisy goodbye to her parents who "wanted to mix outdoors and indoors today", according to her mother, who also wanted to "research ideas for our smaller garden for when we downsize, and don't forget what I said about taking the rest of your books and stuff, Holly".

Wonder where they'll end up, she thought as the train trundled over the river. *Wonder where I'll end up eventually.*

Deciding to remind herself, once again, that she *could* actually write travel articles, she looked at her blog on her phone and randomly selected *New York*.

> *You know when you see images of a place so often that it becomes real to you — you feel like you know it, whether you've been or not.*
>
> *So, I have two words for you — New York.*
>
> *There, I've said it. Now, what do you see?*
>
> *I see the lights of the skyscrapers illuminating the sky as the car emerges from the dark tunnel. I hear myself gasp because, even though this is an image I have seen so many times, I am surprised by the feeling that I am meeting an old and treasured friend for the very first time.*
>
> *And it makes me want to cry with happiness.*
>
> *Hello, I want to say. Hello, Manhattan. Good evening, Annie Hall. Hi there, Moonstruck. How are you doing, Harry? How's Sally?*

Holly put her phone away, frustrated. She felt the same way about London. But the words just hung in the air between her imagination and her Word document.

Stop reading what you have already written and start writing, her inner voice stated assertively. *Contact some of the people who used to ask you to write for them and see if they want more.*

I could earn extra money in a café or a bar, she thought. *Better use of my time. Because what if they just want the stuff about when Ed used to be there? When we used to post about our adventures and I wrote about them?*

Don't look, she urged herself. *Don't pick up your phone and look*.

But she didn't have to. A wave of images flew into her mind as if she were rifling through an album of photographs. A cookery course in Vietnam, Ed riding bareback in Texas, them both giggling in a kayak in southern Spain. Snippets of films posted on to social media from a train, a pedalo, a café, a mountain.

The train eased to a stop and the doors opened. Holly got up without thinking and strode on to the platform. She had no idea where she was until she saw the sign. *Gloucester Road*, it said. All she knew was that if she was lost, she'd make her thoughts useful by focusing on finding her way home instead of fixating on the past.

And when she got home, she put on *Notting Hill* for a while, then climbed wearily into bed followed by a noisy Isabella, who spent fifteen minutes purring loudly into her ear before falling asleep.

CHAPTER SEVEN

Holly woke to silence. There was no purring next to her ear or mournful meowing from the end of the bed. Moving her feet to see if they were attacked from over the duvet elicited no response whatsoever.

'Isabella?' she called sleepily. 'Isabella?' Then she looked at the clock in case she'd slept in.

'Eight o'clock! Eight o'clock? Oh, what?' Almost falling out of bed in a panic, Holly hurried to the bathroom and had a short, sharp shower to wake herself up, then grabbed the first dress that fell on to the floor while she was rifling through the wardrobe and put it on. Then she rushed to the kitchen, took the box of cat food out of the cupboard, filled Isabella's bowl and shook it loudly to try to get her attention. Hurriedly putting her make-up on, Holly then brushed her hair, cleaned her teeth and grabbed her bag.

'Isabella?' she shouted again to the silent house, then began to check in all the cupboards, wardrobes and behind the furniture. 'I'm late. I'm going to be late. I can't be late. Isabella, where are you?'

But as Holly swept around the rooms, a sick feeling in her stomach began to overwhelm her. Since their very first day together, Isabella had been a constant presence every morning.

Even over the long days of the previous three summers, the cat would never go out before she had eaten. She'd often follow Holly around the garden each day, and used to watch for her when she returned from her trips into the village. 'Please don't be lost,' she said softly. 'Just please don't. I've only started letting you out recently. I should have kept you in for ever . . .'

Opening the patio doors a crack, she squeezed out and closed them behind her in case the cat had been hiding very cleverly and was preparing to launch herself into the garden. She stood for a moment and looked around, then started calling, shaking the box of food as she did. 'Isabella? Isabella?' Holly shook the box again. 'Isabella! I've got to go to work!'

She waited for a second. And then she heard it. A loud meowing wail coming from somewhere in the vicinity of her garden.

'Oh, thank goodness.' She sighed, relieved.

Following the noise, Holly hurried to the bottom of the garden, grabbed a plant pot and stood on it, trying to see over the high bushes that obscured the view. She could make out a large, red-brick building at the far end of a concreted yard. It stretched almost two houses' width on either side. A window on the bottom floor was open, but only very slightly. 'Isabella!' shouted Holly. A plaintive meow came from inside. 'I'll come and get you.' Holly jumped down from the pot, ran through the house, where she picked up her bag and phone, and almost cantered out of her front door into the street.

Opening Google Maps on her phone, she tried to get an idea of where she needed to go, but the internet signal was so poor she couldn't get a connection. 'Oh, I'm late and my cat is trapped!' she shouted into the air.

'Trapped where?' Caleb was dragging a bright-yellow shopping trolley on to the pavement from his doorway. 'Don't look at me like that — this is the best way to collect my very rare and very delicate records from the delivery place down the road. No one would expect to find treasures like that in this, would they. And you're in no position to comment, anyway. You're dressed in yellow, too.'

84

Holly glanced down at her dress. 'Oh. I hadn't really noticed.' And then she looked back up at him. 'I hadn't noticed the colour of your shopping trolley either. I have no comment to make. I'm under pressure. My cat is gone.' She could feel her voice beginning to wobble slightly, so she bit her lip and stared into the space above Caleb's head in order to calm herself down.

'How long for?' Caleb seemed to be trying to sound concerned but it was difficult to read his expression, given his beard, sunglasses and hat.

'I don't know. I went out yesterday — and the cat flap . . . I forgot to lock it before I went to sleep and—'

'I'm sure she'll come back. She's a cat.' He turned and began to walk towards the road.

Holly walked behind him. 'I know where she is! In that big, red-brick building on the other side of the fence. I can hear her.'

Caleb slowed down a little. 'That? It's always locked up,' he said without looking back.

'There's a window open a little bit on the ground floor.'

Caleb stopped and turned around. 'If you turn left next to my house, there is a very narrow lane that leads to the other side of that building. I think there's a notice with the number of the company that looks after it if you need someone to get her out for you.'

'Oh, thank you!' Holly threw her arms around him.

'Wasn't expecting that,' he muttered flatly.

Holly stepped back. 'Sorry. I forget that not everyone is as tactile as me.'

'Don't tell anyone else about that lane.' He turned around again and began to drag the trolley behind him. 'I don't want people using it, for obvious reasons. It's our secret,' he shouted just before he disappeared around the corner.

'Right you are.' Holly hurried down the path. It wasn't really a lane, just a very narrow gap between gardens, and at one point she had to turn sideways to edge around a wild rose draped over the fence from Caleb's garden. Eventually, she squeezed between the red-brick building and another one . . . and found herself looking at Farthing Street.

Momentarily confused, she glanced back. *How is this here?* she thought. *All this time it was behind my house? It doesn't make any sense.*

'Have you come back for the green dress?' Bev was putting out some clothes rails at the front of her shop. 'Love the yellow, by the way. But there's—'

'I've come to rescue my cat,' Holly blurted out. 'She's in the Bollington?' Her voice rose at the end as if she was asking a question.

'How did she get in there?'

'No idea.' Holly pushed the front door, just in case it would open, then stepped back.

Viktor bellowed over. 'Is everything all right, my dear?'

'Her cat is stuck inside,' shouted Bev in response.

'Ah, I see.' He walked over and stood next to her. 'How are you going to get it out?'

'There must be the number of a keyholder around somewhere. Do *you* know who it is?' She looked at him hopefully.

Viktor walked over to the dry-cleaner's and stuck his head in the doorway. 'Do you know who has the keys for that old building?' he called. 'Holly's cat is stuck inside.'

'Oh dear!' Marialena's voice grew louder as she joined him outside. She was holding a skirt in one hand and a coat hanger in the other one. 'Your poor kitty. She must be so frightened. I think there's a sticker with a number on the door somewhere.'

The sight of Viktor in his apron and Marialena with the skirt reminded Holly she was going to be late for work, so she sent a message to Claudette and Jack. *Many apologies. I'm going to be a bit late today. My cat has got stuck in an empty building near to my house.* Hastily sending it, she scanned the door, trying to find the number, with Bev trying to help.

'Can't see it anywhere,' Bev muttered, peering at it. 'Hang on, my glasses might help.' She put her hand in her pocket, pulled them out and put them on. 'Still no.'

Holly's phone buzzed. *Oh, your poor cat. I hope you get her out of that place soon. And don't worry about work, Holly. It's Sunday. Claudette*

Holly almost laughed. And then her phone buzzed again. *It's Sunday. Jack*

And then, *Do you need some help? I'm still in Richmond, but if you need me, I can jump on the Tube. Jack*

Holly read that message twice. A surge of what felt like happy butterflies flittered around her stomach for a moment. She put her hand on it as if it would stop them. She hadn't felt like that since Ed had caught her eye at the end-of-term disco.

No, she said to herself sternly. *No!* A single butterfly continued to dance. *He is my workmate. He is my workmate*, she repeated to herself in her head. *He must not make me feel like this.* The butterfly stopped. She imagined it sidling away, embarrassed by its misplaced enthusiasm.

It's Sunday?! she began to type a reply. *Silly me! Thank you for your offer, but I've got some friends here who are helping.* She pressed send then responded to Claudette. *Oh dear! I overslept and got the days mixed up! Have a lovely weekend.*

'It's Sunday.' She looked up at Bev. 'I thought it was Monday. Got up in a panic, rushed out of the house.'

'Ah, that would explain it,' Bev said gently. 'Your lovely yellow dress is on back to front and inside out.'

Holly looked down, and then up. 'Oh dear.'

Viktor waved at her. 'I've found the number. Look!' He pointed at a tiny white note stuck to the left of the doorway, next to a sticker advertising a club night at a nearby bar.

'Oh, thank you!' Holly hurriedly called the number. 'Hello? I need to get access to the Bollington. My cat has somehow got inside and can't get out . . .' She looked up at Bev and Viktor. 'They've just put me on hold.' She sighed.

'When you've spoken to them, come over to the café for a coffee.' Viktor's booming voice got slightly quieter. 'And you can put your dress on the right way round.'

* * *

Sitting down at a table after dressing herself properly in the café bathroom, a cup of steaming hot chocolate was placed in front of her, topped with marshmallows, a chocolate flake and some sprinkles.

'Oh.' Holly looked up at Paulo. 'I think this is someone else's order.'

'No, it's for medicine. A latte isn't good enough for this kind of stress. I mean, you should have seen yourself when you were standing over by that building with the wrong-way-round dress and the odd shoes.'

Holly looked down at her one yellow sandal and one blue sandal, then put her arms on the table and allowed her face to crumple into them. 'Oh . . . no!'

He nudged the hot chocolate closer to her. 'You see. We know what you need. When will they come and open the building?'

'They said it would be any time within one and two hours, so I'll just have to wait.'

'Your little kitty will probably just be having a nap.' Marialena walked past holding a takeaway cup and a pastry. She waved it at them. 'Breakfast! My boss says I have to open on Sundays as the week is so bad for business at the moment. No time for food shopping!' She went back inside the dry-cleaner's.

Paulo went to serve another customer and Holly swirled the flake around in the drink before taking a bite of it. Her phone buzzed again.

Are you sure? I had a cat called Tabitha once and I cried for three days when I thought she was lost. I was seventeen. She came back. But I understand how you must be feeling. Jack

Holly read the message and wanted to cry. *How lovely*, she thought. *How thoughtful.* Her hand hovered over the phone. *Careful*, she warned herself, pondering for a moment so she could send an appropriately worded "you are my work colleague and I appreciate your concern" kind of text.

It's okay. I'm being looked after. Thank you, though. She typed the message and pressed send, then repeated the mantra *work and personal life separate* over and over again in her head until Viktor walked past. 'How's the hot chocolate?'

Holly smiled and took a sip. 'Delicious!' The drink was going down very quickly, and in a couple of minutes, she'd finished it.

A white van pulled up. *Keith's Keys — we'll let you in, we'll let you out, as long as it belongs to you, of course* was written on the side in big green letters.

'I think the cavalry has arrived,' commented Paulo.

'That was quick.' Holly stood up, and he leaned forward, handing her a paper serviette.

'Traces of hot chocolate around the mouth,' he smiled. 'You are doing everything in a hurry today, Holly.'

'Oh God.' She accepted the serviette, cleaned her face and followed the man she assumed was Keith over to the Bollington.

'Hello,' she said. 'I'm Holly Merriweather. It's my cat that's stuck in there.'

'How did it get in?' He looked surprised. 'I checked it the other day and it was all locked up.'

'I think a window was open — I can see it from my garden.'

Keith looked irritated. 'I keep telling the owner to double-check if they feel the urge to go in.'

'Who?' Holly was looking at the keys he was holding in his hand, which he seemed in no hurry to use.

'The owner of the building who likes to keep their identity secret, thank you very much.' He glanced at Holly's feet. 'You've got odd shoes on.'

'I've been rushing around this morning since I realized where my cat was trapped.'

'Bought two pairs of the same type in different colours? My partner, Rosita, does that. She's taken over my shed with all her shoes. Says it saves money in the long run.'

'A woman after my own heart.'

'Yes. Well.' He looked at the floor and grinned. 'She's got mine. Otherwise, I wouldn't put up with that shoe mountain. Right.' He waved a key at her. 'Let's get in, shall we?' He put the key in the door, which opened slightly, then he pressed a code into an app on his phone. 'Security alarm. How your cat didn't set that off, I'll never know.' Pushing the door open, he lowered his voice. 'The owner has told me that you must keep what you see to yourself.'

Holly's eyes widened. 'What kind of place is this?'

Keith looked away. 'A sad one, if I'm going to be honest, but what can you do?' He walked inside and beckoned her in. 'Right — off you go.' He closed the door firmly behind them.

'Isabella!' shouted Holly. 'Isabella!' They were standing in what looked like a reception area, with an old-fashioned till on a desk in front of them, next to a cloakroom. Behind that a wide doorway opened into a very dark, very large room. Holly walked through to it. 'She was somewhere at the back, I think.'

'Dressing rooms,' mumbled Keith.

A loud, wailing meow echoed from close to what Holly assumed was the stage. 'Can you turn the lights on?' Holly edged forward and bumped into a chair. 'I can't see anything.'

'You'll be all right,' Keith shouted from the foyer.

'Isabella?' Holly felt her way around a table. 'How can this place be so dark?'

'Blackout blinds,' responded Keith.

Isabella meowed again, then began to chatter more loudly.

'Getting closer, aren't you?' Holly stepped forward and tripped over the leg of another chair. 'Ow! Please turn the lights on.'

'Okay, but remember what I said before.'

'I won't say anything.' Holly sighed irritably. 'Isabella!' She picked up her cat as she rubbed against her at the same time as the room was suddenly flooded with light. 'You silly thing. Are you all right?' She nuzzled against her head as the cat purred loudly. 'Right, best get out.'

But as she began to move, she couldn't help but start to notice her surroundings. One of the walls was decorated with what looked like a mural of people in bright clothes, dancing together. Several round tables and chairs stood next to the bar, and a small wooden platform in front of a stage was set up as if a band had been rehearsing on it recently. There was a mic, two guitars, a keyboard and a drum kit. She also noticed that the bar seemed to be fully stocked.

'I thought this place wasn't used,' she said to Keith.

'It's not,' he shouted. 'Now, I'm glad you've got your cat. Cute little thing, isn't she? My son has a massive Bengal called Phil . . . but we've got to go.'

Holly hurried out towards him, and as soon as she stepped into the foyer, he switched the lights off. 'Thanks for coming out,' she said, then knocked a pile of flyers off the desk. She picked them up with one hand while holding a still-purring Isabella with the other. They were advertising a gig by the Lights in 1981.

'Oh,' she murmured, surprised, and instinctively put one in her pocket.

'The owner told me to expedite the request. He . . . or she or — I mean, they told me to get a move on in other words. And remember not to tell anyone about what you've seen.'

'Has anyone been practising in here? Is it opening soon?'

'No and no.' Keith ushered Holly and Isabella out and closed the door behind them. 'See what I mean about sad, though?'

'It feels sort of left behind. Or stuck somehow.' Holly pulled Isabella closer to her.

'Like I said, sad.' Keith locked the door, set the alarm and began to walk back to the van. 'Have a nice day now.'

'Thank you again,' called Holly.

Keith had opened the doors at the back of his van and was rummaging around for something. In the process, he knocked over a guitar, which twanged melodically. 'It belongs to my brother,' Keith said when he saw her still watching him. 'He happens to be in a band and I drive him to gigs sometimes.' He pointed at her sternly. 'He is not the person who owns the Bollington. Like I said, forget everything you saw.'

She nodded as Keith closed the doors and got into the van. Then she hurried back round to the hidden lane so Isabella couldn't escape again, got her in the front door and sank down on her sofa, trying to make sense of what she'd just seen.

CHAPTER EIGHT

'I'm telling you, but you can't tell anyone else.' Holly had taken the Tube to Embankment and was on her way to a meeting, or "catch-up", with Jack at a café on the South Bank, having given herself a "he is just an attractive man you happen to work with so get a grip" pep talk while brushing her hair the next morning.

'You can't say that to me. I've got some kind of syndrome about keeping secrets.' Melissa's voice was low. 'I'm also on the train stuck at Clapham Junction and surrounded by people. How am I supposed to react?'

'What syndrome?' Holly paused for a moment on the bridge and stared at the river, already busy with traffic. 'I'm always surprised that the Shard looks so close and then I remember the river has bends in it.'

'Is that what you were going to tell me?' Melissa was beginning to sound irritated. 'And I don't actually have a syndrome. I'm just bad at keeping secrets. I'm like a leaky tap.'

'Sorry. Got distracted.' Holly carried on walking. 'I went inside the Bollington yesterday.' The steps leading to the Southbank Centre were full of people walking towards her. 'Where's everyone going?'

'What?'

'Again. Distracted.'

'Do you mean that old venue?'

'Isabella had got stuck inside and I had to get a man with a key to let me in. He said I wasn't to tell anyone what I'd seen. But I have to tell someone, and I'm meeting Jack for a "catch-up", as he called it, and I really don't want to tell him.'

'I think you can breathe now,' Melissa said. 'Go on.'

'It was set up for a gig. But there are no gigs. There was a bar, and flyers, and it looked like a sort of sad museum that nobody's allowed to visit.' Holly was standing in front of the café now. She saw that Jack was already sitting at a table inside working on his laptop. He scratched his head absent-mindedly. Holly's stomach fluttered pleasantly, although it was completely unwanted.

'Oh no,' she muttered.

'Are you all right? The train's moving again, so I'll lose signal in a minute. Happens every time I pass through Vauxhall.'

'Flyers! I picked one up and now I've forgotten where I put it.'

'I sense a story, Holly.'

'But I'm not supposed to tell anyone about it.' She glanced at Jack again. 'If there was something, it would be great publicity for the guidebooks, wouldn't it? And it could help the traders in Farthing Street.'

'Exactly. Got to go. But, before I forget, you're coming out with me and a work colleague. He's very nice. You need to practise speaking to attractive men. We need you out in the wild again. I'll sort out a date. Speak soon!'

'What?' Holly looked at the handset. 'I don't want to.' She pushed the door open. 'And I'm *really* not supposed to tell anyone about the Bollington,' she said to the silent phone before putting it in her bag. 'Hi.' She waved at Jack 'Want a coffee?'

'No, thanks.' He stood up to greet her. 'I've got one already. And it's on me. It is a business meeting, after all.' He nodded at his table. 'Take a seat. What would you like?'

'Latte, please. Oat milk or soya.' Holly sat down and looked out of the window. Maybe she should leave the Bollington well alone? Whoever owned it clearly didn't want anyone around. So, that was best. Yes. That was definitely best.

'Here.' Jack put the drink in front of her. 'You do have a very expressive face. You look worried. Are you all right?'

'Oh, yes,' lied Holly. 'Thanks for the coffee.'

He smiled, and for a fleeting moment their eyes met. Then they both looked away at the same time. Jack began to study something on his laptop and Holly started to take hers out of her case.

'Why did you want to meet here rather than the office?' A pen had got stuck in the lining of the case and she was concentrating very hard on that.

'There's another leak.' Jack was staring intently at a notepad he had put next to his drink.

'Oh dear.' Holly glanced at him. 'The office is lovely, but . . .'

'In need of some TLC. Yes.' He looked at her again, his face serious. 'Can I be honest with you?'

Holly shifted in her seat. *This doesn't sound good.* Her inner voice sounded unusually wary.

'The office block is owned by a company owned by an old friend of my parents. We've been there for years and pay mates' rates rent, basically. We've gradually leased less and less space as the company shrank and were about to go, until we found the guidebook proofs.'

'Ahhh.'

'But we think they want to sell and are doing the bare minimum to maintain it.'

'Okay.'

'And . . . I think you may have realized that we're not on top of things business-wise.'

Holly began to wonder if she should start looking for a new job.

'Please don't worry.'

'I'm not worried,' she said too quickly.

He smiled again, kindly. 'Your face is sort of saying that you are.'

Holly shrugged. 'I really must do something about that.'

Jack leaned closer. 'No, don't do that. It's very helpful.'

'I'd never be able to play poker or anything like that, would I? Or commit a crime.' She laughed, then realized what she'd said. 'Not that I'm thinking of committing a crime.'

Someone cleared a couple of plates from the table next to them just as a little girl started to giggle in the corner.

'Not ideal for a business meeting, but as it's last-minute,' Jack sighed, then nodded. 'And to work — right — I've found someone for you to interview. They've lived above the bookshop they own since just before my father wrote about the building. It's beautiful. Near Angel. And every other thing around them has changed. Another old friend of the family. Mum asked them. I've sent you their email address and I've told them you'd be in touch.'

'Oh, brilliant!' Holly began to feel excited again. 'Something to write about. We can use it to get some publicity — I'll speak to Melissa.'

'No.' Jack put his hand up to stop her. 'We aren't ready for that yet. Just gather the interviews. That's the stage we're at.'

An image of the dilapidated office with only three people in it floated into her mind. 'But it's a crowded market now, and this is such a lovely project. People need to know Fambridge Books is doing this.' She could hear her voice begin to rise in frustration.

'As I said, we aren't ready.' He looked at his computer. 'It's more complicated than you think.'

'Right, well.' Holly felt her enthusiasm ebb away. 'How are the other members of the team doing?' she asked, trying to sound professional.

'The team is a good way of putting it. I'm not sure we are what you were expecting.'

A tiny Paddington Bear was flung into the air and landed dangerously close to Holly's latte. 'I genuinely wasn't expecting that,' she laughed, picking it up and returning it to the little girl in the corner who was now in floods of tears. 'After his little trip, he decided he missed you, so he asked me to bring him back.' Holly crouched down. 'He wants you to look after him.'

The little girl stared at her for a moment, then smiled shyly.

'What do you say, Mary?' her mother whispered. 'We say thank you, don't we?'

'Thank you,' the little girl squeaked.

Holly sat down opposite Jack again. 'I've seen some things on my travels, but that's the first flying bear.'

'Would you like another latte to help you with the shock?' Jack was already standing up. 'Then we can compare where we are research-wise?'

'Yes, thanks.' Holly checked through her notes. *Just don't look directly into his eyes*, she reminded herself.

* * *

On the way home, Holly decided to visit Farthing Street. The green dress in Bev's shop was calling to her, and she really enjoyed sitting outside the café watching the world go by, albeit very quietly.

'And how is Holly today?' Viktor bellowed as Holly moved her chair slightly so the sunshine warmed her face. 'And your Isabella? She is over the shock of being locked in there?' He pointed at the Bollington.

'Oh, she's fine. It's just another adventure for her.' She smiled up at him. 'Can I have a jasmine tea?'

'Of course.' He turned to go, then leaned in closer. 'What was in there?' he asked in a loud stage whisper.

'Oh, nothing really. Of note,' Holly lied. 'It's a pity, though, isn't it, that a lovely building like that would just stay unused and unloved?'

'Forgotten,' sighed Viktor. Holly didn't respond because she'd already realized it was anything but forgotten. By someone, at least.

Caleb was closing up his shop while Mabel jumped around him, barking. 'She is still very energetic.' Marialena was standing in the doorway of the dry-cleaner's. 'It's so hot in there today,' she complained, holding a tiny electric fan in front of her face. 'Hardly anyone has come in all afternoon.'

'Business will pick up,' mumbled Caleb.

'I hope so.' She walked back inside and he came and sat at a table next to Holly. 'Your cat was staring into my kitchen window so I assume you got her back,' he said. 'The usual, please.' He waved at Viktor to get his attention.

'Yes, thanks for the tip about the lane.' Holly took a sip of her tea.

He tapped his nose with his finger. 'Like I say, keep it to yourself.'

'I won't say a word.' Holly put her cup on the table. 'What a lovely building the Bollington is.'

'Never really thought about it.' Caleb picked Mabel up and put her on his lap. 'It's been like that ever since I can remember.'

'It's owned by someone who likes to keep it looking nice — on the outside, at least.' Holly was trying not to say anything about what she'd seen. 'I really thought you might know something about it as you have a record shop.'

Could the mystery owner be somebody around here? she wondered, just as Bev walked past them carrying a guitar. 'Off to play a few tunes at the old people's home.'

'Oh, sounds lovely,' said Holly.

Caleb leaned back. 'As I've already told you, I don't know anything about that building. It's no big deal, is it? People play music everywhere — pubs, cafés, in the streets, on stages, in theatres.' He nodded at Bev's back as she disappeared around the corner. 'Old people's homes . . . venues come and go. That's life.'

Paulo placed his espresso on the table and rubbed Mabel's ears, then walked back into the café.

'More people need to come to Farthing Street,' Holly said firmly.

'Obviously. But they aren't.'

'I want to help.'

Caleb grunted but couldn't seem to help giving her a small smile. 'It may be all right as it is, Holly Merriweather. But it's a very kind thought.'

CHAPTER NINE

The following Thursday, Holly left her house and purpose-fully walked to Chalk Farm Tube station on her way to meet the owner of the independent bookshop who Jack had asked her to talk to. Her laptop was packed in her rucksack, along with her phone and some ideas she'd noted in the new pink-and-green notebook with *Today is YOUR time to shine, Gorgeous!* written in curling, silver lettering along the top.

Even though it was only 9 a.m., it was already hot and sticky. Holly stopped at the coffee vendor on the railway bridge, bought herself an iced tea, then strode towards the road with a spring in her step, because today was the day she was going to do her first interview in almost four years.

Getting on to the first train that arrived, then realiz-ing she was on the wrong line, she got off at Camden and spent nearly ten minutes in front of the map, trying to work out which of the two platforms she needed. By the time she alighted at Angel, she could feel a sliver of sweat sliding down her back, and her hair, beautifully styled and dried that morning, was already limp and straggly.

Checking the map on her phone, she crossed the road, following it up past a shopping centre, then rows of smart Georgian and Victorian townhouses as the street became wider and quieter. She paused for a moment at the entrance to a pretty square, with a small fenced garden in the middle, to get her bearings. 'Where am I?' she mumbled, looking at the map again. 'Right, yes, Gibson Square — so don't go down there, Holly. Turn left.'

Crossing the road again, she came to a halt outside a florist, then stepped back and scanned the street. 'Aha!' she said loudly, as a tortoiseshell cat sitting next to a lamppost watched her disinterestedly. 'There it is.' She directed the comment to the cat, who promptly stood up and sauntered off.

Barney's Books stood between a betting shop and a veterinary practice, its window display a riot of brightly coloured children's books with a stencil of a unicorn jumping over a snow-covered mountain as a frame. Holly pushed the door open and an old-fashioned bell rang, sending a satisfying shiver down her spine.

A tall man with long dreadlocks looked up from behind the counter.

'Barney?'

'Yes, that's me.' He raised an eyebrow. 'Are you the Holly who messaged me about an interview?'

'Yes, I am.' She shook his hand and he smiled.

'I was expecting someone in green with red, glossy hair and shiny earrings. Like Christmas. Because of your name. But you look like summer.'

Holly touched her hair absentmindedly 'Oh. No. I was born in April. My parents named me after Holly Golightly from *Breakfast at Tiffany's*. Not sure she's the best role model, though.'

'I expect they were thinking of Audrey Hepburn,' he said kindly. 'Would you like a cup of tea?'

'No, thanks. But I'd love some water. It's sweltering out there and it's only ten o'clock.'

'It's going to be one of those hot city days.' Barney beckoned her into a room behind the counter. 'Let's settle in here,' he said as she followed him in. 'That way, I can still hear when anyone comes in.'

'Thank you for allowing me to interview you.' Holly sat down opposite him.

'Oh, anything for Claudette and Jack.' He smiled at her. 'I've known that family a long time.'

'They seem very nice.'

'They are.' He leaned towards her and lowered his voice. 'Although I'm surprised at this new endeavour. Last I heard they were selling up. Another company was buying the rights to the brand for the future, they were going to get a cut, and then they were leaving the rest of it behind. Moving on. I sort of feel Seth would have wanted that for them after eight years.'

'Ah . . . well, they seem to have had a change of heart.'

Barney stood up and took a bottle of water from a fridge in the corner, handing it to her. 'This "then" and "now" thing's catching on.' He sat down. 'I heard that someone else is doing it about . . . wait a minute—' he looked thoughtful — 'old sports grounds. What they represent, what they are now. I've got a small publishing company myself, although we mainly only do local history, so I keep up with what's going on.'

'Oh?' Holly took a swig of her drink. 'Do you know the name of the company doing the sports books? I need to tell them back at the office.'

'No, sorry. But if I do remember, I'll let you all know. But—' he leaned forward again — 'I'm not sure their hearts are in this, Claudette and Jack. I think they think they're helping each other, but they aren't. I think they are keeping each other stuck.'

'Ah.' Holly didn't know what to say.

'That is reading between the lines, though. They've not actually said it out loud to me. As such. Just snippets.'

'I see.'

'Still. I thought money-wise they were okay, but now I'm not so sure. I can't work out whether this is a proper business enterprise or a sort of hobby . . . I hope they're not throwing all their cash at it, anyway.'

'Oh. Well, it's more than a hobby to me,' Holly said quietly, feeling an anxious knot in her stomach again.

'But like I say, I've known them a long, long time. I worry about them. And I probably shouldn't have said any of that.' He looked at her apologetically. 'Anyway, what do you want to know?'

Holly rummaged in her rucksack and took out her pad and her phone. 'Do you mind if I record this and take notes?'

'Not at all.' Barney beamed.

Holly put the phone on the table between them and tapped the record button. 'So, you've been here a long time?'

'Oh yes. Since 1979. My parents bought the shop and the flat above it, and I've been here ever since.'

'A lot must have changed since then in this street?'

'Ah, yes. It wasn't at all gentrified then. They just sat tight and it all sort of grew. I tell you what, I'll get my photograph albums out and we can go through them so you can see for yourself.'

'Wonderful!' Holly managed not to clap her hands excitedly. She just smiled and watched Barney open a door at the back of the room.

'I'll just go upstairs to get them. I'll be back in a minute. If you hear the bell, just go out on to the shop floor and say hello.'

Holly switched off the record button, then put her hand in her rucksack to find some mints. But instead of the sweets, she pulled out a rolled-up piece of paper and smoothed it out.

It was the flyer from the Bollington.

'Oh! There you are,' she said.

'Who?' Barney backed into the room carrying a pile of albums and put them down on the table.

'It's a flyer from somewhere. I picked it up accidentally, then lost it.'

Barney glanced at it. 'The Lights! Well, I never. I was at their last gig at the Bollington in, what was it, 1987 or 1988?' He laughed. 'There was a terrible fight. It was the last performance they did. Pity, though.' He picked the flyer up.

'This is for 1981. Early days.' He looked wistful. 'What are you doing carrying around an old flyer from 1981?'

'I found it somewhere.' Holly sat on her hands, as if that would stop her telling him what she'd seen. Barney handed it back to her, so she folded it away and filed it in her purse.

'You're going to love this.' He opened a glossy, green album and pointed at a photograph on the first page. 'There is Seth Fambridge with my father outside the bookshop.'

'So, there you are, Seth,' she murmured. 'I've only seen the photo on the back of all of his books.' The two men were laughing at whoever was taking the picture, and Seth was holding a book in his hand.

'He'd brought his first book over and handed it to my father in person. He was a real force of nature, was Seth.'

Holly studied it closely. She wanted to put her arm into the photograph and shake his hand so she could tell him how his books had changed her life.

'No wonder Jack cleared off to Central America. Wanted to be his own person. Not just be in the shadow of his dad.' The doorbell jingled at the front of the shop. 'Have a browse.' Barney stood up. 'I'll be back in a minute and we'll do the interview properly.'

Holly picked up the album and began to flick through the pages, the past slowly coming to life before her eyes.

* * *

Leaving the shop at the end of the interview, Holly was practically skipping as she formulated in her mind what she would write and how it could help publicize the new books. Whenever Barney's words about Fambridge Books being a "hobby" threatened to encroach, she hummed "Always Look on the Bright Side of Life". Ducking into a coffee shop to escape the midday heat, she began to put her notes together, then uploaded the interview and began to transcribe it. Her fingers felt like they were flying over the keyboard, and in her head "The Typewriter Song" played in the background, so that when she'd finished writing, she pressed the last key dramatically, then closed her laptop and smiled.

'Right,' she said to herself as she walked out on to the street. The sun was now comfortably warm, the buildings bright and pedestrians smiling as they strode past, clearly their moods uplifted by a perfect London summer's day. Her excitement had turned to restlessness, and when she got to the Tube station, she checked the map and decided that she'd carry on writing under a tree on Parliament Hill and watch the sun begin to set over the city.

Alighting at Gospel Oak, she checked the messages on her phone. There was one from her father.

> *I've found you someone to talk to from an old music venue that's something else. He was at the gig in Richmond and we chatted. Mentioned what you're doing. Not sure if it was in one of those books already or not, but it's worth a go. Finally rang me back today! Sent you an email. Love Dad xx*

'Ooooh,' she squealed, checking her emails, then scrolling through to the one sent by her father. 'Thank you, Dad. That is perfect.'

Underneath it was a message from Jack.

How did it go with Barney?

Very, very well. I'm about to celebrate by sitting under a tree on Parliament Hill and enjoying the view — while working, of course!

She pressed send, then walked happily on to Hampstead Heath, which was full of people sunbathing, playing ball games, walking dogs, chatting, laughing. It felt like the whole of the city was there. And she loved it.

Identifying a suitable spot, Holly sat down under a tree and got out her laptop. She leaned back and stared at the view for a few minutes, the old and the new of London spread out in front of her like a long landscape postcard. She imagined the names of the buildings hanging in the air above them as if they were in a guidebook — the Shard, the London Eye, Westminster Abbey. Then her mind drifted as she wondered what font would look most effective suspended in the sky.

Two women jogged along the path. A child began to laugh. A dog barked. And Holly closed her eyes, letting the evening sun warm her face for a moment.

Then, taking a glug of water, she wiggled her fingers dramatically above the keyboard, allowing them to hover for a moment. 'Now, edit!' she said out loud, before focusing her mind, opening the first document and beginning to work.

'Holly!' She heard her name and looked up, confused. 'Of all the places in all the world, fancy bumping into you on Parliament Hill.' Jack was walking over from the path, smiling. 'Is this your office for the evening?' He pointed at her laptop.

'Oh . . . hello.' Holly felt the familiar butterflies and moved her hand over her stomach as her way of telling them to calm down.

'I've been following Dad's trail in Highgate and decided to cut across the Heath before I grabbed the Tube home.' He sat down next to her. 'And when you told me you were here, I thought I'd see if I could spot you and say hi. Don't mind if I join you, do you?'

'Of course not. This particular office is quite spacious.' She grinned. 'But it does get very busy, so you're right to arrive after the crowds have gone.'

'I'm just passing through.' He put his rucksack down next to him and leaned back against a tree. 'I've been out of the country for so long that I feel like I'm catching up with all the friends and all the years I've missed. I'm quite the social butterfly at the moment.'

Holly folded up her laptop and put it on the ground. 'This is just stunning, isn't it?'

'I love these long summer days. I just want them to go on for ever.'

'Me too.'

The sound of drums punctured the air for a few beats.

'There's a gig at Kenwood House, I think.' Jack got out his phone as a few chords from an electric guitar floated across the Heath. 'It's an eighties bonanza, it says here.'

'I'm surprised my parents aren't there.'

'Maybe they are.'

'Oh!' She turned to him, suddenly animated. 'I've just interviewed Barney and have almost written it all up. And,' she beamed, 'my father messaged me earlier. He was speaking to someone at the gig they went to in Richmond. You remember when you met them?'

'When I fell off my paddleboard? Oh yes, I remember.'

'Well, this person was the manager of a pub in Wandsworth that was a well-known music venue. It's now a community centre. And I've checked — your father wrote about it. One of the things it offers is free music lessons for children who can't afford to pay for them. And he's in charge.' Holly stopped talking, realizing she hadn't taken a breath.

'Wow!' Jack grinned at her. 'Not only are *you* proactive, but your parents are, too.'

'Yes, they are.' Holly said proudly. 'Anyway, he lives in Richmond now, but he's happy to do an interview in Wandsworth. So, we need to organize it.'

'We? I presume you mean the royal "we"?'

'Oh no, I mean you and me. Me because my dad will be there, because he's a music nerd, and you because this man is fan of the *London: How I See It* guidebooks and wants to meet you.'

'Ah, a fan of my father's?' Jack stared into the distance. 'Well, thank you to your dad and to you,' he said eventually. 'Just let me know when it is and I'll be there.'

'Great.' Holly glanced at him, confused. *He should be a bit more enthusiastic*, she thought. But before she could say anything else, a familiar song swept across the Heath.

'What's that?' She glanced above her as if she could see the notes in the sky.

'Um.' Jack looked thoughtful for a moment. 'I know — wait a second — I know it. It's Aswad. "Don't Turn Around".'

Holly closed her eyes. 'How perfect is this?' she said quietly. 'It makes me want to dance.'

'My legs have gone to sleep.' Jack began to massage them.

Holly lay on her back. 'Have you tried lying down dancing, like in *Gregory's Girl*?'

'What's that?' Jack looked down at her. Holly resisted the urge to put her arms up and pull him towards her by waving them around in time to the music.

'The film. Where they lie in the park under a tree and dance to music they can't hear. Unlike today.'

'Oh yes. I think I have seen that.' Jack laid down next to her and began to move his arms and legs in time to the music.

'And the sky is golden as the sun sets over the rolling hills.'

'It's a bit early for that here.' Jack sighed. 'But, it's still extremely lovely.'

'Indeed, it is.' Holly sighed, too.

'Have you done this before, Holly Merriweather?'

Holly stared at the branches of the tree hanging above them. 'Yes, I confess I have. A long time ago.' She felt Jack's eyes on her. 'Just after Ed and I started going out. He's my ex.'

'Ah.' She sensed Jack shifting his gaze away from her.

'Oh, it's okay. It had run its course. Sadly.'

'Things do,' Jack said slowly.

'We met at school. We were sixteen. I remember us walking to the park the first summer we were together and I made him do this.' She laughed. 'He said I was mad but that's why he loved me.'

'Nothing wrong with mad.'

'Hmm.' Holly was expecting an image of her and Ed in the long grass on the hill listening to the music in their heads and laughing. But nothing came. Just her thoughts, but no pictures, and a sadness. Not because she wanted him back, she realized, but because they had loved each other and now they didn't.

She glanced towards Jack, who had his eyes closed. He began to sing and she joined in without thinking about it. 'How do I know all the words?' she mumbled.

'Absorbed through constant radio plays, I expect.'

'So, I'm here making a new life for myself after my one and only long-term relationship ended.' Holly felt like she was making a declaration.

Jack leaned over. 'You do have the air of someone who is determined to move forward.'

'Do I?' The music finished and Holly sat up.

'In a very good way.'

'Hence the vibrant trousers and colourful clothes.' Holly looked at her yellow shoes. 'It's like I'm wearing a manifesto.'

'I was married.' Jack was looking ahead at the London skyline. 'It ended two years ago. Quite amicably. But . . .'

'But?'

'We were in business together at the beginning. And for some reason, we let the business bit slip when we sorted all the money out. It was naive of us.' He sighed. 'We were friends. It gave her a bit of an income when she was making a new life.'

'We started to work together, too.' Holly closed her eyes. 'We didn't start like that. I travelled the world working where I could and blogging. And then Ed would meet me wherever I was, and we'd post things about what we were doing, too.' She opened her eyes again and watched a plane soar above the rooftops. 'So, I suppose it became about *our* experiences, not mine.'

'And I needed to come home, because eight years after my father died, I finally realized my mother needed me to be closer. For a while at least. And I had to sell the business.' Jack went quiet for a few moments. 'Now it's messy with my ex. And definitely not friendly.' His expression turned troubled. 'And it was both of our faults.'

'Then we really went into business together. And it went wrong. And so did we.' Holly closed her eyes again. 'So, whereas when we met, I was Holly Merriweather, and then I was Holly Merriweather, who was travelling and working — and I was writing about it and earning money from that, too. Then it was Holly and Ed, who had their own lives but posted about the things we did together.' She took a breath. 'And then we were the Cheese Cottage.' Holly pulled up a handful of grass, rubbing her fingers through the blades absentmindedly. 'So, there was no me and no him. There was just that. And then we both somehow disappeared.' A dog barked in the distance, and they both fell silent for a few moments. 'And I never want to feel like that again.' She managed to make her voice sound calmer than she felt.

'I want to move on, but I keep having to sort out money in Costa Rica, plus the legal stuff, and it's dredging up the past. I feel stuck.' Jack said quietly. 'Never again. No mixing work with pleasure. It's too painful.'

I feel stuck, too, thought Holly. *And I'm frightened no one will want me, now it's just me.*

'I'm sorry, Holly. I don't love you anymore.' Her mind drew her back to the previous winter. Ed had been unloading the van while she'd been going through emails in the kitchen.

She had looked up, not quite understanding what he was saying.

'Maybe we aren't suited to being together all the time, and we've found out the hard way.'

'I don't understand.' Holly heard her voice come out thin and confused.

'It was all so exciting when we'd meet up in all those exotic locations but now . . . it's not enough, is it?'

She had stared at him, unable to speak for a few moments. 'Is there someone else?' she'd asked eventually.

'No.'

'Is it because I said we were bleeding money and we should find a way out of the business?'

He'd paused for a beat too long. 'No.' He looked over her head and out of the window. 'I keep waiting for you to move on, to plan something else. That's who you are. You're always moving. It's putting me on edge. Just waiting.'

Holly felt her voice begin to wobble. 'Where is this coming from? I'm committed to you. To the business. You're making me sound disloyal. And immature.'

Ed stepped back. 'I still like you. Very much. But . . . you know, there's no hurry? There are leases to get out of, and we have to do something with the business. Let's keep it . . . friendly?'

'Okay.' Holly's head was swimming.

'I'm right, though, aren't I?' He sounded weary and sad.

Holly couldn't speak as random thoughts began to flood her head. *I'll pack up and go travelling again. If he thinks I can't settle, I'll just go. He obviously can't stand being with me for more than a month at a time.* Isabella ambled past Ed and jumped on to Holly's lap. She stroked the cat's head gently.

But deep in her heart she knew she didn't love Ed anymore either.

The first few bars of "Do You Really Want to Hurt Me?" floated across the Heath.

Holly stared at the sky, as she pulled back into the present. She shook her head as if it would get rid of the memory, bit her lip, and from somewhere deep inside, a giggle erupted. And she couldn't stop it. 'Is someone listening to us?'

Jack sat up. 'I think I said too much.' He looked embarrassed.

'No. I think I did. I'm sorry. I didn't mean to laugh, but I was remembering something really very sad, and then that song started up, and well . . .'

He smiled shyly. 'You didn't say too much at all. And as for the song?' He began to laugh, too. 'Perhaps it will help our working life if we know a bit about each other's history.' He looked around. 'There's an ice cream van over there. Shall I treat us to a 99 before I have to head off? It'd be a pity to miss this free music.'

'Lovely.' They both stood up and Holly watched him amble over to join the queue. *Seems like we're all a bit stuck*, she thought.

* * *

The following day Holly sat at her desk in the office enjoying the sound of the busy *tap*, *tap*, *tap* of her fingers on the keyboard. Claudette had headphones on and would hum every few moments to an unidentifiable tune, which made Holly smile.

She pressed save on the document entitled *Barney's Books* and put it in the shared folder, then opened her emails so she could let Jack know it was there.

There was one new message in the inbox.

FROM: Jack Fambridge
SUBJECT Re: Publicity ideas as there are other businesses doing "then and now" travel content
Hi Holly,
Thank you for your email.
I don't think we need to be too concerned about the other companies at the moment as the "then" and "now" travel book is not a new idea.
I have read the document your friend Melissa sent over regarding modernizing the way we reach our readers with interest, and agree there are some things that we can do.
Also, your ideas about TikTok, Facebook, Instagram and YouTube content, as well as contacting the press to get some publicity in advance, are all sound, although I think it's too soon.
Regards,
Jack

Holly sighed, her fingers beginning to drum irritably on the desk, and decided not to respond for a moment. It was his business, after all. She was only a writer. Actually, she was the *only* writer.

And then her phone rang.

Ed's name moved across the top in bold white letters. *ED'S PHONE. ED'S PHONE. ED'S PHONE.*

She felt sick. It may as well have said, *Are you going to talk to him? Are you NOT going to talk to him? Go on, ARE you going to talk to him as any adult would?*

Holly put the phone on the table and waited for it to stop ringing. There was a pause until the voicemail alert buzzed, and when it did, she stood up and walked into the kitchen to get herself a drink. Her mind began to chatter frantically. *What does he want? I don't want to speak to him. I have to speak to him. I don't want to know what he wants. I probably should listen to the voicemail. He wouldn't have rung me if it wasn't important.*

'But I don't want to!'

'Are you all right?' Claudette followed her in. 'You look a bit pale all of a sudden.'

'Oh. I'm fine.' Holly smiled as brightly as she could.

'You have a very expressive face, Holly.' Claudette touched her arm. 'And I got several emotions from when the phone started to ring to when it stopped, and not one of them said, "I'm fine".'

Holly picked up a glass and filled it from the water cooler. 'It's just my ex. It'll be to do with something practical we need to sort out, and I'm not in the mood.' She took a gulp of her drink. 'The past and all that.'

'Ah, yes. The past.' Claudette took a biscuit out of the packet of chocolate digestives on the counter. 'Just when you think you're dealing with it and moving on, it raises its some-times-ugly head again.' She held the biscuit in front of her and examined it. 'This, for instance — our lives were fuelled by these when we were setting up the business. Sometimes I wonder why I don't just let it go and buy some Rich Tea or bourbons.' She took it into the office and Holly followed. 'And sometimes I see them and feel nothing, apart from the feeling you get from deciding to eat a biscuit, but there are other times . . .' She sat down. 'Out of the blue, I'll remember a conversation, or a laugh, or a look, and I'll be back in a happy past I can't have anymore.' She put the biscuit on her desk and looked at it. 'And sometimes I just want something new. And then I feel guilty. Honestly, every visit to the crisp and biscuit aisle of the supermarket is a complete emotional lottery.'

Holly sat down opposite her. 'Working here and updating the guidebooks — is that like the chocolate digestives?'

Claudette smiled. 'Yes. But don't tell Jack. All of this is so important to him to reconnect with his father in some way. I just wish we could do it faster. But on a shoestring, it takes a bit longer.'

'I think we need to push the publicity.' Holly could feel her heart starting to race a little. The only thing she and Ed talked about in any depth towards the end of their relationship was money. She didn't want this job to disappear before it really started.

'You're probably right. But Jack has his reasons for holding back, I expect.'

As she spoke, a polystyrene ceiling tile floated elegantly to the floor.

They both looked at it, and then at each other, and then began to laugh.

'But at least the rent is still cheap!' Claudette took a bite out of her biscuit and turned to her keyboard while Holly walked to her desk and looked at her phone.

'I'm just going to deal with this,' she said assertively. 'I'll pop outside.'

Opening the door, she began to walk down the stairs, listening to the voicemail as she did.

'Hi, Holly.' Ed's familiar deep baritone pulled her back in time to the day they took charge of their business. He was like a puppy, excitable and happy, reading out excerpts from the instructions the previous owner had left for them with a wide grin on his face.

Holly smiled at the memory, but then continued to listen.

'I hope all is top-notch with you. I'm settled in here nicely. Can you call me? I've had an email from the accountant about some money we owe that's outstanding.'

Money. Holly felt sick. *I really haven't got very much left*, she thought, stepping out on to the pavement then across the road to sit on a bench next to the park. Taking a deep breath, she made the call, her heart beginning to speed up uncomfortably as it rang out.

'Holly!' The sound of his voice made her smile again. Even though she didn't want to. 'How are you?'

'I'm okay, thanks. What about you?'

'I'm good. This change is doing me good.'

'Great.' Holly tried not to sound disappointed. He should be missing her, shouldn't he? Even though she was not missing him at all. The thought surprised her and she felt her anxiety begin to subside.

'I'm sorry to call you about boring financial things, but there's an outstanding amount left over we need to pay for winding up the business.'

'Right.' She tried not to think about her bank account and the small amount of money she now had in her savings.

'We owe £2,000. I can pay it all now if you want me to, and you can pay your half back when you can?'

Holly paused for a moment, thinking about Claudette and the chocolate digestives and a past that she wasn't able to let go. 'I'll pay my half today,' she said firmly.

'Oh, excellent.' He sounded relieved. 'Thank you. So, how's the new job going?'

'Really well.' She didn't want to tell him she was worried that the wonderful company that had published the books that inspired her to write about travel in the first place was floundering. Or, despite the fact she could find another job to pay the bills, she wanted to help Claudette and Jack for irrational reasons she couldn't quite put her finger on.

Well, you can, she reminded herself. *His name is Jack.*

Holly coughed. 'I've got to go. Lovely to speak to you.' She stood up.

'Okay, you too.'

'Oh, wait.' Holly remembered the envelopes addressed to Ed that were still on the hall table. 'I've got all these official-looking letters for you — they arrived at the cottage after you left, and you haven't returned my messages asking for your new address.'

There was a pause.

'I'll text you my address. Probably marketing letters.'

'Probably. But I'll still send them on. I could open them to check?'

'No! No . . . that's fine. Just send them on.'

'Okay. Bye, Ed.'

'Bye, Holly.'

The phone went dead, and Holly walked back across the road, trying not to think about the very large dent that £1,000 was about to make in her savings.

CHAPTER TEN

Watching the money fly out from her account, Holly imagined it dropping into Ed's and disappearing — another connection cut from the last almost sixteen years. No more financial interweaving, no house to deal with, no shared assets, just a rental property that had gone and a failed business that had disappeared.

'Which,' she said to Isabella who was fast asleep on the sofa, 'is, I suppose, a good thing. Not much to show for all that time together. But.' She stood up and poured herself a glass of water. 'But. I don't know what the "but" is, but there is a but.'

A wood pigeon was sitting on the branch of a tree in a garden a few doors down, the breeze blowing it around, so it looked as if it were clinging on to a fairground ride. Holly's mind clicked back to Ed swinging through the trees and clipping the leaves as he did while hanging from a rope at an outdoor pursuits centre in North Wales. Her hand reached automatically for her phone and she opened her photographs, scrolling through them till she found the one she was looking for — Ed's mouth in a perfect O, to match his round, startled eyes, as a squirrel launched itself from the top of a tree in front of him.

'Watch out, flying squirrel!' someone had shouted.

Holly had tried to capture the moment, but she was a second too late, and the only proof that there had been wildlife in the way was a tuft of the squirrel's little, grey tail in the bottom left-hand corner.

She stared at it for a while and tried to feel sad. And she did a little, but mainly because all that had gone. Not because she wanted Ed to come back.

'I am feeling scared though, Isabella.' She sat down next to the cat and stroked her ears. 'Because now it's all down to me. And I'm not sure what I'm doing.'

A notification pinged on the phone and she absent-mindedly clicked on it. Ed had re-posted a photo of himself on Instagram.

Woodturner Ed moved into the Commune, and within two months has crafted a brand-new line for our unique wooden cookware and sculptures. What a star! #woodturning.

It had been posted by someone called Kirsty.

Holly opened Kirsty's page. She was standing next to Ed. In fact, she was standing very close to Ed. Or was Ed standing very close to her? She had her arm around his back, he had his arm draped over her shoulder. It looked very cosy.

Holly felt a surge of anger and stood up, dropping her phone next to Isabella as if it were on fire. Then she began to pace around the room. *We're not together. It's fine. I don't love him anymore. But he only moved out four and a half months ago. You said you needed breathing space, Ed Purcell. You've only left enough time for a sniff!*

She paced into the kitchen. Then out again. Then she thought of the money she had just sent him and, although she owed it to him, she got annoyed.

'I don't like cheese!' she shouted at the cat, who opened her eyes briefly and went back to sleep. 'But I do like hand-crafted wooden cookware. Why couldn't we have invested our savings into that?'

The phone buzzed again and she picked it up angrily, expecting another post about how wonderful Ed was.

It was a text from Melissa. Holly sat down and read it.

Don't forget — 6.30 p.m. at the Dog and Whistle. Franc is looking forward to meeting you.

Holly reread the message and smiled faintly. 'Thank you,' she said to the screen. 'Not sure if I'm fully on board with this, but thank you anyway.'

Digging something out of the freezer without really looking, she put it in the microwave, while almost jumping up and down with frustration. No one was listening to her about the books and, judging by the photo, Ed was obviously moving ahead, very quickly, with his new dreams of a new life. And Kirsty — who, according to her bio, was a weaver — looked rather thrilled about it, too.

'I kept telling him about the money, Isabella.' She gazed out of the window. 'But it was all "it's okay, Holly. Don't worry, Holly. You get on with the marketing and stuff, Holly. Budgeting was a big part of my job for the hotels, Holly." Well, it was my money, too, Ed!' She opened a drawer and pushed it shut dramatically.

Isabella sat up.

'Sorry!' Holly scrolled through her list of itineraries for all her travel adventures on her laptop, opening one with the title *Peru, Costa Rica, Galapagos, Ecuador, Chile*.

She clicked on the sub-folder called *Travel Atlas*, reading the notes she'd made on transport links, with screenshots of information about flights, ferries, trains and cars. Then she moved on to information from blogs and guidebooks and admin — what paperwork do I need to travel? What paperwork do I need to get a job if I'm able to work? Looking at the pile of books filed randomly against the living room wall, she walked over and ran her finger along the spine of the *Travel Atlas*. 'My life was in you,' she murmured.

She moved back over to her laptop just as the microwave pinged.

'I did all of that.' A chaffinch that was sitting outside on the table looked at her. 'I researched it, I planned it, I organized it, I booked it and I did it. I budgeted for it. I made money on what I wrote about it. I asked other people for advice, and I *listened to them*!' She surprised herself at the force with which she'd said the last three words.

Closing the laptop, she took the tray out of the microwave, opened the film and began to eat, images of that Latin American trip rolling colourfully through her mind.

Isabella jumped on to the floor and began to drink from her bowl.

'But no one is listening.' Holly took another bite, but this one didn't taste or feel like the last one. She began to chew slowly, then swallowed and poked her fork into the meal a few times. Some of it was quite hard.

'Oh no.' She got up and threw the remnants in the bin, unable to face trying to reheat it. 'I didn't defrost it properly, Isabella!'

The cat ignored her and carried on drinking.

'Thanks for your support,' she muttered, taking a couple of slices of bread out of a packet and putting them in the toaster. 'I didn't eat much, but I have no intention of poisoning myself.'

Then she ate her toast while staring out of the window. The garden outside was bright and luscious — she wished she could find the words to describe it, but she was so frustrated that she just couldn't.

* * *

Holly checked her reflection in the mirror, then stepped back and scrutinized her dress. It was white with tiny pink-and-green flowers dotted over the top. Behind her on the bed was a pile of discarded clothing that she had rifled through irritably, knowing she had to go and meet this man, but not really wanting to because life was easier as it was now. Not that good. But easier.

120

Glancing down at her shoes to make sure they were a pair, she picked up her bag, closed the front door with a satisfying bang behind her, then made her way to Farthing Street for a cup of tea to steady her nerves.

'You're looking very nice.' Viktor sat down next to Holly. 'Even nicer than usual. You always look nice.'

'That's very kind.' Holly took a sip of her drink and checked the time on her phone. 'I've got to be somewhere at half six, so thought I'd pop in before I head off.'

'What's this? A date?' Marialena was closing the dry-cleaner's and had overheard their conversation.

'Not as such,' Holly muttered. The nervous knot in her stomach was now unravelling. 'How can you tell?'

'Instinct.' She laughed and sat down opposite her. 'Lemon iced tea, please, Paulo.'

'I left the house in a hurry and somehow found my way here without thinking.'

'To be among friends.' Marialena waved at Bev.

'Yes, yes, I suppose I am.' Holly smiled at Caleb, who was dragging a barking Mabel over towards them. She briefly wondered if he was the secret owner of the Bollington. Then she dismissed the idea as it was only really because he liked records.

'She needs a good run,' he muttered irritably. 'I suppose I have to join all those other dog owners on Primrose Hill in a bit.'

'It's a good way to meet new people.' Marialena patted Mabel on the head.

'I don't want to meet new people,' he grunted, sitting down. 'So, what's this I hear about an event then?' he asked as Paulo brought over Marialena's tea.

'We're having a midsummer party. Next week. On the twenty-first.' Paulo's face brightened as he spoke. 'Viktor has given in and we are opening late. Well, till nine o'clock. We're doing afternoon tea, but it will be in the evening, so we are going to call it something else.'

'Oh, that sounds exciting.' Holly finished her drink. 'Was it one of Melissa's ideas?'

'No. She had lots of ideas but this one is ours. Mine, actually. We had to decide in a hurry. More unexpected out-goings on broken kitchen equipment last week. We have to try something.'

'What if it rains?' Caleb looked down and gave Mabel a dog treat.

'It won't.' Paulo sounded a little bit defensive. 'It's mid-summer. But we are organizing marquees.'

'What about some music?' Marialena nudged Caleb. 'Know any bands that would do something? Or could you do a DJ set?'

'No. I don't and I can't,' mumbled Caleb.

'But it would be good for Farthing Street.' Bev sat down. 'I've closed early today — it's been so quiet in the shop, I've almost forgotten what a human being looks like. Although I don't like too many people in. They keep interrupting my day.' Holly glanced at her, remembering the day she saw her carrying a guitar to the old people's home. *Mmmm*, she thought. *But again, owning a guitar could mean nothing . . . apart from owning a guitar.*

'My boss says if it doesn't get better soon, we will have to close.' Marialena bit her lip.

'Oh dear.' Bev put her arm around her. 'I'm sure it *will* get better.'

'I hope so,' Marialena sniffed, clearly trying not to cry. 'It's all complicated by the fact that I live above the shop, too. I don't know where I'll go. I can't afford to live anywhere else.'

Caleb shifted uncomfortably in his seat. 'Okay, I'll think about the music,' he said eventually. 'But it may not be me. I don't like people much.'

Bev gently kicked his leg and laughed. 'Yes, you do.'

'No, I don't.'

Holly smiled, almost wishing she could stay at the table rather than meet Melissa and her colleague for "not a date" as Melissa had described it.

She stood up and felt a little bit sick. *Honestly*, her inner voice whispered. *It's just a little meet-up. It shouldn't be making you ill. Get a grip.*

122

'Got to go. See you soon.' She put some change on the table, took a deep breath and walked purposefully towards Camden Lock.

* * *

The pavements were thronged with the early-evening drinkers at the pubs and cafés peppering the route. The warmth of the day seemed to be buoying everyone up, and the chatter was almost orchestral as Holly walked to the bar on the canal where Melissa and Franc were waiting. Pushing the door open, she whispered to herself, 'This is not a date. This is a step in the right direction.' Then she plastered a smile on her face, before waving at Melissa and a man with a kind face, who she assumed was Franc.

Still smiling very widely, she weaved around the tables then plonked herself next to them a little too enthusiastically. 'It's lovely out there, isn't it? But absolutely rammed.'

'Yes — couldn't get any seats outside, everyone is so excited by the sun. As we always are.' Melissa pushed a glass towards her. 'I've taken the liberty of ordering you a wine spritzer. Is that okay?'

'Marvellous. Thanks.' Holly turned to Franc. 'Hello. I'm Holly. Nice to meet you.'

'It's very good to meet you too, Holly.' His voice was warm and lilting, with what sounded like a slight Nordic accent.

'So!' She began to relax. *He seems nice,* she thought. *And looks nothing like Ed. In fact, he is the anti-Ed. Blond, like a Viking, and tall. Well, he looks tall, given the distance the top of his head is from the table.* She took a sip of her drink. And then she began to sweat.

'Franc is the Head of New Business at work.' Melissa nodded at him, and then at Holly. 'Holly is a travel blogger and she's working on guidebooks at the moment.'

'How very interesting.' Franc leaned forward and looked directly at her with his blue eyes. 'Melissa tells me you've been friends since school?'

123

'Yes.' Holly tried to speak, but her forehead felt cold and clammy. She was suddenly feeling *very* sweaty, but also a bit chilly. But she nodded and took a deep breath, hoping that whatever this was would ebb away within moments. 'We've barely seen each other over the past ten years, though, as I was scooting around the world while Melissa was building her amazing career.'

'Have you ever been to Stockholm?' Franc turned to Melissa. 'That's where I'm from. Did I tell you that?'

'I think you mentioned it.'

Holly's stomach began to gurgle. She swallowed slowly and watched Melissa and Franc talk, trying to focus, but the sweatiness and clamminess seemed to be getting worse.

'Are you all right?' Franc leaned towards her. 'You're looking very pale.'

Her stomach churned and she felt a bead of sweat trickle down her back. 'I think I need some air,' she mumbled and stood up, picked up her bag and hurried out of the door, taking long gulps of air when she got outside. Leaning for a moment on a railing next to the canal, she tried to calm her stomach down, but it was lurching and churning at the same time now.

Home . . . home . . . Got to get home. Holly began to walk, and then trot, weaving around people who were ambling in front of her — far too slowly, in her opinion — and then there were the cyclists and the people on the little boats. Why were they there enjoying themselves and laughing when she felt so terrible? And why was she the only one sweating and feeling clammy? They all looked healthy and happy, and she didn't, she knew she didn't. *Oh God, that half-defrosted thing at lunchtime*, she thought, running up the steps on to Regent's Park Road.

Her phone began to ring in her bag, but she couldn't answer it — she was too busy walking determinedly back to her house, counting the steps to take her mind off the churning and the rumbling and the sweat, until she eventually found herself outside her door. Fumbling around in her bag for her keys, she finally managed to open the door, then slammed it firmly behind her.

A bit ill. Sorry, she messaged Melissa, then threw her phone on to the table.

* * *

There was a ringing in her ears. A musical ding-dong. It stopped for a moment and then started again. Holly opened her eyes and rolled over, the strap of a handbag tangled around her ankle. She was vaguely aware of a pile of clothes scattered on the floor.

There it was again, the bell, but she couldn't quite remember where she was. It wasn't the bedroom in the cottage. This room had high ceilings and wooden floors and rich-green walls. 'Ah,' she mumbled as the bell rang again, then she rolled on to the floor and pulled herself to her feet before shuffling to the hallway. 'I'm coming,' she shouted. 'I'm on my way.' Pushing her hair behind her ears and straightening her dress, she opened the door wide enough for a cat to be pushed in.

'Your cat has been eating my dog's food,' Caleb said grumpily. 'For the past two days.'

'Two days?' Holly croaked wearily, as Isabella stalked in and sat down in the living room. 'Two days?'

'I sensed something wasn't right. And Mabel is so soft, she just let her eat all of it. I mean, your cat is an animal.'

'Two days?' Holly edged the door open a little wider.

'Oh dear.' Caleb edged back slightly. 'Something hasn't been right, has it?'

'Not really.' Holly wanted to go and lie down again. 'Food poisoning, I think.'

'Have you been drinking enough water? You need to drink water to rehydrate.'

'I will.' She began to close the door. 'Thank you for Isabella. I'll feed her now.'

Caleb put his foot in the doorway so she couldn't close it. 'Have you got any food, Holly?'

'Probably.' She sighed, the urge to throw herself on to her bed and go back to sleep almost overwhelming. 'But I don't want any, currently.'

He moved his foot away. 'If you need anything, just knock on the door. Or send your cat round with a note in her collar.'

Holly managed a limp smile. 'Will do.' She closed the door and dragged herself back to bed. Isabella jumped on top of her, immediately beginning to purr loudly, and Holly fell back to sleep.

* * *

There was the ding-dong sound again in the distance. And this time there was banging, too. And someone shouting. And a cat meowing angrily.

Holly opened her eyes reluctantly, allowing the ceiling to come slowly into focus. 'Oh . . .' she muttered. 'This again.' Then she rolled over and locked eyes with Isabella, who was staring at her and not moving. Just staring and breathing. Then she started meowing again in time to the doorbell and the banging.

'Coming,' croaked Holly, who didn't have the energy to walk, so crawled to the door, grabbed the handle to pull herself to her feet, then opened it a crack.

Viktor was on the doorstep holding out a large bag. 'Oh, Holly. You look terrible,' he boomed. 'It is time to eat. Not a lot. Little but often.' He touched her forehead. 'You haven't got a temperature. You're getting better.'

'Am I?' She felt herself sway slightly.

'You're weak.' He pushed the bag into her hands. 'Chicken soup. Homemade. Fresh bread from the baker's, and a flask of camomile tea.'

Holly felt a tear trickle down her face. 'I'm sorry. I'm overtired and overemotional.' She rubbed it away and sniffed.

He smiled kindly. 'I have to go. Paulo is on his own — although we don't have any customers — but I'd better get back, anyway. Caleb told us you were unwell.'

'Thank you.' Holly wanted to close the door before she burst into tears for no reason.

'Viktor's prescription is this,' he pointed at her sternly. 'Eat slowly, sleep, eat slowly, sleep, watch old films, eat slowly, sleep, and when you wake up in the morning, you will be yourself again.'

'After all, tomorrow is another day,' Holly murmured weakly. 'Scarlett O'Hara. *Gone with the Wind* . . . never mind.'

He guffawed. 'You see, you are feeling better already.' Then he turned to go. 'If you need us, just call.' He blew her a kiss and began to walk up towards the road.

Holly watched him, her heart surging with emotion. *Because I'm ill*, she thought. *Get a grip.*

Closing the door, she took the bag to the kitchen and gingerly opened the carton of soup. Isabella stuck her face in the bag, so Holly moved her and gave her some dry cat food. Then she poured half the soup into a bowl and warmed it up, before sitting down on the sofa, turning on the television and choosing the first old film Netflix had to offer.

After *Minnie Saxonbury and the Lost Diamond*, which Holly enjoyed, although she had never heard of it before, she made a list of films she was familiar with and knew would make her feel better. Then she sent a message to Melissa saying she was fine and to thank her for all the concerned messages, and then to Claudette and Jack to tell them she wouldn't be in the next day due to ill health, but would try to be in on Tuesday. Then she ate a little bit more chicken soup.

Scrolling through her list, she began with *Jerry Maguire*, to be followed by *Pride and Prejudice* and *Roman Holiday*.

* * *

A car horn blared angrily in the distance and Holly woke up with a start. *Jerry Maguire* had somehow morphed into *Whisky Galore!*, and her phone was sticking out from under a cushion. The screen had frozen on to a Facebook page called *The Lights Fans For Ever*. She studied it woozily, trying to work out why it was there, then looked at Isabella, who was sitting on the coffee table staring at her.

'Have you been using my phone?' Holly asked hopefully. 'Because I don't know why I'd be on a page like that.'

Isabella stretched, displacing a piece of paper, which floated to the floor. Holly leaned over and picked it up, realizing it was the flyer for the Lights gig at the Bollington in 1981.

'God, I must have been researching in my sleep,' she muttered, standing up slowly and opening the patio door. The cool evening air was a welcome respite from the heat of the house, and she padded out barefoot on to the grass, wiggling her toes and taking long, deep breaths. A jasmine bush on the back fence had begun to flower, and she stood for a while enjoying its delicate, summery scent. The mystery guitarist was playing "American Pie" somewhere above her, but she still couldn't work out exactly where they were, so she just paused and listened.

Isabella skipped out and began to skitter around the garden, just as Holly wandered back inside. Picking up her phone, she read a text from Claudette.

Oh, my goodness. Let me know if you need anything. C

And then one from Jack:

Poor you. If you need anything, let me know. I'm in my flat in Rotherhithe this weekend so I can jump on the Tube and get to you if you need me. J

Holly smiled. *Lovely people*, she thought. *Even if a little bit stubborn.*

There was one notification from the Lights' Facebook fan page from somebody called Fergus Jones. She opened it warily.

I was at the 1981 gig and the 1988 gig at the Bollington. Great venue. Didn't know it had closed down. If I'd have known the 1988 gig was the last time I'd ever see the Lights perform live, I would have stopped that bloody fight myself and made them do it again. I've always thought that was such a pity, given what happened to Lawrence Mandrel not long after.

Holly read the post above it.

I'm doing research on the Bollington and wondered if anyone had seen the Lights there in 1981?

The post was from her account.

She sat down. 'I don't remember writing that,' she said to Isabella, who was now lying across the doorway. Then she noticed her notepad on the floor under the coffee table. She picked it up and rifled through it until she found a page with the previous day's date scrawled untidily at the top.

Things to do:
Make time to research the Bollington but without asking anything specific — don't want to upset the owner.
Find out about the Lights. Haven't looked into it properly till now as it just seems too sad.
So sad. Someone is just so sad. And stuck. Like me.
Come up with plan — may be difficult — owner not happy. Why?
Fambridge Books needs help and no one's listening to me!
Think about how the publicity can help them.
Don't want them to go out of business — this is my job!
Farthing Street needs help too! Bollington could be the key!
I'm tired.
Love Holly

'Oh!' She laughed. 'Sleep writing? I hope that's all I did.' She flipped through the rest of the pad to check. 'Nope, nothing else. Thank goodness.'

Picking up her laptop, she opened it up and googled "The Lights":

Lead singer: Don C. Peterson — 1960–
Guitar: Lawrence Mandrel — 1959–1989
Bass guitar: B.B. Jones — 1960–
Drums: Charlie Thomas — 1959–2018
Keyboards: Francis De Paul 1961–
Formed in 1975 at Harps Valley Comprehensive School, Chelmsford
Genre: Punk/new wave
Last album: Live at The Bollington 1988
Five number ones between 1982 and 1988
Four top ten hits
Broke up in 1988, shortly before death of Lawrence Mandrel in an avalanche in Colorado in January 1989.

Holly shut the laptop. 'Does the Bollington belong to a fan or a member of the band?' she asked Isabella thoughtfully, thinking about the venue frozen in time from 1981 — paused before the beginning of one particular gig, it seemed. 'I can't just ask around because, as I noted down in my fever-fuelled research, someone clearly is very, very sad about something.'

Isabella jumped up and laid down next to her. 'My brain hurts,' whispered Holly, switching on the television. '*Pride and Prejudice* next, cat. I need to rest before the big interview day for our first music venue feature.'

CHAPTER ELEVEN

Holly went into the office to do some research before heading to Wandsworth to record the interview because her internet connection kept dropping out when she tried to log on at home. The office was empty, apart from a plumber trying to fix a leak under the sink, so she messaged Claudette and Jack to tell them she was there. Then she got to work. She was looking forward to gathering another story and hoping that, if the interview went well, Jack might give in and start to do some pre-publicity.

Her phone buzzed just as she was standing up to get ready to leave.

I can give you a lift to Wandsworth if you like? Jack. She felt her heart begin to race pleasantly at the thought of sharing a car with him.

No! yelled the rational part of her brain. *Do not allow yourself to think like that!*

'I won't!' she almost shouted at herself.

'Did you say something?' The plumber poked his head around the door.

Holly waved the phone at him. 'I was talking to someone. Sorry to disturb.'

Another message arrived. *It'll be quicker than getting public transport from the office. But I've just got to collect something on the way. The van is parked outside right now.*

Holly looked at the time. On the one hand, being in such close proximity to Jack was a very good thing. On the other hand, it was a very bad thing. However, she realized she should have probably left half an hour ago anyway, so decided to take the risk and just try not to look at him, or talk too much to him, or lean too close so that she wouldn't be seduced by that nice aftershave he wore.

Her phone buzzed again. *Hurry up! I'm on a single yellow line and I sense traffic wardens nearby . . . is it a yes or no?*

On my way, she typed, grabbing her bag and her laptop, and hurrying out of the office and down the stairs.

Jack was revving the engine as she opened the door of the van and climbed in.

'Hello, thanks for the—' Jack put the van into gear and pulled out into the road before she could finish the sentence.

'Sorry,' he muttered. 'Borrowed this from a friend, so getting used to it. I usually drive an automatic. And I don't want to get another parking ticket.' He glanced at her and smiled.

Holly smiled back, then stared straight ahead, determined not to get pulled into his orbit or whatever it was that made her irrational side rear its head — that "all or nothing" bit of her she hadn't realized was within her until Jack had climbed up from the floor on Tower Bridge all those weeks ago. Holding on to her bag tightly, she tried to replace the image with that of a horse. Which Jack was riding towards her like Mr Darcy. Biting her lip, she looked out of the window and focused on a delivery driver on a moped waiting at the junction ahead in front of a burger bar . . . only this time it was Jack all Gregory Peck-like in *Roman Holiday*.

'I watched too many films when I was sick. Too many.'

'Did you say something?' Jack changed gear.

'I was dictating something to my phone for later — for my blog.'

'Ah, how's that going?'

Holly could feel him glancing at her again. 'A bit slow, to be honest. Lots of thoughts. Not much in the way of actual writing.'

'You need something to motivate you — something to spur you into action.' They turned out on to the main road opposite Borough Tube station.

'Where exactly are we going?' Holly checked her phone to see what time it was again. 'Are you sure we'll get to Wandsworth on time?'

'Oh, yes. I've just got to collect an electric bike and a generator from a mate's lock-up in Kennington.'

'A generator?'

'It's a long story. He needs somewhere to store it. The lease on the lock-up is up for renewal and he's moving. So, it's going in my mother's garage.'

'Ah, so are we dropping it off in Richmond before the interview then?'

'No, don't think so. We'll have to see how much time we have. Traffic's bad though, isn't it?'

'I know I'm something of a country bumpkin, but I assumed the traffic was always bad in London.' Holly risked looking at him for a moment. Her worry about being late had allowed her rational side to take control, so all she felt now was slight panic and vague irritation.

'Right, I'm going to go round the houses so I don't get sucked into the Elephant and Castle road system. I swear that when I first learned to drive, I drove round and round there for eight hours before I found my way out.'

'Oh dear.' Holly glanced at her phone again. 'Shall I message my dad? He'll be on his way down. It was really tricky to find a time Mr Bright could do, apparently.'

'I was joking about the eight hours.' Jack checked the satnav. 'We'll be fine. No red lines. All clear.'

'Okay.' Holly sat back and tried to relax, but the mention of Richmond seemed to have triggered an unwanted memory of Jack on a paddleboard on the Thames. Holly noticed a man struggling with a unicycle at the side of the road, so focused on that instead.

'London!' Jack laughed, nodding in his direction. 'Most of this you actually couldn't make up.'

Holly then started to fret about the speed at which they were moving. *And*, whispered her inner voice, *don't pretend you're just worried about being late — you're also worried about doing this interview properly, writing it up and publishing it, as you've made such a big thing about it. Honestly, the "jumping in with both feet" bit of you can get a bit overexcited sometimes.*

'Oh, for God's sake!' Jack sounded panicked. 'Not this.'

'What?' Holly looked at him. He looked panicked, too.

'The satnav's brought me to Elephant and Castle.' He leaned closer to the steering wheel. Holly wasn't quite sure, but it appeared that he wasn't blinking.

'Just follow the directions — it'll guide us the right way. Maybe there's worse traffic somewhere it's taking us away from?' She tried to sound upbeat and positive.

'Do you know, I've driven in Costa Rica, Peru, across the Alps. I got through Bangkok in an old SEAT completely unscathed. But here? The Elephant and Castle road system is my Achilles heel.'

'Okay.' Holly felt her voice take on its "I'm actually really happy, regardless of what I look like I'm feeling" sing-song quality. The car was now in the middle of five lanes of traffic. 'It'll be fine.'

'The last time I drove this way, my dad was in the car and eventually *he* had to take over and drive. It was so humiliating . . . and now I've heard myself say that, it's clear I need counselling.'

'You were only young, though.'

'I was twenty-five.'

'That's sort of young.'

He ground the gears of the van noisily, took a breath and forced his way into the left-hand lane. 'According to this rubbish satnav, there's a road on the left. I'm going down that. I'm making my own decisions.'

'Good idea.' Holly tried to sound supportive. 'Pity there isn't a setting on the satnav that says "Avoid toll road, bridges and Elephant and Castle".'

Jack manoeuvred away from the traffic and turned off, then he pulled over to the side of the road and re-set the satnav. 'There! We can get there if we go that way.'

They set off again. Holly checked her phone for the time. She decided not to say anything.

For a full five minutes, they drove along in silence but with sense of purpose, until Jack eased to a stop at a set of traffic lights. 'No!' He hit the steering wheel. 'Not this again! It's here again! The Elephant and Castle road system.'

'Shall we just go with the flow this time?' sang Holly. 'Maybe we just need to grit our teeth and push through the anxiety.'

Jack didn't respond. Instead, he started to breathe in through his nose and out through his mouth, then when the traffic lights turned green, managed to force his way into the right-hand lane. 'I'm going to try this way now,' he muttered.

'Are you sure you didn't add "Definitely via Elephant and Castle" to the settings?' Holly forced out a laugh.

Jack churned the gear stick again. 'Should have hired an automatic instead of trying to save money and borrowing this,' he shouted. Then he turned to look at her. 'Sorry . . . It's just there's more to this than me just getting lost here.'

'Ah, okay?' Holly smiled at him expectantly, but he just veered off on to a road on the right, then parked up, re-set the satnav again and began to drive until they reached some roadworks, took the diversion and found themselves back heading southwards around Elephant and Castle. Jack seemed to grit his teeth, turned left, then left again, parked the van, got out and stood on the pavement.

Holly undid her seat belt and climbed out to join him. For some reason, she instinctively moved her arms to hug him, but he stepped away.

'Shall I drive?' she asked after a while. 'I don't mean because I'd do any better, but you seem stressed.'

'It was the last time I was with my dad before he died.' He was looking at a lamppost behind her. 'We drove round and round and round. I was trying to impress him — you know — I'd just come back from trekking in Nepal. He couldn't tell me anything, could he? But I got myself in such a knot.'

'Oh, so this has reminded you of that? I get it,' Holly said gently.

'In the end, I got out of the car, he drove us to my mate's house and dropped me off. Me and my mate, Marco — he's the one with the lock-up — were supposed to be driving off into the distance around Europe for another adventure. My dad didn't make a fuss. He was just kind and assertive and in control and got me there. I was very, very embarrassed and behaving like a stroppy teenager.'

Holly touched his hand reassuringly.

'I got out of the car, took my rucksack out of the boot, slammed it shut and walked away. I didn't look back, you know?' He looked at her, his eyes watery. 'How stupid was I? He died a week later. Unexpected heart attack. Out of nowhere. And that's the last time I saw him.'

It's like looking at a different person, thought Holly. He seemed smaller suddenly, like he'd shrunk in on himself.

'What was it like when you saw him before you both got in the car that day?' It was the first thing that came into her mind.

He looked up at her, surprised. 'Well, we grabbed a drink from our local coffee shop, sat on a bench and went through the route Marco and I were planning to get to Berlin.'

'What did he say?' Holly looked at a coffee van just behind them and began to move towards it.

'He said he was very envious. That he'd love to take off with Mum and have another adventure. That the route looked great — he had a few suggestions of how to do it better — and he showed me a few links to articles people were writing about their own travelling. One, in particular, he loved — "Keep an eye on this person, they really can write," he'd said. "Maybe you'll want to do that one day."' Holly joined the queue for coffee and Jack followed her, still speaking. 'I remember reading it and thinking, *wow, this is so vibrant and relatable, and with a unique voice too, and I will never be able to create anything like that. He will never, ever be proud of me for writing like he did.* And guess what—' he took a breath — 'I found a part of that article in one of his folders at Mum's when I was helping her sort stuff out on that day you saw me on the river. He kept examples of writing he liked. Half of it was missing, so I have no idea who wrote it, but I remembered it vividly from that day.' He looked at her. 'Maybe that's why I'm so stressed — it's dredged up the past. Again.'

They edged forward as the person in front of them was served.

'I knew then that I needed to do something different from him. And finding those old articles reminded me of that. It's not because I didn't love him. But he was such a force of nature, I felt I'd just be in his shadow.' He sighed. 'And yet here I am. In publishing.'

'Coffee?' Holly asked, pointing at the board. 'I think I need a bit of caffeine.'

'Ah.' Jack almost smiled. 'An Americano, please,' he said to the barista.

'And a latte for me.' Holly turned back to him. 'He must have been proud of you.'

'Oh yes. He said that. Just as we got in the car. "I'm very proud of you. Getting out there. Doing your own thing. Being brave." I'd just come back from my travels — worked on a project in Sumatra before I went to Nepal.'

Holly paid for the drinks and handed Jack his coffee. 'So, he was very proud of you. That's a wonderful thing to remember.'

'Yes, I suppose so. What a difference an hour being lost in a car can make.' Jack looked at the floor.

'Shall we change the route? You can arrange to get the stuff from your friend's lock-up another day? Or if we have to get it today, put Waterloo or something into the satnav, then find our way to Kennington from there?'

Jack took a sip of his coffee. 'Excellent idea — but I have to pick up the equipment today. Oh, and thanks for the offer to drive, but you're not on the insurance.'

'What a pity!' Holly laughed. 'I was looking forward to that. Not!' Jack opened the van door, but Holly couldn't help clutching his arm for a second. 'Before you get in — remember, your dad was very proud of you. He said that. Maybe we rewrite the negative bit. Get in the car, or van, this time and take a different route.'

'Oh.' He looked at the cup he was holding. 'I see what you've done: had the coffee, talked about the route — clever woman, Holly Merriweather.' He held her gaze for a beat too long, his dark eyes sparkling with life again.

'I just want to help,' she said quietly, looking away. 'Shall we get going? Wandsworth is still quite a way.'

* * *

'Here we are.' Jack turned into a small industrial estate just off Kennington Lane and parked the van in front of a lock-up garage, beeping his horn several times as he did.

A tall, lean, red-headed man walked towards them, waving. 'Oi oi, Jack!' he shouted. 'Bit on the tardy side, mate, but I forgive you.'

Jack got out, so Holly did too. 'We had a bit of a navigational issue.' Jack shook his friend's hand. 'This is Holly, by the way. She's just joined the company and we're on our way to an assignment.' He turned to Holly. 'And this is Marco. We were at university together and haven't been able to get rid of each other since then.'

'Cool.' Marco smiled and looked directly into Holly's eyes. 'Good to meet you. Sorry we've got you involved in shifting this equipment.'

'I'm not sure I . . .' Holly looked around, confused. 'I'm not sure I'm up to helping move a generator.'

'Ha! Just kidding.' Marco winked at her. 'It's on wheels. And I've got a ramp. Also wheeled. It's a fully wheeled operation here.' His face became serious. 'You can try lifting it if you want to, though?'

Holly laughed. 'No, your way sounds most effective. Thanks for the offer, though.'

He opened the lock-up and pushed the generator out. 'The ramp is at the back there.' Marco nodded at Jack.

'Oh, I'll get it.' Holly wanted to help, partly because they were running late for the big interview.

'You don't have to.' She heard Marco shout after her. 'But if you do—' The rest of his words were drowned out by a lorry driving noisily past.

Spotting what looked like a ramp propped up against the back wall, she turned it on to its wheels and began to drag it outside, proudly placing it at the back of the van. 'Do you want me to attach it?' she asked, pushing her hair behind her ears, then scratching her nose.

Both men stared at her silently. She couldn't quite work out their expressions. They both looked like they wanted to say something but weren't sure how to formulate the words.

'I can do it.' Holly bristled. 'I mean, I've helped build toilet blocks at a school in Ghana. I can attach a ramp to the back of a van.'

Jack touched his cheek and opened his mouth to speak but nothing came out. Marco looked like he was about to step forward, but he didn't seem able to move.

The three of them stood, looking at one another for a few moments in silence, until Jack moved a wing mirror and nodded at Holly, then edged back to the front of the van.

Holly peered in. Her face was covered in black, greasy stripes. *Oh God, I look like a black-and-white Adam Ant*, she thought, turning back around to look at the men. Their expressions were still unreadable until Holly burst into peals of laughter. 'Oh no!' She guffawed. 'Oh no, oh no . . .'

'I tried to warn you.' Marco took a grubby handkerchief out of his pocket and tried to give it to her. 'Will this help?'

Holly waved it away. 'No, I think it may just add to it.'

Jack was rummaging around in the glove compartment of the van. 'I've got something — wait a minute.' He reappeared and handed her some damp kitchen roll. 'It's been there a while,' he muttered. 'A water bottle leaked on it on the way here, too.'

Holly stared at it with distaste, trying not to wrinkle her nose. 'Thank you both. But it's fine. Is there a bathroom? I just need a sink.'

'It's broken.' Marco sighed apologetically. 'The rental of this place is ending today, so it's not being fixed till I go.'

'Ah.' Holly glanced at her phone. 'Well, I'm sure there's a supermarket en route I can clean myself up in.' She tried to sound positive but was beginning to panic. They were running late for the interview, and she was in danger of arriving looking like she'd just left a survival course. The unusual kind, where you also wear a green-and-yellow sundress and flip-flops.

'Yes, yes.' Jack put the kitchen roll back in the van. 'Let's sort this out, shall we?' He looked over at Marco. 'Can I borrow the ramp so I can unload it all at Mum's?'

Marco nodded and the men began to work quickly, trying not to make eye contact with Holly, who was by now almost hopping from one foot to another impatiently, but with a bright and positive smile painted on her very dirty face.

Wish there was CCTV to record this! Her inner voice sounded delighted.

Ten minutes later, the van was loaded and they were waving to Marco as Jack began to drive out of the estate.

'Right.' He glanced at her when they got to the junction of the main road. 'Let's get to that Tesco on the way. You can clean your face there.'

Holly bit her lip. 'You are allowed to laugh, by the way.'

'Are you sure you don't need the kitchen roll? I ripped another piece off ready for you just in case.' He leaned forward and used it to brush her cheek very gently. 'There was a spot there.'

140

They held each other's gaze for a second too long. Holly looked away first and stared out of the window.

'Before I forget,' Jack said brightly, 'Marco was asking if you were single.'

'Oh?' Holly picked her phone out of her bag and began to scroll through the messages with great concentration, even though she wasn't really reading them. 'I suppose I am. It's the first time I've been asked that since I've actually been single.'

'I can give you his number if you like? I have his permission.'

Holly felt like she was being edged out of her comfort zone. *Should I say yes to prove to myself that I can go on dates with someone other than Ed?* 'That's very flattering,' she said eventually. 'It's no reflection on him, but I'm new to all this, so can I let you know another time?'

'Sure.' Jack's voice was expressionless. Then he looked at the clock on the dashboard. 'Oh,' he said. 'Um.'

Holly followed his gaze. 'Oh.' She looked up at the queue of vehicles snaking along the road in front of them, then noticed the red line on the satnav. 'That means there's lots of traffic on the way,' she muttered. 'We're going to be very late.'

'It's fine. It's okay.' Jack smiled reassuringly at her. 'We'll find a way.'

Holly held her hand out to Jack. 'Can you hand me that kitchen roll,' she said firmly. 'This is important and we need to look professional. And that means not being late.'

'If you're sure.' Jack nodded at her then revved the engine.

'I am.' Holly began to wipe her face, trying not to notice the grey, sludgy marks she was making on the paper. *But*, she thought, her anxiety returning, *he really shouldn't have collected that equipment on the way, should he? I mean, the meltdown couldn't be helped. However, I'm not sure he's taking this as seriously as he should.* Holly cleared her throat, trying to shove the negative thoughts away.

'All okay?' Jack was turning left. 'I know a shortcut that will get us there quicker.' He looked at her briefly. 'Don't worry

— the Elephant and Castle incident is now a distant memory.' Then his face changed and he stopped smiling. 'Well, it isn't. It was very embarrassing. But my navigational mojo is now back.'

'Nothing to be embarrassed about,' Holly said softly. Her mind was lurching between irritation, panic, kindness and a desire to touch Jack's face. She pulled another piece off the kitchen roll and began to rub it on her cheeks vigorously, focusing her energy on how awful she looked instead.

Jack switched on the radio halfway through "The Long and Winding Road". 'Oh God, I hope not,' he muttered, changing the station. They were greeted by the opening bars of "Bright Side of the Road".

'Let's keep that on!' Holly looked straight ahead and tried to remain composed, even though it was difficult with grease smeared on her face. 'Maybe it's how the rest of the day will go.'

The van paused at a roundabout with six exits. 'Yes,' said Jack, assertively. 'Positive thoughts, because it feels a bit like Groundhog Day.'

* * *

Holly's father was leaning against a wall outside the venue with his headphones on when they arrived, but he began striding towards them when he spotted them, seemingly in time to whatever music he was listening to. 'Holly, my lovely!' He beamed, holding his arms out. 'What a brilliant old place. I remember coming to this venue in the late seventies. Hasn't changed much. Hang on.' He stared at her. 'What's happened to your face? It's all grey.'

'Is it?' Holy felt her stomach lurch nervously. 'It's a long story, Dad, but maybe there's a bathroom inside I can use before I meet our guest?'

Jack banged the van door shut and shook Gary's hand. 'Nice to see you again, Mr Merriweather.'

'Likewise.' Gary began to laugh. 'I'm pleased you've got clothes on this time.'

'Ha ha.' Jack patted him on the back in a very manly way. 'I only dress like that when I'm paddleboarding, thankfully. Shall we go in?'

'Yes, our guest is there already.' He opened the door. 'No time for the bathroom, my dear, but it's quite dark in there, so maybe we won't turn the lights on and your weird face won't stand out.'

'Thanks, Dad.' Holly took a deep breath. *I shall transcend this setback*, she chanted to herself. *I shall make the most of it.*

'Are you that Holly Merriweather that posted on the Lights' Facebook fan page?' A wiry man with long hair tied back into a ponytail shouted from the back of the room.

'Um . . .' Holly was confused. 'I did. Yes.'

'Why are you interested in the Bollington?' He turned the light on. 'And what's happened to your face?'

'Long story,' Holly muttered.

'The Bollington?' he said again.

'I live near Farthing Street and wondered why the Bollington had been closed for so long. That's all.' She glanced at Jack, hoping he wouldn't ask why she was digging around.

'It's weird that one. I remember it closed down in February 1989, and do you know — it's never been used since? I assumed it had been repurposed or knocked down. But when you put that post up, I was very surprised. So, I did a bit of research and it turns out the Lights were the last band to play there. Ever. The place was trashed after their gig and that fight.' He looked at Holly's father. 'What a loss to music, eh? I thought they had a lot more to give.'

Gary shook his head sadly. 'I saw them there, you know? Before Holly was born. It was life-changing. The energy they had. When they played "In the Dark and the Shade", the room went silent. It was — I can't describe it . . .' He trailed off, his voice strangely emotional.

'What happened to the Lights?' Holly remembered the sadness that had permeated the building when she'd been there.

'After Lawrence Mandrel died, they split up. Immediately. It was on the cards, anyway. That massive fight at the last gig was partly because he was eyeing up Hollywood. Different direction altogether. And there was a rumour that Don was having an affair with the keyboard player's girlfriend.' He shook his head sadly. 'Rock and roll, eh?'

'What about the rest of the band?' Holly wondered if she could contact them and ask a few questions.

'Disappeared off the face of the earth. Not one of them carried on in the business. Which is unheard of, isn't it? And then the drummer died a few years ago in an industrial accident. Turned out he'd been living on a smallholding in Cheshire all that time.'

'So very sad. They were heartbroken about Lawrence, weren't they?' Gary sighed. 'I reckon.'

Jack cleared his throat. 'That's very interesting. But aren't we here to talk to you about this magnificent place?'

'Oh yeah.' Mr Bright shook his head. 'I get a bit lost in the past sometimes. Anyway, let me show you around. And my name's Leo by the way. You'll need it for the article.'

CHAPTER TWELVE

Holly sat at her desk in the office with her headphones on to block out the steady drip of another leaking pipe into a bucket. She had taken on the responsibility of emptying it as it was closest to her. She'd also downloaded the Lights' *Greatest Hits* out of curiosity. Their sweeping guitar riffs and punchy rhythms were loud enough to cover irritating noises, and she found their songs rather upbeat and beautiful.

Saving a document about some research she had done in Russell Square, she added it to the shared drive folder and took her headphones off.

'I *am* taking it seriously.' Claudette's voice drifted from Jack's office. 'This project is hugely important for the business. Without it, we don't have a business.'

'I'm beginning to wonder if we should have sold it when we had the chance,' Jack responded with a sigh.

Holly had the headphones in her hand, hovering between the table and her ears, knowing she shouldn't be listening, but also wanting to know what was going on.

'I understand. But Barney said it was a bad deal, and when we found those old guidebooks, it felt like a sign we should carry on.'

'It's just that we're leaking money as quickly as that leaky pipe is leaking water.' Jack sounded disconsolate. 'Maybe we should have let the past be? I'm an outdoor pursuits instructor, Mum. Not a publisher. Or a writer.'

'And I'm an artist. I was ready to let go, you know? But finding those books when we did, it was as if your father wasn't ready.'

'His other travel books would have had another life with that company, though. I just don't want to let you down, Mum. Or him.'

'This is the right thing to do!' Claudette almost shouted. 'I'll find the money.'

'I don't want you to do that. We need to be cautious.'

'Well, maybe we should listen to Holly and bring some money in via the website before the books are published. It's about more than money, Jack. It's putting a line under the past. For us both.'

Holly held her breath.

'Maybe. I'll think about it.'

Holly breathed out. She felt frustrated and confused. What was holding him back? Didn't he trust her? She put the headphones back on and opened up another document, typing *Regent's Park Road* on the top. 'Oh well, at least Viktor and Paulo are doing something to help themselves at Farthing Street tonight,' she mumbled, opening a Facebook event inviting everyone to the *Midsummer Evening Tea — cakes, drink, music and stalls to celebrate summer!*

Claudette walked out into the office and sat down. 'Oh, it's so hot, isn't it?' She smiled at Holly. 'I could do with a swim.'

'That's a good idea.' Holly looked at her. The smile wasn't real. The sadness she'd noticed when they'd first met was there again. 'I've just this moment decided I'm going to swim in the mixed pond on Hampstead Heath tomorrow morning. Do you want to come? You said you'd like to a while back, but we never actually did it. I can book for you?'

Claudette suddenly looked as if she were about to cry. 'Oh . . . no! I know I said I might do it last time you mentioned it. But I'm not sure. I haven't done that for so long. It's the past,' she added quickly.

'Well, so are these guidebooks, really.' Holly looked out of the window. 'It will be gorgeous — plunging into a cool pool on a hot, hot day.'

Several drips drummed loudly in the bucket.

'No. You're right.' Claudette stood up. 'I'm living with the past every day, so why not? Yes. Yes, please, Holly. Tell me the time and I'll meet you there.'

'Okay — I'm going to a little street party this evening, too, near where I live. You're welcome to come to that.'

'That's very kind of you, but I'm at a gathering in a friend's garden this evening to celebrate Midsummer's Day.' She also glanced out of the window. 'There's not a cloud in the sky. Except one or two!'

* * *

The rain started when Holly was on the bus — almost just a scattering of mist from an unseen cloud. As they drove over Tower Bridge, it began to pitter-patter rhythmically on the window from a sky that was beginning to turn a depressing grey from the east. To the west, along the river, it remained an optimistic warm and sunny blue.

She rummaged around in her handbag to check she had her umbrella. 'Just in case,' she said to herself. 'Because it can't rain, can it? That would ruin the party and that just *mustn't* happen.'

Suddenly, the rain fell harder, looking like someone was spraying the bus with a fierce garden hose. Holly closed her eyes and decided it would definitely have stopped by the time she got to Primrose Hill. Then she put on her headphones and began to play *The Lights Live at the Hollywood Bowl, 1986*. She smiled as she listened to the lyrics of the song "Summer in Your Eyes".

I don't want you to know it
I'm trying not to show it

Hiding it all away
But there's summer in your eyes

The crowd began to join in as the song rose to an anthem-like crescendo.

Summer
Summer
Summer
Summer
In
Your
Eyes

By the time she got off the bus outside Camden Tube station, she was almost skipping through the puddles.

I can't stop it, I can feel it
And all I want to see is
Summer
In
Your
Eyes

The music stopped and she heard someone shouting her name above the sound of the traffic. 'Holly! Holly, wait!'

She turned around, still caught up in the melody. Jack was waving at her from outside the Jazz Café, sheltering from the rain in the doorway.

'Hi!' She waved back, the butterflies in her stomach dancing around excitedly. *Stop it*, she thought. *It's the song you were listening to, not the sight of Jack that's causing this.*

Isn't it? Isn't it!

He crossed the road, weaving around the stationary traffic, with the rain now almost cascading from the sky. 'I wasn't expecting to see you here,' he said, putting on a raincoat with a hood hurriedly. 'Where has this rain come from? It wasn't forecast.'

'No.' Holly glanced at her sodden feet. 'I'm definitely dressed for a midsummer day.'

'Are you heading home? I was meeting a friend for a drink, but he's just cancelled. Bad flooding just outside King's Cross station is blocking the lines, apparently.'

'I'm going to a party in Farthing Street.' The rain was now hammering down on her umbrella. 'I think they've hired marquees so it should be dry.' She suddenly had a thought — *maybe if I get him there, he'll see why I want to do something on the Bollington? Once I've worked out how to do something without upsetting the owner, obviously.* 'Do you want to come? It's where that music venue your father wrote about is.'

'Ah.' He hesitated, checked his phone and looked up at her again. 'Why not? It may be raining but at least it's warm!'

'I do have to nip home and change my footwear, though. Do you want to meet me at the party?'

'Is it all right if I follow you? I don't have to come in. I'd just rather go with someone who knows, you know?'

Holly panicked. She mentally scanned every room for mess, underwear strewn over the back of a living room chair, or unwashed plates, and decided that there was nothing to be really ashamed of. 'Yes. It's only a few minutes' away. Come on.'

They began to run along the pavement, darting around pedestrians and hurrying across roads until they arrived at her house. 'Come in.' Holly pushed the door open. 'You can't stand in the rain. I hope you like cats.'

Isabella launched herself at Jack's feet as soon as he stepped inside. Holly tried to pick her up to stop her. 'It's all right.' Jack laughed. 'I had to leave my cat behind when I split up with my ex, so I'm happy to have the attention.'

'Right!' Holly ran into her bedroom, grabbed the first pair of shoes she could find, put them on and then joined Jack back in the hallway. 'Ready then.' She looked down. They were bright red. 'I'll be easy to spot!'

149

'You're always very summery.' Jack picked Isabella up and stroked her head. 'And your cat is a real sweetheart.' He put her down and followed Holly outside.

It was still pouring with rain. Holly looked up, then along the street as the drops almost bounced off the cobbles, then at the secret path that led to Farthing Street.

'Follow me,' she whispered. 'But don't tell anyone about this. It's a secret.'

'I don't really know where I am.' Jack shrugged. 'So, it's a secret from me, too.'

They scurried along the narrow lane, the branches heavy with wet leaves brushing Holly's arms as she passed, just as a loud clap of thunder banged in the distance.

'Here.' They stopped and Holly gasped. 'I thought they had marquees!' She looked at Jack, then at the tables outside the café huddled under their parasols, set for a midsummer tea. But there was no one there. "Never Gonna Not Dance Again" by P!nk blasted out of a sound system set up just inside Caleb's record shop, and Bev had pulled her clothes rails under the awning outside her shop.

Melissa was standing inside the café talking to Paulo and Viktor. 'You needed more time to organize an event like this,' Holly heard her saying, as she and Jack walked over to join them. 'I mean, where are the marquees you needed?'

'They let us down.' Paulo was looking disconsolately at the floor. 'My friend's brother's friend's uncle gave us a good deal. He was highly recommended.'

'Who by?' Viktor's voice was even louder than normal.

'My friend's brother's friend,' Paulo almost whispered.

The song changed to "Ray of Light" by Madonna. 'Oh, Holly.' Viktor grabbed her hand when he noticed her. 'This is very bad. So very disappointing.'

'It's fine, it's fine. We can organize something better, can't we?' Melissa turned her attention to a stocky man wearing a leather jacket.

'Absolutely,' he said. 'Great spot.'

'This is Geraint.' Melissa almost pushed Holly towards him. 'We work together. He's in events. I'm thinking of branching out.'

'Hello, Geraint.' Holly shook his hand. 'I thought you wanted to be a teacher,' she said quietly to Melissa.

'I'm exploring many ideas.' Melissa changed the subject quickly. 'You remember Franc, Holly? Well, he's been seconded to the New York office. Geraint here is recently single, so I thought I'd get him out and about. Holly is also recently single. You have a lot in common.'

'Oh . . . right.' Geraint leaned forward. 'Horrible out there, isn't it?'

'I don't know.' Holly didn't know what to say. 'I'm not really . . . out there . . . currently.' Jack cleared his throat behind her. 'Oh, yes — this is Jack. We work together. We just bumped into each other by accident.'

'Well, hi!' Melissa almost pushed Holly out of the way. 'Nice to meet you, Jack. Did Holly send you my ideas about publicity for the books? I've been in Dublin working so haven't had time to check in with you.'

'Oh, is this the guidebook man?' Viktor boomed. 'This is very bad. Farthing Street is a wonderful place. Please don't judge us on this waste-of-time, wash-out English summer's evening debacle.'

Jack didn't say anything for a moment. In fact, he looked a little startled. But then he composed himself. 'Hello, Melissa. Nice to meet you. And, yes, she did. And thank you.' Then he turned to Viktor and Paulo. 'And it's not that kind of guidebook. You have absolutely nothing to worry about.'

'Have you shown him the Bollington yet?' Melissa almost clapped her hands together and turned to Geraint. 'There's this old music venue next door that's very famous. No one uses it. But someone looks after it.'

Holly waved her hand in front of her mouth to try to get Melissa to stop. 'We know it's an old music venue. As for the other part, Melissa — we don't know that, do we?' She nodded at her. '*Do* we?'

'Ah, no.' Melissa fumbled in her bag and pulled out her phone. 'Sorry about that. I got a bit carried away.'

'The Bollington?' Geraint's eyes lit up and he took his hands out of his pockets, waving them around enthusiastically. 'I thought it had been knocked down years ago. Where is it? I used to dabble in music journalism before events, you see.'

'It's next to the clothes shop.' Holly glanced outside. The rain was now hammering on to the road. She decided to stay where she was.

'Holly, lovely!' Holly looked up to see her father hurrying across from the record shop followed by Caleb, who was dragging a reluctant-looking Mabel.

'Dad?' Holly waved at him. 'Why are you here?'

'Heard so much about this place and wanted to see the Bollington again. Was at a loose end and drove in. Fully intended to call you, but I got carried away with talking when I popped into the record shop.' He darted into the café, dripping water on the floor. Caleb eased himself inside and put down his umbrella.

'Why's everyone so interested in that place all of a sudden?' Caleb sounded almost sullen.

'Me and Caleb here have been chewing the fat about music. What a collection of vinyl he's got. I'll be spreading the word to my fellow enthusiasts.'

'Where's Mrs Merriweather today?' Melissa kissed his cheek.

'Hello, my dear! She's at an eight-hour-long yoga retreat near Hemel Hempstead.'

'Are we going to give this up then?' Caleb peered outside as "It's Raining Men" began to blast from the speakers. 'I think this is it for the night. And I told you so.' He sat down at a table. 'Pity for the food to go to waste, though.' He looked at Viktor. 'I'll have the Midsummer Madness Special, please.'

'Absolutely.' Holly's dad sat down next to him. 'Me too. Come on, everyone.'

'I'd love to get into that place for a look around.' Geraint became animated again. 'Music history and all that.'

Holly bit her lip. Viktor's shoulders were hunched. Marialena was trudging sadly from the dry-cleaner's. She noticed Bev closing her shop. Then she remembered all the empty tables and chairs in the Bollington, ready for something that was never going to happen. Unused, not neglected, but sad and somehow lonely.

'I think,' she said loudly over the chatter around the tables, 'that the Bollington may hold the key to helping get more people to Farthing Street. Even if we never go inside. And . . .' She turned to Jack and caught his eye for a moment. When she did, it felt as though an electric shock had almost knocked her off her chair, and she quickly glanced at the floor to shake the feeling away. 'And,' she looked up and focused on his left ear. 'It will help with pre-publicity for the books.'

'We don't need to use an old building like that to get people here. I say leave well alone.' Caleb leaned back as Mabel shook the rain from her back. 'It's been like that for years. It's just old bricks and mortar.'

'But it isn't.' Gary almost leaped up. 'Think about the bands that have played there. And there's the Lights. Their first and last gigs, and they've completely disappeared. Completely. It's one of the great rock mysteries of all time.'

Jack smiled at Holly. 'Your father is a real fan, isn't he?'

'Surely it will help you, Caleb?' Paulo placed a plate of sandwiches and cakes in front of him. 'I mean, you *do* have a record shop opposite that place.'

'I do very well as it is. I'm happy with how things are.' He picked up a pink fondant fancy and began to eat it quite aggressively.

'I can speak to some old contacts?' Geraint sat down next to Caleb.

'You don't have to.'

'It's worth a try?' Viktor boomed.

'Not sure if we should jump in with the publicity for us, though,' Jack said slowly. 'Maybe we should wait.'

Holly's phone rang. She ignored it. Then it rang again. And again. *Who's that?* she wondered, trying to work out who the number on the screen belonged to. 'Sorry. I just need to get this.' She went outside and stood under a parasol. The rain was easing slowly. 'Hello. Holly Merriweather.'

'I'm phoning from Leested and Grange about an unpaid debt on a business you recently wound up.' The man's voice was deep and business-like.

Holly felt like someone had thumped her. 'What? I didn't realize we had any debts.'

'You were in partnership with Edward Purcell?'

'Umm, yes.'

'Well, you should be aware then that there were three separate loans taken out eighteen months ago that have been defaulted on and, despite our attempts to contact Mr Purcell, they have remained unpaid and have accrued interest.'

'What?' she repeated, putting her hand on to the parasol as if it would keep her from collapsing on to the floor.

'Do you know where he is? You are both liable to pay.'

'I didn't sign anything for any loans.' There were so many thoughts running around her head that she couldn't focus on any of them. 'I don't know about any loans apart from the business support ones we took out three years ago.'

'I believe you are no longer residing in Yorkshire. We have visited the premises and the new tenants gave us your number.'

Holly felt sick again, imagining the nice family who had moved in after her having to open the door to someone chasing her for Ed's unpaid debts. 'Have you contacted Mr Purcell?' she asked.

'Yes. But he's not responding to our messages. And, as I said, you are both liable for the debts.'

'How much?' She didn't want to know.

'£18,500.'

'*What?*'

'And there will be more interest to be paid if they're not settled within four weeks.'

Holly felt her breathing begin to quicken and her head begin to thump.

'And it will proceed to court if it remains unpaid.'

'I . . .' She swallowed. 'I was completely unaware of this.' Then she remembered the envelopes she'd asked Ed about on the hall table. *That's why he hasn't sent me his address.*

'As I said, we have tried to contact Mr Purcell, but he's not answering and we do not have an address for him either. We have one for you, however.'

'Leave it with me.' Holly felt suddenly angry. Her heart was beating fast, but now it was because she wanted to shout at Ed. Stubborn Ed. Ed who wouldn't listen to her when she told him the business was struggling. She could see him now, walking towards her with his arms outstretched, smiling.

'Hol, Hol, trust me,' he'd said. 'We're getting there. It's February — everything is quiet in February. Just a few more months and things will pick up.'

'But we're almost out of money. I don't want us to get into the kind of debt we can't get out of.'

He pulled her into a hug and begun to stroke her hair. 'You worry too much. Trust me. I'm keeping an eye on the cash flow. It's you and me. Like it always has been. A team. Together. We've got this.'

'Miss Merriweather?' The voice on the end of the phone dragged her back into the present.

'Yes. I will contact Mr Purcell.'

'We have been trying to contact him for some time without success.'

'Some time!' She felt her voice get louder. 'He moved away four months ago. He ran away and left me with these debts?' *He was getting those letters for months. Is that what he was reading the day he told me I should be writing instead of just thinking about writing?* Now she just wanted to cry.

'I don't know. That's none of my business, Miss Merriweather.'

'Right,' she said limply. 'Goodbye.' She switched the phone off and stared into the distance. 'He didn't listen to me. I was right,' she muttered. 'He didn't listen to me. And then he ran away.'

She looked at her phone then rang him, her still heart racing as the rain turned to drizzle around her.

The phone rang out so she left a voicemail. 'Ed,' she said, trying to sound calm. 'I have had a debt collector on the phone just now. He said we owe money. And that you knew that when you left. We don't owe the money. You owe the money. You must ring me back immediately. *Immediately*.' Putting the phone in her bag, she stood up and watched the people in the café chatting and laughing despite the rain, but she knew she couldn't join them again now. Turning towards the road, she began to walk home.

'Going so soon?' Bev smiled at her as she walked past.

'Yes, just a bit tired.'

'They still talking about the Bollington?'

'Oh yes.'

'Honestly. Someone obviously just wants it to stay the way it is, so what's all the fuss?' She shrugged her shoulders. 'See you soon then, Holly.'

'Yes, see you soon.'

* * *

Holly lay down on the bed and tried to ignore her phone, which was ringing and pinging with messages for about an hour. She eventually wrote a message — *Sudden migraine, sorry* — sent it to everyone and stared at the ceiling, her mind swirling. She was fighting the urge to get on a train, travel to Scotland and shout at Ed in person.

Isabella sat next to her all night, listening when Holly cried. 'He ran away and left me. He ran away. And he knew. And I was right, I was right. He didn't listen. But I was right,' she kept on repeating.

At 1 a.m., she climbed out of bed and made herself a cup of camomile tea, then sat in the living room and put on the TV, switching between the channels until she found an old black-and-white film starring Judy Garland and Mickey Rooney in which they put on a fundraiser to help out some financially strapped relatives. Holly thought about the money Ed owed and the little money she had left, her friends in Farthing Street fighting for survival, and Claudette and Jack struggling to keep Fambridge Books afloat.

'I'm going to be out of a job soon if I don't do something,' she said to Isabella, who was now curled up next to her on the sofa.

She opened her laptop and found some photographs of Ed standing outside the cottage next to their delivery van. Her heart began to pound angrily. She picked up the phone and stared at his number, desperate to wake him in the middle of the night so he would feel as stressed as she did. Then she stared at her laptop.

'Right. Right,' she muttered, opening a Word document. 'If you lot won't listen to me, maybe somebody else will.'

CHAPTER THIRTEEN

The alarm buzzed insistently, rousing Holly from her restless sleep. Opening her eyes, it took a moment for her to remember the phone call from the previous day. When she did, the tears came again. Tears of anger, fear and betrayal. The man she had loved and trusted had run away, dismissing her questions and stamping on her heart. That's what he had done — he had stamped on her kind and open heart.

Opening her laptop, she read what she had written in the early hours of the morning. One new article for her travel blog about Farthing Street and the Bollington, which she had dashed off hurriedly and published before she could change her mind, and another post on the Fambridge Books rarely used social media accounts.

> *The hidden gem that is Farthing Street is protector of a precious musical nugget. A place that hosted some of the most famous bands in the world at the beginning of their careers — the Bollington. It isn't something else now. And it hasn't been knocked down or redeveloped. It's just as it was. But seemingly locked away from the outside world, watching over the shops and cafés that surround it — those independent businesses that strive to keep our high streets and town centres thriving.*

They are all delightful, delicious and special — and those that are in Farthing Street are particularly so, in my opinion . . .

'I *do* know what I'm doing,' she muttered, getting out of bed. 'And I'm doing this for me. And them. But mainly me.'

Picking up her phone, she called Ed again, but it went straight to voicemail, so she sent him a text instead.

You need to call me, please. I've had a call from a debt collector. Hoping it's a mistake. But it was very frightening.

Then she had a shower, got dressed, packed her swimming costume and towel, and set off in the rain to meet Claudette for their swim at the mixed pond on Hampstead Heath, desperate for a little respite from the constant commentary in her mind about Ed and his debts.

* * *

Claudette was waiting for her outside Fenton House, almost hidden under a large, striped umbrella. 'I was hoping for less rain and more sun,' she said as Holly got closer. 'But I really feel this is something I need to do.'

'You don't have to do it.' Holly remembered Claudette's description of the chocolate digestive. 'If it's going to upset you. It's just swimming.'

'I woke up this morning with this feeling that coming today was absolutely necessary.' Her tone was firm. 'So, I will enjoy it. I definitely will!' Grabbing Holly's hand, she turned in the direction of the Heath. 'Come on — before I decide that enjoying myself is not worth the effort.'

The rain got heavier as they trudged into the park. 'We're going to get wet anyway, aren't we?' Holly tried to sound jaunty but her feet were feeling very damp already.

'Oh, yes, swimming in the rain is one of my favourite things,' Claudette almost sang. 'They should have written a song about that too. You know . . . "I'm swimming in the rain".' She laughed loudly, then went very quiet as they turned the corner.

'I haven't been here for so many years,' she murmured eventually as they stood on the path overlooking the pond, then she put on her sunglasses and touched Holly's arm. 'Come on. I used to love it then. I'm sure I'll love it now, too.'

Holly wiped some rainwater out of her eyes. 'Yes, you will.' *I'm not sure I will, though*, she thought, striding purposefully towards the gate.

'I have swum here in the summer, in the winter, in the rain, in the snow.' Claudette seemed to be talking to herself. 'I have swum on autumn mornings when the mist floated above us, covering the trees like cobwebs, and we'd stay so long the sun would slowly burn it away. It was like watching the sunrise twice.'

Holly pushed the gate open. 'That sounds absolutely magical.'

'It was so very inspiring. In fact, it's those experiences that motivated me to paint. The first thing I sold was a watercolour of the Heath in the mist.' Claudette pulled out her phone as the woman checking the tickets smiled at them. 'Here we are. Two for 11 o'clock.'

'The changing rooms are over there,' said the woman. 'And the pond is over here.' She smirked as she pointed to the end of a pontoon.

Claudette looked up and touched the leaves of a tree overhead. 'Look at the raindrops — hanging like tiny glass baubles from the branches . . . and the light — it's such a gorgeous, wistful silver-grey, don't you think?'

The rain pitter-pattered relentlessly as they walked to the wooden changing rooms. 'Shout when you're ready.' Holly opened the door to her cubicle. 'Then we can make a run for it together rather than one of us standing getting drenched — before we actually want to get drenched, that is.'

'Good point,' muttered Claudette, slamming the door shut behind her.

Holly hurriedly changed, stuffing her clothes into the rucksack, then knocked on the dividing wall. 'I'm done.'

'Can you hear that?' Claudette whispered.

'Hear what?'

'Exactly. It's stopped raining!'

Holly opened the door and peered outside. 'Yes, you're right. Shall we run towards the water very, very quickly in case it starts again?'

'Yes! One, two, three . . . let's go!'

They both giggled as they hurried towards the pontoon, then stopped.

'Oh, my goodness,' breathed Holly. A watery sunlight was glowing palely over the empty pond. 'It's like a film set.'

'You and your films.' Claudette climbed up to the steps. 'Best get straight in and not think about how it will feel.' She paused for a moment and took a long, deep breath. 'It's been over thirty years.' Holly watched her as she dropped herself into the water, then swam over to one of the grassy banks. As she watched, she imagined Seth and Claudette splashing around in the lake and laughing while discussing how to describe the scene in his books. She waved over at her. 'Come on in, it's absolutely lovely.'

Holly gingerly climbed on to the ladder and began to allow her body to sink into the pond. She shivered, expecting the water to send a cold, uncomfortable frisson from her feet to the top of her head. But it didn't. It was warm and somehow welcoming. And then she began to swim, but it didn't feel like swimming — it was more like floating, gliding effortlessly across the pond, weightless and free. 'I feel like I'm flying through the water,' she whispered to Claudette as she drew closer. 'It's—'

'Don't even try to work out why, or what.' She pointed up. 'Look, there's blue sky, and there's a shaft of sunlight illuminating the water like an arrow, and the only people here are us.'

Holly grabbed on to a pontoon platform and sighed happily. 'It's as if this were meant to be.'

'I threw myself into my art when Seth died . . . there, I said it — the word "died".' Claudette turned and floated on her back. 'But it's been flowers and faces and not what I really love, which is landscapes.' She gazed at the sky. 'I was in the middle of planning, the day I got the call telling me he'd been rushed to hospital. He'd been out jogging and collapsed in a park near our house.' She paused for a moment. 'I threw the canvas away. Every time I looked at it, I'd remember the phone ringing and me tutting and walking over to answer it — I was mid-flow and didn't like being interrupted. But it kept ringing and ringing, and then I decided I never wanted to paint a tree or a lawn or a lake again. But now . . .'

'Now?'

'I'm going to paint this, how it looks and how it feels today.' She pushed her hair back behind her ear, her voice becoming more animated. 'I shouldn't stop doing something I love because of the pain of the past. I wouldn't have wanted Seth to stop doing what he loved if I'd been the one to die. And for some reason, I feel he's been trying to tell me the same thing for so long. If only I'd been listening. I've not been living. I've been treading water.' Then she burst out laughing and it rang around the lake, joyful and uninhibited. 'And I had to go for a swim to realize it!'

'And I'm going to write about it,' said Holly. 'Not as well as Seth did, obviously.'

Claudette turned to face her. 'It will be just as good, but different. Your way. Remember.'

'Yes, my way.' Holly watched as one of the lifeguards helped an elderly man climb down the steps. The man then plunged in and began to swim his first circuit while a moorhen landed like a seaplane on the surface of the pond, slowly and elegantly easing to a halt.

'It's so amazing that this is in the middle of a city,' she remarked.

'It really is. Thank you for this, Holly. I was so worried about coming back. I was frightened it would pull me into the past and I'd feel guilty for moving on. Letting the grief go. You know, I feel like I'm stuck — I'm scared to leave it behind, but I'm scared not to . . . but . . . but . . .' She moved her arms backwards and forwards in the water, sending ripples across to the bank. 'It's just made me happy. Suddenly! Magically! I can't have what I had. But I'm glad I had it. And I can have something just as good. But different — like today.' She began to swim again. 'So, that's why I'm going to paint it again,' she called back. 'It'll be London how *I* see it now. Through different eyes.'

Holly watched her go, then floated on to her back, observing the grey clouds slowly disperse above her, flickers of blue and white illuminating the sky.

'As if someone were turning a light switch on and off,' she mumbled. 'Must write that down.'

After their swim, they dressed and meandered across the Heath towards Hampstead and Claudette's car. 'You don't have to give me a lift, honestly, if it's out of your way. I can catch the Tube home.'

'It's absolutely fine.' Claudette smiled 'Get in.' She started the car and pulled down the sunroof. 'I haven't been to Primrose Hill for a few years, so I can drop you off and have a little wander about.'

Holly stretched her arms above her head. 'What a treat — an open-topped Mini on a warm summer's day in London.'

'And I can have a peek at your house and meet your cat?' Claudette asked. 'Purely personal — not guidebook-related at all. Music?' She turned on the radio, then turned it off again. 'Let's have the Spice Girls, shall we?'

"Spice Up Your Life" began to blast from the car speakers as she edged out into the traffic and drove towards Chalk Farm.

* * *

'Oh, this is a lovely little mews.' Claudette got out of the car. 'How did you find this?'

'My friend Melissa's cousin owns it.' Holly also got out, shutting the door behind her. 'He's gone off to New York for a couple of years, so I've got it at a reduced rent. Something to do with tax. Otherwise, I'd never be able to afford it.'

'That was a stroke of luck.' Claudette turned slowly around and surveyed the street. 'Now, this is like a scene in a Richard Curtis film, isn't it? No wonder you love it!'

'Again, entirely accidental, but you can only imagine how excited I was when I arrived — I hadn't been down to see it before saying yes. The photos were enough to get me on board.'

Isabella jumped over the fence from the garden and immediately began to weave around Holly's ankles, purring loudly. 'Hello, you.' She picked her up and snuggled her. 'You're like a fur cushion, aren't you?'

'Your cat has been tormenting Mabel. Standing in the garden and looking in the window. It's been almost impossible to drag that dog away. And I'm in a hurry.' Caleb had stepped out on to the street and was locking his front door, while Mabel ran around in circles on the end of her lead at the sight of Isabella.

'I'm sorry. She's just very difficult to keep in. She gets quite agitated until she can go out. Then she wants to come in again.' Holly put the cat down just as Caleb turned to face her and Claudette. They stared at one another for a moment.

'Hello,' said Claudette, breaking the silence.

Holly raised her eyebrows. *That's not Claudette's voice*, she thought. *It's much higher than usual.*

'Hello.'

Holly waited for Caleb to say something else, but they just continued to look at each other. Mabel began to bark loudly. Holly glanced from one to the other, but still neither of them spoke. She nudged Claudette. 'This is my neighbour, Caleb. He owns a record shop in the road I was telling you about.'

'Ah.' Claudette moved forward slightly, her arm outstretched. 'How very nice to meet you.' Her voice was very measured and regal. Holly realized she sounded a bit like Audrey Hepburn in *Roman Holiday*.

'And this is Claudette. My boss.' Holly gently grabbed Caleb's arm to guide it towards Claudette's so he could shake her hand. He eventually took it.

'Come and see my record shop. Any time. Just whenever. I don't have regular opening hours. But I'll open it for you. Any time.'

'Oh,' sighed Claudette. 'What a lovely idea. I really like records.'

A bird began to chirp high on a tree in a nearby garden and was joined by others in a kind of late-morning chorus.

'I have got a lot of records.' Caleb's voice became uncharacteristically animated.

'Perfect.' Claudette was still holding his hand.

A car drove past the end of the street with "Is This Love?" booming out as it went.

'Ah,' murmured Holly. Mabel barked again and jumped up at Caleb, who looked down at his dog as if surprised she was there.

'I'm just showing Claudette my house.' Holly began to open the door. *If I go inside, I won't be witness to whatever is about to unfold*, she thought, as Isabella skittered into the hallway in front of her.

'Who was that?' breathed Claudette, eventually following her in.

'Caleb. I just told you his name! Why didn't you stay outside for a chat?'

'The dog ran around his legs and got him tangled in the lead, so I thought I'd remove myself to save him any embarrassment,' Claudette said sinking on to the sofa. 'He's very enigmatic, isn't he? I mean, there's something about him. You can tell . . . despite the hat and the glasses and the beard.'

'It's like he's in disguise, I think,' said Holly. 'But he's quite nice. A bit irritable. And not very helpful. But apart from that—'

'And record shop?' Claudette interrupted her. 'Oh, is he the one who's not very forthcoming about the Bollington?' Claudette seemed to be pulling herself out of whatever hypnotic spell Caleb had somehow accidentally put her under.

'Yes, that's the one. Fancy a cup of tea?'

'No.' Claudette stood up. 'I must be on my way. Lovely place.' She hugged Holly quickly and walked out of the door.

CHAPTER FOURTEEN

A ray of morning sunlight shone on Holly's face as Isabella jumped from the bedroom windowsill, the curtains moving slightly as she landed on the floor.

'Lovely way to wake up,' she murmured at the cat, opening her eyes slightly. Reaching her hand out to her bedside table, she picked up her phone and checked to see if Ed had responded to her messages. *Nothing.*

'Is there any point?' She sighed wearily. Scrolling through her phone contacts, Holly found her mother's number and stared at it for a moment, then turned the phone over and put it back on the table so she couldn't see the screen.

'Mum will get on a plane and hammer his door down, Isabella. She would if she knew his address, anyway. So, let's not tell my parents unless I have to.' She scrolled down to Ed's parents' contacts and sighed. 'If I tell them, their already fraught relationship will get even worse . . . Oh Holly. Stop being so nice!'

Getting out of bed, she padded barefoot into the kitchen, enjoying the feel of the cool, wooden floor on her feet. Then she put the kettle on and opened the door to the garden. Guitar chords drifted in the air, and she stepped outside and sat down to listen.

'It's "Summer in Your Eyes",' she whispered to Isabella, who jumped on to her left foot and nipped her toe. 'I'll get your food in a second, cat!' She scanned the nearby houses for an open window so she could work out who the musician was.

As the song ended, all that was left was the comforting chirping of the birds and the background thrum of nearby traffic, so she stood up and walked back into the house, followed by Isabella skipping behind her.

* * *

After a quick trip to the supermarket, Holly stopped off in Farthing Street. The green dress Bev had tempted her with a while back was on a hanger outside, so she picked it up and held it against her.

'Aha!' Bev paused in the doorway, a cup of coffee in her hand. 'It's finally getting it's wicked way with you.'

Holly smiled. 'It is lovely.' She looked at the price tag. 'Hopefully it will be here on payday.' She put it back on the rail. *And hopefully you won't have used all your money to pay for a debt you knew nothing about*, she said to herself.

The first few bars of "Summer in Your Eyes" began to drift out from the back of the shop.

'Gosh, I'm hearing that a lot at the moment,' Holly said as she turned to go.

'It takes me right back to happy times.' Bev took a slurp of her coffee. 'Music can do that to you, can't it?'

Holly glanced at the Bollington. The tiny, white notice with Keith the keyholder's number on it caught her eye. 'It certainly can.' She thought for a moment. 'I'm off to get a coffee myself, but I think I'll just get the number of the man who let me into the Bollington again.' Holly took a photo of the notice with her phone.

Bev watched her as she took a long gulp of her drink. 'Some things are best left alone,' she muttered under her breath, then walked back into her shop.

Holly watched her go. *Is the Bollington something to do with Bev? Or does she just like music and a quiet life?* She briefly wondered whether to follow her and ask a few discreet questions, but decided she was too distracted by her money worries to do anything properly, so reluctantly sat down at the café and stared at her phone for a while, wondering what to do about Ed. His silence felt like a punch in the stomach, and every time she thought about it, it was as if she were being punched again.

'We've been going through the list of ideas your friend Melissa sent us.' Paulo sat down opposite her. 'There are some very good ones. We have to do something.' He waved his arm towards the empty tables nearby. 'It's getting worse every day. And I just heard from the man who took over the convenience store from Sven that he may be shutting up shop.'

'You just need to let people know you're here again, Paulo. This is such a lovely street.'

He stood up and nodded. 'That music venue. You're both right, you know? It's the key to getting us all back on track.'

A notification came up on her phone from her bank. *One more direct debit flying out*, she thought. *All my careful financial plans for the next few months laid waste by Ed.*

The anger started to seep uncomfortably around her body again, so she scrolled through social media and found three more photographs of his woodturning efforts, just to make sure she didn't calm down.

You can post those then, can't you, Ed? So, you've got signal.

She read the caption above the photos.

Let me design and create something unique to you. My new website is up and running. Just send me a message and we can start making your dreams come true.

She clicked on the website link and almost threw the phone on the table. The site was glossy and professional. It had probably cost a lot of money.

'Is everything all right, Holly?' Viktor was passing with two plates of food for customers at another table.

'Oh, yes. I just need to sort something out.' Her breathing began to speed up and her heart started to beat faster, so she tried to slow it down by counting and staring at the birds flitting around in the trees lining the street.

Take some control, Holly. Take control of it.

Picking up the phone again, she searched for community groups near the place Ed had moved to. Then she composed a post.

> *Hello. I wonder if anyone can help me? I'm trying to get hold of Ed Purcell. I'm an old friend of his and have an urgent issue I need to discuss with him. I can't seem to connect with him, so if anyone knows Ed, can they ask him to contact me as soon as possible? Many thanks.*

Her hand hovered over the "post" button for a few moments.

The cheese business was his dream, she thought. *Not mine. And the woodturning is his dream. Not mine. So, it's time he dealt with the fallout. Not me.*

Pressing send, she put her phone in her bag, finished her drink and stood up.

That's the last time you get caught in the middle of anyone else's ambitions. Her inner voice sounded positive. *From now on, it's all about you.*

'The hardware store definitely is closing down.' Marialena touched Holly's arm as she walked past the dry-cleaner's. 'Kwan told me this morning.'

'Oh dear. That's a pity.' Holly squeezed her hand. 'When's it happening?'

'He didn't say.' Marialena looked like she was going to cry. 'Just said he'd had enough. It was too stressful.' She grabbed a handkerchief from her pocket and dabbed her eyes. 'I'm scared, Holly. What if my boss really does close the dry-cleaner's down? What will I do?'

'Do you want a cup of something from the café? I've just had a drink, but I can pop back before I go.'

'Yes. Yes, please.' She turned to go back into her shop just as a middle-aged man in a T-shirt with *Are you ready to rock!* written across it in blue letters strode towards them.

'Hello. Excuse me. Can you tell me which building the Bollington is?'

'Over there.' Marialena pointed at it. 'But you won't get in. It's not occupied.'

'I know.' He looked over at it. 'I read a bit about it on a blog that someone had written and posted on the Lights' Facebook page.' He smiled at them both. 'I'm a self-confessed music nerd. I assumed the Bollington would have been knocked down after all this time or redeveloped. So, when I found out it hadn't been, I had to come and have a look.'

'That's funny.' Marialena put her handkerchief back in her pocket. 'Someone was here yesterday afternoon asking the same thing. He had a proper camera with him, too.'

'I'm going to take some photos and post them so my friends can see them,' the man said. 'Thanks for your help. I asked the guy in the record shop and he wasn't very helpful at all, and the woman in the clothes shop was very vague.'

A little burst of excitement was making Holly smile more widely than she assumed she could in the present circumstances.

'Are you a fan?' he asked her.

'I like some of their stuff,' she said. 'Hang on . . . is someone playing . . . ?'

'"Summer in Your Eyes!"' the man exclaimed. 'It's coming from the dress shop. Is it?' They all looked across the road as Bev poked her head out of the shop.

'You're playing it again!' Holly called over.

'What?' She ambled towards them. 'How do you mean?'

'"Summer in Your Eyes" is coming from your shop,' said the man.

'Oh? It's the radio. I changed stations and it's playing on that one now. That's all. What's up, Marialena?'

171

Marialena began to cry, so Holly hurried over to the café as Bev began to comfort her while the man sauntered over to the Bollington. 'Perfect,' she heard him say. 'What with the Lights' most well-known song playing in the background. I'll film it, too. The guys will love it.'

'Can I have a latte and a green tea to go?' she asked Paulo, who was cleaning the tables. 'Marialena is upset.'

He sighed. 'I heard. This is bad, Holly.' He peered back inside the café. 'Even Viktor is down about it. He's not even humming that horrible, tuneless song he normally drives me mad with.'

She glanced over at the man in the T-shirt. 'Maybe something will happen. Something to bring new people into Farthing Street.'

'Maybe.' He sighed. 'I'll get your order.'

Holly sat at a table while she waited and logged on to her blog, then on to the Lights' fan page, where she read the comments on what she'd posted.

What a shame. Such a great old place and it's going to waste.

I'm too young to have seen the Lights live, but if I could just see that place where they last performed, I'd be thrilled.

Successive governments have failed to protect our cultural heritage. Another example. Fuming.

It's just an old building.

The Liiiiiiiights! Ya Ya Ya!

Can anything be done?

'Here you are.' Paulo handed her the drinks. 'You're looking happy all of a sudden. Anything to tell?'

Holly took the cup. 'No. Just work. See you later.' She hurried over to Marialena. 'Here you are. Hope you get better

172

news soon.' Then she headed towards the main road so she could catch the bus to Oxford Street and enjoy London from above ground. *Things may get better*, she thought. *They just might.*

* * *

'The two drafts of your interviews are very, very good, Holly.' Claudette looked over at her from her desk. 'I'm sure Jack will agree.'

'Oh, thank you!' Holly glanced up. 'I'm just putting together a route for tomorrow around Chancery Lane. How are all the other routes doing?'

'Sporadic. Everyone else is fitting all this around their day jobs. But we're getting there.'

Holly's phone lit up with another notification about a direct debit heading out of her account, then she checked for any messages about the note she'd put on the community groups to find Ed. There was nothing there. 'How are things going generally?' She stood up and walked to the kitchen to get a glass of water.

'Oh, you know. Jack's out wheeling and dealing. And then he's doing some intrepid rock climbing with Marco for a few days in Scotland.' Claudette stared at her screen. 'It's all slowly falling into place.'

'I honestly think that some pre-publicity would make a difference.'

'You're probably right.' Claudette suddenly appeared a little distracted. 'How is your grumpy neighbour, by the way?'

'Caleb? He seems the same. Are you going to take him up on his offer to visit the shop?'

'Oh no!' Claudette made a big show of clicking on a file, but Holly was sure she was blushing. 'Although . . .' She looked up at Holly shyly. 'There was something about him.'

'You could just visit and look at the records? Then you could see if there really *is* something about him.'

'Yes. Maybe.' Their phones rang at the same time. 'I'll just get this.'

Holly didn't recognize the number on her phone. Perhaps it was Ed. Perhaps he'd got a new phone. 'Hello, Holly Merriweather here.'

'A man's been banging on my door looking for you.' It was Caleb. 'He said he's a debt collector. I don't appreciate my day being interrupted with someone else's problems, and I'd like you to sort this out. Thank you.' He put the phone down.

Holly walked into the bathroom and began to cry. *Neither do I*, she said to herself. *Neither do I.*

* * *

Holly tried to work hard for the rest of the day, attempting to focus her energy on writing.

The café in the gardens of Russell Square itself . . .

. . . what am I going to do?

is a delight . . .

. . . should I borrow the money to get rid of the debt collectors?

as are some of the inscriptions on the park benches.

. . . should I get on a plane and fly to Scotland to confront Ed? But that would cost more money!

The surrounding buildings, stately and . . .

. . . should I tell Mum and Dad? And Ed's parents?

stately and . . .

. . . No!

stately and . . .

An arm moved into view holding a packet of chocolate digestives. 'Medicinal biscuit?' Claudette pulled up a chair and sat down at Holly's desk.

Holly took one and put it on the table at the same time as Claudette slid a takeaway latte in front of her. 'You didn't even notice me leaving the building, did you?'

'God, I'm so sorry. I'm just very distracted.'

'I would say there is a little cloud hovering above your head.' Claudette took a bite of a digestive. 'Actually,' she said after a moment, 'it's more like its own weather system.' She studied the area above Holly's head intently. 'There's been thunder, lightning, very, very grey clouds and a tornado.'

Holly gave her a weak smile and picked up the coffee. 'You know that you feel stuck in the past?'

'Yes, I do. Sometimes I feel there's a wide-open door, full of sunlight and happiness and newness, and I just stand there, just inside, in the left-hand corner of a dark room holding on to the handle, looking at it, but just staying there. And I can't walk through it.'

'Well, I feel I walked through into that garden, but somebody's grabbed a long pole with a hook on it and dragged me back into the dark room. Their room, actually. Not mine.' Holly bit half the biscuit and chewed it, feeling some kind of relief that she'd actually said that out loud. 'Although, if it's raining *above* my head, it doesn't make sense that I'm inside a room, does it?'

Claudette smiled. 'Mine is all to do with my late husband. Is yours anything to do with your ex-boyfriend?'

'I should never have told myself it was an easy and clean break — that it had run its course and there were no bad feelings.'

'No bad feelings?'

'There weren't. But there are now!' Holly realized she'd raised her voice. 'It's about money,' she said more quietly. 'And debts he's run up for our business I knew nothing about.'

Claudette stood up. 'Well, the question is, what are you going to do about it?'

Holly looked at her. 'And the question for you is, what are *you* going to do about it?'

'Quite.' Claudette walked over to her computer and switched it off. She nodded at Holly, who switched her computer off, too. 'I've got an appointment with some old photographs I'm going to discuss my future with,' she said.

'And I've got a few phone calls to make.' Holly grabbed her rucksack. 'And then I've got to do something about that really good idea I had.'

CHAPTER FIFTEEN

The top of Primrose Hill was busy with what felt like the whole of humanity talking, lazing in the sun, listening to unidentifiable music on headphones, walking dogs and taking photographs. Holly had stepped off the Tube at Camden and allowed her feet to take her to where they felt she needed to be.

And this was the place.

A perfect London view on a perfect summer's day.

Finding a spot under a nearby tree, Holly closed her eyes for a moment. The smell of freshly cut grass acted as a catalyst for her to get on with the job in hand. Opening her eyes, she took her phone out of her bag, rang Ed and left another voicemail.

'Hi, Ed. It's Holly again. Hopefully you'll get this and be able to respond. I know it's all been a bit fuzzy with the breakup and everything, but I'm being hassled by debt collectors about a loan you took out that I knew nothing about. One of them has even been talking to my neighbours. I'm sure you can imagine how distressing and worrying this is. Can you call me back as soon as possible? If I don't hear from you, I'll contact your parents to check I've got the right number and email address. Thanks.'

She then sent a similar message via text, WhatsApp, Facebook Messenger and email.

'Stop hiding,' she said, imagining the messages growing wings and flying determinedly to Scotland. Then she opened the photograph she had taken of Keith the keyholder's contact number.

'Right.' Holly stood up and called Keith's Keys, then began to absentmindedly walk around the tree as the phone rang out.

'Yes?' Keith's voice sounded irritable. Holly nearly cut the call there and then, but forced herself to sound chirpy before beginning to speak.

'Hi, Keith. My name's Holly. We met when I had to rescue my cat from the Bollington.'

'Oh, that lovely little fluffy, black cat?' He sounded a little friendlier now.

'Well, I'm trying to get hold of the owner and I wondered if you could help me?'

The line went quiet.

'I know it's a long shot, and whoever they are obviously wants some anonymity, but Farthing Street needs a boost. Places will be going out of business soon. I just feel like the Bollington has such an interesting history, and we could all collaborate in some way.'

'The owner is not happy about that article or whatever you wrote, Holly.' Keith sounded strangely weary. 'Although, to be honest, it's not like I disagree with you.'

'Oh?' Holly wasn't expecting that. 'I'm glad you don't disagree.'

'But the owner is cheesed off that people are now coming and taking photographs and asking questions.'

'There's something I need to say . . .' Her voice trailed off nervously.

'Go on.'

'It felt so sad in there. It was full of unfinished business. And I think it's been like that for a long time.'

'And?'

177

'I don't want to upset whoever owns it. Clearly, they are still grieving for something. I don't know what. But they own a building in a community of other people, and I thought that perhaps . . .' She could feel her voice slowing down. 'That thinking of the other people in Farthing Street, who are their neighbours, may encourage them to consider . . . something.'

The line was quiet again for a while. 'It will also be helping you and that book company though, won't it, Holly?' Keith said eventually.

'Of course, it — wait! How did you know where I work?'

'I don't hold out much hope, but I'll pass your message on. Bye, Holly. And say hello to Isabella for me.'

Holly hadn't realized her heart was beating uncomfortably quickly until the phone went dead and she had stopped doing circuits around the tree. She sat down.

'Goodness. Being positive and assertive can sometimes be quite exhausting,' she said to a pigeon that had landed in front of her and begun to peck at some grass. It looked up at her briefly before carrying on its search for food.

Holly leaned back against the trunk of the tree, sighing. 'Oh well. Now I just wait for everything to happen.'

* * *

'Geraint asked if he could have your number.' Melissa leaned forward gleefully. 'Holly Merriweather, you have still got it!'

Holly slurped her drink through a multicoloured straw until it made a satisfying gurgle. 'He seemed very nice, but I'm not sure I'm ready to go out on a date yet.'

'Well, it's better than going all gooey-eyed over that colleague of yours.' Melissa waved at the barman. 'Can I have another one of these, and another of those for my friend, please?' She looked back at Holly. 'Although, actually, your colleague *is* film-star handsome.'

'I'm trying hard not to be gooey-eyed. I am *not* getting involved with anyone I work with, or for. As you know.' Holly sighed. 'He is gorgeous, though. But I can admire him in a purely superficial way, as you would a painting or a nice cake.' The drinks arrived. 'I shouldn't really.' Holly took a long gulp despite her better judgement. 'I'm so stressed about bloody Ed and the money. And I'm worried that my job is going to go down the drain, too. You know that Jack has gone off on holiday, in the middle of all this! I heard him and Claudette talking the other day — maybe they've got loads of money and what I'm doing is just a little sideline. Maybe I misheard that conversation about Claudette having to find the money — she could have meant finding which of her many bank accounts was the best one to take it out of. I mean, sometimes I feel like I'm working on their hobby. I wish they weren't so lovely and I didn't like them so much.'

'Firstly, I don't think I've ever heard you talk so loudly or so fast, so I'm glad you've stopped for a breath. And secondly and more importantly — bloody them and bloody Ed.' Melissa smiled kindly. 'Hasn't he called you yet?'

'No.' Holly felt a heaviness descending on her. 'It's not like we split up with any bad feeling. It just ended. So, why is he ignoring me now?'

'Maybe he's embarrassed.' Melissa stood up, walked around the table to Holly and pulled her into a hug. 'And he's stupid. What are you going to do?'

'I've done my sums and spoken to the bank. I may have to get a loan to pay off his loan. But it could be tricky because now my credit score has plummeted. I've tried Citizens Advice but I can't get an appointment for a month. And the debt collectors are keeping in touch, of course.' Holly tried to laugh, but it just sounded more like a cough.

'Have you spoken to your parents?'

'I don't want to. I'm not a child. And I'm not sure what they'd do to Ed if they found out.'

Melissa sat back down and took a long, thoughtful slurp of her drink. 'I'd phone his parents and shame him.'

Holly didn't answer.

'He's being vile, Holly. Don't let some misplaced loyalty stop you from looking after yourself. Talking of which—' she got down again from the bar stool — 'should you need any freelance work to keep you going, if your dream job becomes not a job, we've got plenty.' Picking up her bag, she pecked Holly on the cheek. 'Must rush. The last train to Surbiton waits for no man. And I have a fiancé who has just got back from a work trip to Hong Kong. Happy days!' She winked and walked off.

Holly watched her go and finished her cocktail, then checked her phone to see if Ed had called. But there was still nothing. So she walked out of the door and ambled home, hoping not to bump into any debt collectors or Caleb when she got there.

The evening was still and warm, the scent of honeysuckle floating gently from nearby gardens as she walked, but Holly couldn't shake off the anxiety. Every time her phone rang, her heart raced in case it was another call from the debt collectors. For the last few weeks, each time a letter had arrived on her doormat she'd worried it was another demand for money. And now someone had even been to her house.

Turning into the mews, she stared straight ahead, hoping no one was lurking there. Thankfully, it was quiet — just the sound of a guitar being played again, filling the street with music. Looking around, Holly tried to work out where it was coming from for the millionth time, but every window was open in every house except for hers, so it was hard to tell.

Isabella jumped at her as she opened the door. She picked her up and carried her to the kitchen, putting her down next to her bowls. 'You must be hungry if you're not outside on a night like this.' She shook out some cat food.

After pouring herself a glass of water, she opened the patio doors, went into the garden and sat down next to the table, closing her eyes and breathing in the night air.

The last few bars of "Summer in Your Eyes" faded away, then another song drifted towards her — but this time, someone was singing. She couldn't quite work out whether it was a man or woman's voice, but she caught the lyrics.

I was hiding in the shade
Scared to step outside
But your sunlit soul

The music briefly stopped, then started again.

I was stuck in the shade
Scared to step outside
Then sunlight stood in front of me
You made the bad things start to fade . . .

The mystery musician played a few more chords then began "Summer in Your Eyes" again.

Holly stood up and looked around. 'Who is that?' she said out loud as a bird flitted on to the branch of the cherry tree at the bottom of her garden. Beyond it, she noticed a window in the attic of the Bollington was open a crack.

'Oh, my goodness!' She hurried inside, picked up her keys, then almost flew down the secret lane to Farthing Street.

She pushed the door of the Bollington gently, hoping it would open. When it didn't, she rang the bell. Then she banged on the door. 'Hello?' she shouted. 'Hello?'

'What's up?' Marialena leaned out of the window of her flat above the dry-cleaner's. 'Is everything all right?'

'I think someone's in the Bollington. Can you hear the music?'

Marialena looked around. 'No. I have company.'

A man popped up behind her in the window and waved. 'Everything okay?' he called.

'I thought I could hear music, that's all.'

He held up a guitar. 'I was practising this afternoon.' He grinned at Marialena. 'I'm more than the nephew of the owner of a dry-cleaning empire. I had dreams too once!'

Marialena giggled flirtatiously. 'My mysterious man.' He stroked her hair and then they disappeared from sight.

Holly stood back and looked up at the Bollington. 'There aren't any lights on. I was just sure I heard music coming from an open window.'

'Maybe you did.' Marialena was back now and blew her a kiss. 'I have to go. The phone is ringing. *Boa noite.*'

181

'Good night.' Holly turned to leave, taking one last look at the Bollington. *Maybe I just wanted it to be from there*, she thought as she walked back through the lane, glancing up again at the attic window, which was now definitely shut.

* * *

The following day, Holly worked from home in the morning. Eventually, she decided to pop to the café to get a takeaway coffee before catching the Tube to the office to finish her shift there, but as she turned the corner, she saw a film crew standing outside the Bollington.

'Wow!' She waved at Viktor as he bustled past with a tray of drinks for them.

'It's very exciting!' he beamed. 'At last. People may come back to Farthing Street!'

'I will bring you your coffee in a moment.' Paulo was getting another order ready. 'They arrived first thing this morning. I don't think they've even filmed anything yet.'

'I assume it's about the Bollington?'

'Apparently. Not only because it's a famous music venue, but because it's untouched after so many years.'

'I hope the person that owns it doesn't mind,' Holly found herself saying, the image of the empty room full of sadness making her slightly uncomfortable. 'But I think it's important people know it's there.'

'Holly!' Bev swerved around the crew and a small group of people watching them work. 'What do you think of this then?'

'Who'd have thought you lived next door to such a famous place?' Holly smiled at her, searching her face for a clue she might be connected to the mystery.

'I don't like fuss. I like things left alone.' Her face was creased into an uncharacteristic frown. 'I mean, I need more business. But this is people asking questions and all sorts.'

'Questions?'

'Who owns it? Does anyone go in it? What do I think about it? Did I know any of the Lights? Is it a good thing? Is it a bad thing? What do I want to see happen next? I mean, I don't want to see anything happen next.'

'Well, it is good for business for us,' Viktor cut in.

'You're not the only business here,' Bev snapped, then hurried away. 'Someone's going in the shop — bet they don't buy anything.'

'Caleb isn't happy either.' Paulo handed Holly her drink. 'They tried to get in his shop earlier, and he threw them out then slapped the closed sign on the door.'

'Yes, but he is unhappy most of the time.' Marialena walked over and joined in the conversation. 'Well done for writing that article, Holly. At least something fun is happening as a result.'

Holly heard her phone buzz in her rucksack, so took it out and looked at the number as it flashed over the screen. It was Keith. 'Hi, Keith,' she said quietly and a little nervously.

'Well, Holly. What have you done?'

'I've done nothing very much. But I hope the owner is all right?'

'The owner is not happy but has asked me to make sure you won't say anything to anyone about what you saw inside, even if they offer you fame and riches for it.'

'Of course, I won't. I only wanted people to know about Farthing Street, really. The Bollington is an interesting feature.'

'I knew you wouldn't. You're a good person. I could tell — I could tell from your face when we rescued your cat.'

Holly paused for a moment, then said quickly, 'I don't know whether this is the wrong time but—'

'I have mentioned your thoughts. They have not been responded to yet, so I wouldn't get your hopes up.'

'Ah, okay.' She felt mildly disappointed.

'But as I've said. I think you're right. Something needs to be done. For my friend, AKA my client, mainly. But people, eh? Can't make it up, can you?'

'No, you can't.'

'Look after yourself now, Holly.'

'Thank you, Keith.' She put the phone down as Caleb walked towards them, his face like thunder.

'I've had to take Mabel home. She kept whining with all the fuss. And as for that lot.' He pointed at the camera crew. 'Tried to force their way into my shop and ask all sorts of intrusive questions.'

'They're only doing their job,' Marialena pointed out.

'I'm fed up of everyone thinking that, just because I own a music shop, I know everything about everything about . . . music . . . and that place!' he almost shouted. 'I don't like all this. I want it to stop. And it's your fault, Holly.'

'I was only trying to help.' Holly backed away, confused. 'I'm sure it'll all blow over soon.'

'Don't be like that to her,' Viktor protested. 'We need some publicity. This has helped. Why should some rich developer be sitting on the Bollington, leaving it to go to rack and ruin, and then complain when we, the neighbours, get a little bit of help from it actually being there?'

'What makes you think it's a rich property developer?' Caleb was clearly very irritated.

'Only someone rich can own a place like that and leave it be for so long.'

'Well, I don't like it.' Caleb folded his arms and grunted.

'Well, I do,' Viktor hissed. 'Usual?' He shouted into the shop. 'Usual for Caleb here, Paulo.'

Caleb took out his phone. 'I'm going to do some work here. People keep knocking on the door of the shop.'

'Maybe they want to buy something?' Holly said helpfully.

'This lot don't. They just want to chat. Waste of time.'

'You're being very selfish.' Paulo plonked an iced tea in front of him. 'Sitting around with that miserable face. We need the business. Just because *you* are all online now.'

'Some business is not worth the fuss.' Caleb turned his chair to face the other way.

Holly looked from one to the other unhappily. 'Please don't argue. You're friends and neighbours.'

Marialena touched her hand. 'I don't think they will listen,' she whispered. 'It will all die down soon. You go to work. You did a good thing.'

Holly smiled at her. 'Thanks . . . Bye?' she said to the men, who were busy staring angrily in opposite directions to one another. 'I'll pop over tomorrow.' She turned and walked out of the square, wondering how a simple blog post could cause so much friction, then wondering whether it was Caleb who was the mystery owner rather than Bev, as he did seem very, very angry about the situation. But her mind was still scrambled with Ed and the money, so she made the decision that when she got to the office, she would speak to the bank again — because she felt the need to be in control of something, even if it was sorting out someone else's debt.

* * *

'What a lovely day!' Claudette was standing by the kettle and gazing out of the window. 'Look at the birds skittering about in that tree.' The kettle switched itself off and she picked it up, pouring the steaming water into a mug. 'I just love London in the summer.' She turned to Holly, who was holding her phone and still trying to connect to someone at her bank. 'Is everything all right?' she asked.

'Yes. Just some life admin that needs to be sorted.' Holly stared at the messenger service on the screen, waiting for a human being to get back to her rather than the bot she'd had to deal with first.

'Ah, life.' Claudette sat down. 'Guess what I did? I did a Holly Merriweather.'

Holly looked up. 'A what . . . ?'

'I put on my brightest, happiest clothes, stepped out of the shadows, went to Farthing Street and took Caleb up on his invitation to visit his shop.'

'Oh!' Holly beamed. 'How did that go?' The app pinged. 'Bear with. I've just got to deal with this for a moment.'

185

'Actually, I was just going to nip out to buy some milk. I'll tell you all about it when I get back.' Claudette stood up and walked out of the door, while Holly took a deep breath and tried to organize a loan.

When you find Ed, you really should charge him interest. After you've screamed at him for an hour or so. The voice in her sounded a bit like Melissa today.

She decided to go and sit in the green space opposite the office for a few minutes to create some space between dealing with the fallout from the past and doing her job. Trying to clear her mind, she gazed absentmindedly at the cars and motorbikes driving past, picking up snippets of conversation as people walked by, and then she started counting the number of raised dots on a manhole cover.

She saw Claudette go back into the office building. *Right, back to reality*, she said to herself, just as Jack walked around the corner and followed his mother inside.

Her unguarded heart flipped with relief. *Thank God you're here.* The words flew into her mind unexpectedly, and she sat down again and looked at the doorway, confused.

I barely know him. He's my colleague. He's a nice man. That's why I'm pleased he's back. Calm down and go back to work.

'Okay, once more but this time with feeling — right, back to reality.' She smoothed down the skirt of her pink-and-green sundress, ran a hand through her hair, fixed a smile on her face and crossed the road.

As she got to the door of the office, she heard raised voices from inside, so hovered, wondering whether to go in or head back outside.

'She shouldn't have done it, Mum. I've had a phone call from Susanna all the way from Costa Rica. She saw the post and wants to know what we're doing in case she's entitled to some of the money from it.'

'Why would she do that?'

'I think it's her new boyfriend pushing her to get as much out of me as possible. I'm making sure everything is fair with our old business together. But this is separate, and

I was trying to keep it that way by not formally launching it until all that was settled. I mean, I go off climbing for a few days and Holly does this. Why didn't she wait?'

'Oh — I see, but Holly was trying to help. And it has raised our profile a bit. I had an email from a journalist at a glossy magazine asking to do an interview.'

'And I've had some phone calls from one of our potential new investors asking what we're doing — we weren't finalizing our publication dates till late October, so they wanted to know if we had brought things forward without telling them. They now think we don't know what we're doing. Or not being honest with them . . . either way, I've had to work really hard to keep them on board.'

'I don't understand myself why we're taking so long to decide on publication dates. At least if we know, we can plan, even if we don't tell anyone else.' Claudette sounded exasperated.

'Because we had just about wound the business up before we decided to not wind it up. It's the money, it's the investors, it's the whole thing, Mum. I'm not a publisher. I'm not experienced. I don't want to ruin everything by doing it wrong!'

'You won't do it wrong, Jack.'

'For you and for Dad's memory, it *has* to be right. I don't want to let you down.' There was a pause. 'Marco wanted to start an outdoor pursuits business with me when I came home. I should have done that.'

Holly stepped backwards. *I was just trying to help.* The words rang around her head. *I was just trying to help.*

'Holly should have listened to me.' Jack's voice was getting closer. 'It's not her company. She just gets too carried away with herself. She nearly ruined everything. She's just here to do research. That's all.'

Holly turned towards the stairway, just as Jack opened the office door. They stared at each other for a few moments, his words still hanging in the air.

'Did you hear all that?' Jack put his hand out to touch her arm.

'Yes.' She could hear her own voice, thin and fragile.

He sighed. 'I wish you hadn't.'

'I was trying to help.' Holly began to walk down the stairs. 'I'm sorry if I overstepped the mark. But I heard you talking about money a while ago . . . I thought I could lose my job.'

'That's not going to happen.' Jack began to follow her.

'No? Okay. Good.' Holly couldn't make herself turn back to look at him. She couldn't understand why she felt so betrayed.

There's something of a chasm between "Thank God you're here" and "She's just here to do research". That's why.

She heard Jack's phone ring. 'I'm sorry. I've got to get this. It's business.'

'Right. I'll go and do some research. Field research. So, I don't need to be in the office. Shouldn't have come in, really.'

'Hello, Jack Fambridge here. Can I put you on hold for a second?' She felt him touch her arm again. 'Holly. I'm sorry you heard that. I'm very stressed at the moment.'

Holly forced herself to look at him but couldn't meet his gaze. 'It's work. It's okay. I understand. I'll leave you to it.' Then she walked down the stairs and opened the door, stepping back out to people and traffic. But, despite the blue of the sky and the gold of the sun, the lush green of every blade of grass across the road, it felt as if the lights had been turned down.

* * *

Holly found herself ambling around the stalls at Borough Market, not seeing anything, just moving, trying to get away from the thoughts jumping around in her head.

Everything had gone wrong. And she didn't know what to do.

Finding herself by the river, she weaved through the crowds, putting one foot in front of the other but with no idea of where to go.

Your dream job, she told herself angrily, *has nearly been ruined. By you. You should have stayed and sorted it out with Jack. Like an adult. But here we are. You're running away, just like Ed did to you.*

'I'm not like Ed.' Holly heard her voice and realized she had said it out loud. She carried on walking, past the Globe Theatre, trying not to think, reciting the names of the monuments and the landmarks in her head to focus on anything other than the past few days. *St Paul's to the right*, she chanted, *the Millennium Bridge, Blackfriars Bridge, London Bridge behind me.*

All your savings have gone.

I wonder where that plane is going. Heathrow? Gatwick?

Who's on that boat?

And you're trying to get another loan. Although good luck with that, given you're being chased by debt collectors. What are you going to do now?

Which bridge is this I'm walking under?

What's that song?

Holly looked up, taking in her surroundings properly rather than scanning the path ahead on autopilot.

A tall man in a long, dark coat was standing next to an amplifier singing "The Impossible Dream", his deep voice full of emotion. Holly stopped walking suddenly, caught in the music. She couldn't move. Her feet wouldn't take her anywhere. They forced her to listen, and finally, unable to block things out any longer, she burst into tears.

All those impossible dreams, she thought, hurrying away. *Ed's dream that I thought was mine, too. But all it's done is drag me down with it.*

Fambridge Books. I need to harden my heart. I just wanted to help. Farthing Street — everyone's arguing there now. I just wanted to help. The Bollington . . .

The image of all the empty tables and chairs in the room stuck in time flew into her mind.

'I just wanted to help,' she said out loud. 'And I've made everything worse, haven't I?'

* * *

At 6 a.m. the following morning, Holly sat up in bed and made a decision — she was just going to have to get yet another job on top of her regular job. And she was going to keep her distance from the Fambridge Books office as much as possible.

Picking up her phone, she sent a message to Melissa. *Hey — if you have any weekend freelance work going, let me know. I'm up for as much as possible. H x*

Then she lay back down and had the best two hours' sleep she'd had in a long time.

CHAPTER SIXTEEN

Holly grabbed her bag, put her sun hat on and checked the location of the farmers' market on her phone. Picking up Isabella, she put her next to the food bowl and placed a couple of cat treats in it.

'That's for being a lovely cat.' She gave Isabella a scratch behind the ears. 'Sorry I won't be here much this weekend, but at least I'll have enough money to keep you in cat food. When I sent that text to Melissa earlier in the week, it didn't occur to me I'd be working for her this Saturday!'

Opening the front door, she almost bumped into someone who was on the verge of ringing her doorbell. For a moment, she didn't realize who it was. Until the person spoke.

'Hi, Holly.' Ed's deep voice almost seemed to purr.

'Ed.' That's all she could say, unable to really comprehend he was actually there. Her brain was frozen — all the words she had said to him in her head were stuck somewhere, just out of reach. 'I'm going to work,' is what finally came out of her mouth.

'Can we talk?' He stepped in front of her.

'Only if it is to inform me you have paid off the debts I knew nothing about.' She closed the door and walked around him. 'You have sorted it out, haven't you?'

'I wanted to say sorry.' He followed her as she hurried up along the cobbles, almost slipping as she did.

'Sorry — and?'

'I think I made a mistake.'

They turned right on to the main road. 'A mistake about what?'

'Us.'

Holly's head began to swim, all the things she'd been storing to say to him now swirling around in her mind.

'Are you going to say anything?' Ed tried to get ahead of her to bar her way.

'Us when we were sixteen or us last year?' she said eventually. 'I'm going to be late for my shift, so I'm not going to stop. I'm doing extra work on top of my regular work in order to earn money to stop the bailiffs coming round to my house.'

'I'm going to sort it out. I've spoken to them. I'm sorry. I—'

Holly crossed the road and headed to the square where the market was being held. Ed continued to hurry after her.

'Where have you been?' She could feel her voice rising. 'It's been weeks since I started leaving you messages.'

'I was on a retreat.'

'For all that time?' She waved at Melissa, who was standing with a photographer next to a cheese stall.

'Oh God. Is that Melissa?' His voice started to lose its confident, baritone quality.

Holly stopped and turned, finally facing him. 'Have you any explanation for taking out loans without discussing it with me?'

'I thought you'd say no.'

'Not good enough.' Holly was struggling to keep her voice steady. 'It was our business. Not just yours. You should have allowed me to say no.'

'I know.' He looked at the floor.

'Stop being so nice. I want to shout at you.'

'But I was wrong.' He touched her arm, then reached out and stroked her hair. 'About everything.'

'Holly!' Melissa was striding over to her purposefully. 'Are you all right? We need you to do this interview as soon as possible.' She looked Ed up and down. 'Well, hello, stranger.' Her voice dripped with disdain.

'Hi, Melissa. Lovely to see you.'

Melissa grabbed Holly's hand. 'I'm sorry to be so forceful, but we need to get to work.'

'I want to get to work, thanks.' Holly followed her to the cheese stall, with Ed ambling behind. 'Hello.' She smiled at a woman who was standing in front of it, wearing a white coat and a cream hair net. 'I'm Holly — I'll be asking you questions for the interview for the social media channels. I won't be in the video, though, so we'll make sure when you answer the questions, it will sound like you're just chatting to the camera.'

Of all the things in all the world, it had to be cheese. Her inner voice sighed.

'We could have carried on, you know?' Ed said quietly. 'If you'd had more faith, I wouldn't have gone behind your back.'

Holly could feel the chatter in her head surging angrily again. 'We were bleeding money, Ed. And you lost interest.'

'You were never interested.'

'I was. I'm just not that much of a fan of cheese.' She turned to the stallholder, who was looking at her, confused. 'Nothing personal. I like cheddar and feta, but that's sort of it.'

'I knew it!' He sounded almost triumphant.

'I wanted us to build a life together, which is what you asked me to do on that rooftop in Marrakech, remember?' Holly took the script from Melissa, who was standing next to her and staring furiously at Ed. 'It just happened to be via the medium of cheese.'

'All right, Holly?' Now, just to confuse matters further, Geraint was walking towards them. 'Glad you could help us out today.'

'Who's this?' Ed moved closer to her.

'A work colleague.' Holly glared at him. 'Why are you asking? You don't love me anymore. I remember you telling me.'

'I may have been hasty.'

'You were right, Ed,' she sighed. 'It had ended. Us, the cheese, our dreams. We just let it all drag on for months after that.' She tried to sound nonchalant.

'Who's this, then?' Geraint moved closer to Ed and began to stare a little threateningly at him. 'Is he bothering you?'

'Oh goodness, Hol,' Ed laughed hollowly. 'You and your film fixation — are we going to have a *Bridget Jones* fight now?'

'Oh my God,' muttered Melissa. 'I don't remember you being such a prat.'

'But the films — everything through the filter of fantasy.' Ed's face was turning red. 'Coming to London. All a bit Richard Curtis, isn't it?'

'Your cheese business was a fantasy — what's wrong with that? It's actually called having dreams.' She picked up some Edam and waved it at him. 'There are plenty of films about people starting businesses, Ed.'

'Are you going to pay for that?' the stallholder said under her breath, sounding slightly panicky.

'Yes, yes, sorry. The cheese is a bit of a trigger.' Holly put it back down, then picked it up again and waved it at Ed. 'Are you making fun of me?'

'No!' He stepped back.

'Are you going to pay the debt collectors today and get them off my back?'

He looked at her silently.

'If you don't, I'm going to tell your mum!' She held the Edam up like a bowler about to throw a cricket ball.

Melissa snorted quietly, her shoulders beginning to shake. 'That's the worst threat ever, Holly,' she whispered, grabbing Holly's arm and prising the cheese from her hand.

'Oh dear.' Holly bit her lip. 'I'm so sorry. I don't know what came over me.'

Ed bowed his head, then touched her arm gently. 'Can I take you for a coffee after work?' he asked softly. 'I owe you explanations and apologies, and I was so nervous when I knocked on your door. I've totally mucked it up.'

Holly stared at him. *He's still Ed*, she thought. *The biggest part of my life since I was sixteen. It's time to really let him go.* 'Yes, okay. Let's do it properly. I finish at three. I'll meet you at the café in Farthing Street.'

His face softened. 'I'll find it. I'll see you there.' He turned and walked away.

'Entertaining or what!' Geraint laughed.

'Not the right thing to say,' muttered Melissa. 'Right, Holly. We've got a lot of people to talk to. Shall we start?'

* * *

'Are you sure you don't want us to come with you?' Melissa took her hand as she waited at the crossing to the lane leading to Farthing Street. 'Geraint can come and puff out his chest in a manly way to intimidate Ed.'

'I don't puff out my chest.' Geraint put his hands on his hips. 'Do I?'

'I'll be okay. I've got to speak to him. There are things that need to be said.' Holly put her sunglasses on. 'We pretended it was all so easy when we split up, you know? I've only realized today it wasn't when I was attempting to use that Edam as a weapon.'

'And his mum.' Melissa kissed her on the cheek. 'She would have been the ultimate weapon.'

The lights at the crossing turned red. 'Wish me luck.' Holly squeezed her hand and crossed the road, her strides getting longer and more purposeful as she did. She counted her breaths in and out slowly to make sure she was calm when she got to the café.

Music greeted her as she turned the corner to Farthing Street. A woman was standing in front of the Bollington singing "Summer in Your Eyes", backed by an accordion player and a guitarist. A small group of people were watching her, filming the performance on their phones.

'What's going on?' she asked Viktor as he carried a tray of drinks past her.

'The past few days have been like this.' He looked delighted. 'People coming to look at that place and hanging around outside. This is the first lot who have started singing, though.'

Paulo waved happily at her from inside just as she spotted Ed, who was sitting at a table, nursing a beer and watching the performer.

'Hi.' She sat down opposite him and took her sun hat off.

'Hi.' His voice was quiet. 'I'm so sorry about earlier.'

Holly waited for the happy butterflies to start skittering around in her chest, floating around on the last remnants of sixteen years of love. She braced herself to calm them down. But they didn't appear. Nothing happened.

'Oh,' she said.

'Is everything okay?' Ed leaned in closer.

'Yes, fine. I was just remembering something I should have done earlier.'

'What can I get you?' Ed put his hand up to get Viktor's attention.

'It's fine. I think it's probably already on its way over.' Sure enough, Viktor placed a white wine spritzer in front of her.

'I put ice in it this time. Such a hot day.' He moved on to another table.

'I come here a lot.' Holly picked up her drink just as the guitarist played the first few bars of another song.

'What's this, the Lights' Appreciation Society or something?' Ed looked around at the crowd.

'Oh, it's that old venue — it played a very important part in their career.'

'I'm surprised you haven't written about it.' Ed took a long gulp of his drink and stared at Holly from over the top of his glass.

'I have.' She looked away.

He took a deep breath. 'I'm sorry. I've been awful. Actually, I've been embarrassed and frightened.'

'Of what?' Holly already knew. She just wanted to hear him say the words.

'I knew the business was tanking, but I got those loans because I couldn't bear the thought of all those dreams and that hard work turning into nothing.'

'Why didn't you speak to me about it?'

He leaned forward again. 'Because I knew you'd tell the truth, Holly. And I didn't want the truth. Because when you — positive, excitable, can-do you — says this is not good anymore, you really mean it.'

She took a long gulp of her wine, wondering whether to ask the question, because she realized she might not like the answer. 'Did some of the money get spent on your new website?'

He looked at the table, his foot tapping the floor anxiously. 'Not all of it. I had some of it left after I'd invested in yet more stock we would never be able to sell, and booked us in at some festivals we would never go to. I just doubled down.' He shook his head. 'I didn't want to be wrong, I suppose.'

'What about the money you did ask me for?' Holly looked up at the sky as the light summer clouds floated elegantly past, wondering how the man she'd loved, who was so good at his job with the hotel chain, had lost his way so quickly when the money was theirs.

'That was real. And thank you. I just blocked the loans out. Until I couldn't.'

'I need to tell you this, Ed.' She took his hand. 'I loved you. I wanted to be part of your dreams. I thought they were mine, too. But they weren't, unfortunately.'

'Loved.' He winced.

'You weren't expecting anything else, were you? You said you didn't love me first, after all.'

'No. No turning the clock back.' He picked up his glass again and took a sip, holding it in front of his face as if it were a shield.

'But you got me in the middle of those dreams. And when you applied for those loans behind my back, you got me in the middle of that, too. The last year has been heartbreaking for me. And the last month has been—'

He held his hand up. 'Stop. I know. Like I say, I'm embarrassed.'

'You need to sort it out. But—' she looked at him and caught his eyes, gazing into them deeply for probably the last time — 'I appreciate you coming to see me in person.'

'I have to admit there was a part of me that thought we could try again.' He put his drink down. 'But it was the same part of me that took out the loans because I couldn't let go. Stuck in the past.'

'There's a lot of it about.' She sighed, just as the song changed to a cover of "Thinking of You" by the Colourfield.

They sat in silence for a few moments, lost in their own thoughts.

Then he smiled weakly at her. 'Whenever you hear this song, will you think kindly of me? Of us?'

'I do already.' Holly stood up and kissed him on the cheek, knowing it would be the last time she ever did it. His skin felt stubbly and familiar, and she lingered for longer than she intended, squeezing his hand as she did.

'I'll miss you, Holly,' he whispered. 'I will deal with all the money. I promise. It's not your problem anymore.'

'Thank God they're playing something other than the Lights.' Caleb was walking over, followed by Mabel, who was wagging her tail happily.

'It's bringing a lot of business to the street, though.' Holly sat back down and held up her hand in greeting.

'They're not spending money in my shop.' He pulled a chair over and sat at the next table. 'Just got people coming in wanging on about the eighties music scene and how the Lights changed their lives and on and on and on . . .'

'It's boosting our business no end. I keep telling you.' Paulo hurried past to take another order. 'Thank God. That boiler repair nearly did it for us. It's good to have proper money coming in at last.'

'Mmmm,' mumbled Caleb. 'I think dredging up the past isn't healthy. But there you go. I'm moving forward. Your friend Claudette is helping me. What a lovely woman.'

'Claudette?' Holly was thrilled. 'Have you been hanging out?'

'Hanging out?' He shifted in his seat. 'If you call meeting for coffee once or twice hanging out, then yes.'

Holly glanced at Ed, who was patting Mabel on the head, and wondered if she would ever see him again. She realized she wasn't angry with him. She just wanted him to untangle her money from his and move on. She took a deep breath and was silently thankful for the fact that she didn't love him anymore. In fact, she was romantically free. Completely. *I am absolutely a free agent now*, she thought. *Officially footloose and fancy-free.*

A message flashed up on her phone.

I think I've upset you. It's taken me a few days to pluck up the courage to send this. I can only apologize for taking my frustrations out on you. You are a real asset to the company, and both myself and my mother appreciate everything you do. Jack

Holly read it and put her hand on her stomach to stop the rogue excitable butterfly kicking off again. Then Mabel barked as Ed looked up and smiled.

Holly turned the phone over so she couldn't see the next message that buzzed up. *I am an asset to the company*, she said to herself. *Jack's mother owns the company. He's my colleague. Harden your heart and don't be an idiot, Holly Merriweather. Sitting opposite you is a lesson in what happens when you mix business and pleasure.*

Her hand hovered over the phone for a second, then she rolled her eyes and turned it back over.

I haven't plucked up the courage to actually ring you, though. Hopefully I'll grow up a bit quite soon and do that too. Jack

Holly bit her lip, scrolled through to find Melissa's number and began to type.

Really enjoyed today. If you've got any other bits of weekend work going, let me know. Holly x

The less time I have to think about things other than work the better, she said to herself, then decided to start looking for other job opportunities as soon as possible.

* * *

The following morning Holly took a cup of camomile tea into the garden and sat on a chair under the cherry tree, listening to the birds chattering happily. Slipping off her sandals, she wiggled her toes on the grass, watching Isabella stare at a bee that was clinging to a luscious pink fuchsia. Then she closed her eyes and breathed in the fresh, grassy scent of the garden. She felt lighter again, the money worries hopefully now in the background, and made a mental note to send Ed all the old letters, which were still on the table in the hall. A woman laughed in the distance and Holly looked around. It had sounded a lot like Claudette. Then a car engine thrummed into life and buzzed into the distance. Holly smiled. *If it was her*, she thought, *she sounds really happy*.

CHAPTER SEVENTEEN

Holly spent the next week and a half not going into the office and doing all her meetings via Zoom, often claiming her internet connection was so bad that she couldn't be on video. Her reaction to Jack's overheard negative words were, she had reasoned at around 2 a.m. over several restless nights, not only a surprise but also completely out of proportion, and therefore must have something to do with what had been going on with Ed. And absolutely nothing to do with Jack.

'My only relationship has been with Ed,' she explained to Isabella while pouring herself a glass of cold water at 3 a.m. on the last Thursday she was able to follow that Jack-avoidance-and-denial strategy. She pushed the cat gently away when she tried to drink directly from the tap. 'I just don't know how to deal with whatever all this is. Which is nothing. It's a habit. I have to be professional at all times, and I've frankly been a bit of a twit in my opinion.'

Isabella jumped down on to the floor and stared up at her.

'No, you're right, Isabella. Jack has absolutely no clue about my reaction to the situation, so that is excellent. That is why I must keep my distance, wean myself off, and next time I encounter him, I will behave in a normal way.'

She climbed back into bed and put on a soothing rain-forest background track, but it made her think of Costa Rica, which made her think of Jack and his stubble and his intoxicating, seductive aftershave, which in turn made her feel like an idiot. So, she put on whale music instead, and somehow managed to drift off to sleep.

* * *

The next day, Holly got up and decided she absolutely had to focus on work. So, she packed her rucksack and notes, planning on spending the morning in the area around Broadway Market and London Fields. The member of Jack's family who was looking after the Hackney research was on holiday in Lanzarote and Holly had volunteered to help out. She also planned to visit the lido in her lunch hour for a swim. The July heat was hanging over the city, slowing everyone down and pushing the population outside again, so Holly had booked herself a slot and packed her swimming costume, intending to make the most of the day.

As she was spooning out some cat food for Isabella, her doorbell rang. 'Just a sec,' she shouted, closing the kitchen door behind her before going to see who it was.

Claudette was standing outside her door but was looking at Caleb's front door.

'Hi . . . ?' Holly joined her in looking at her neighbour's house. 'Is everything all right?'

'No. No, it's not, to be honest with you.' Claudette walked into Holly's hallway. 'Can I come in?' she asked a little belatedly.

'Of course.' Holly followed her. 'What's going on?' she asked, guiding her to the living room and sitting down, hoping Claudette would join her on the sofa. Instead, her boss paced around the tiny room restlessly.

'Two things.' Claudette turned to her. 'First — why won't you come into the office? Please come into the office. Jack was really out of order that day, you know? And I don't blame you for feeling a bit . . . aggrieved . . . but it's all this pressure and—'

'I'm just getting on with work. It's not deliberate,' Holly lied. 'Do you want a cup of tea?'

'No, thank you. Kind of you to ask.' Claudette started pacing around again. 'I'm worried about Jack. But then I'm his mother. I'm always worried,' she laughed thinly. 'That's the second thing.'

'I haven't got any medicinal biscuits, I'm afraid. I think they would help. Would you like to pop to Farthing Street for coffee and cake? Would that help?'

'Oh no . . . no!' Claudette seemed to give in at this point and sat on the chair opposite Holly. 'All right.' She took off her sunglasses. 'There are three things. Not two. And this is the third thing.'

'Okay,' Holly smiled encouragingly.

'I am sixty-two years old, Holly.'

'You don't look it.'

'Thank you, but that's not what I meant. I mean, wouldn't you think that at my age, dealing with men would be easy?'

'I'm in no position to comment on that, given my track record.' Isabella jumped up next to her and climbed on to her lap.

'Have you seen Caleb?'

'Not really. He didn't seem happy with all the publicity my article about the Bollington brought the street so I've kept my distance a bit.'

'Well, he's stopped speaking to me.'

'Oh?'

'We went out for coffee a few times, and it was all rather lovely.' She leaned forward. 'And . . . well, not just coffee, to be honest. This is quite new to me. I mean, I've been on one or two dates since Seth died, but this felt different.' She put her sunglasses back on. 'But I must have been wrong because he's gone quiet.'

'I'm sure there's an explanation,' Holly smiled at her. 'He's grumpy but he doesn't seem unkind.'

'It was when we started talking about the past — the way you do. I mean, we're both in our sixties, of course we've got pasts. I don't know anything about him apart from the fact he owns the record shop and Mabel is his dog.' She took her sunglasses off again. 'And he likes music. And, apparently, composes jingles for adverts.'

'Does he?' Holly stood up. 'I think this calls for a cuppa, honestly. I didn't know that!'

'But as soon as we started talking about anything beyond that, he clammed up. It was like someone flicked a switch — and I was only being interested because I'm that kind of person.' Claudette put her sunglasses back on. Holly was beginning to realize it must be a nervous habit. 'What is the protocol around sex for single women at my age, Holly? When I met Seth, it was all very different. I mean what did I do wrong?'

'I'm sure nothing.' Holly switched the kettle on, unsure how to answer.

'And why am I so upset? I'm sixty-two years old!'

'Could it be that you like him? Lemon-and-ginger tea or common or garden breakfast, by the way?'

'What's the point of really liking someone if they make you feel like this?' Claudette sank back further into her chair. 'I can't actually believe that I've come to see you to tell you all this. I feel so very silly.' Isabella walked over to Claudette and jumped up on to the arm of her chair. 'She is really the most delightful cat,' Claudette sighed. 'I blame that swim we had on Hampstead Heath. It felt so cleansing and so meaningful that it sort of made me feel like I was finally able to move on somehow. And then I bumped into Caleb . . . and I probably just got carried away with myself. Stupid woman.'

'Would you like to go to Farthing Street for that tea instead of here? It's a lovely day. I haven't been for a week or so myself.'

'Oh no. He'll think I'm chasing him.'

'Claudette, your car is parked outside my house, which is next door to his house. And you're my boss, so we can say it's a business meeting.' Holly picked up her rucksack and looked at the door. 'What do you say?'

'Yes. Okay. Yes, you're right.' Claudette readjusted her sunglasses and stood up. 'It's lovely to see you in person, Holly. You're such a breath of fresh air.'

* * *

Farthing Street was quieter than the last time Holly had visited. There was no film crew or small crowd watching them, and no one was standing outside the Bollington singing, but there were a few more people on the street and the café seemed to be busier than usual.

'It's lovely here. How lucky are you to live around the corner?' Claudette sat down at a table facing away from the entrance to Caleb's shop. Holly joined her and waved at Viktor.

'Hello, stranger!' he bellowed. 'You haven't been here for days. Is everything all right? I would have come round to see you but we've been run off our feet.'

'I'm fine, thanks. I'm glad you're busy.'

'Yes. That film on the news has got a lot more people passing through. Most of us think that is good.'

'How's Caleb, by the way?' Holly jumped when Claudette kicked her shin.

'Just goes into the shop, puts the closed sign up and goes straight home. He and Paulo have had a few skirmishes about what's been going on.' He looked momentarily weary. 'It's a pity, isn't it? I'll bring you the usual? And you?' He smiled at Claudette.

'I'll have a pot of jasmine tea,' she said.

'You see? Caleb is a bit of an enigma. It's not just you,' Holly said as she looked around. 'London in July. How lovely. Look at the colour of that sky. It's like someone's painted it.'

'Yes.' Claudette sounded distracted again. 'Jack's heart is not in our project. You know it. I know it. And he's pretending he doesn't know it,' she blurted out. 'And I don't know what to do. I wish I'd never found the proofs of those books.'

'I'm sure it will be fine — it's early days, really.' Holly tried to sound like she meant it but she wasn't all that sure either.

Bev wandered over. 'Hey, Holly.' She sat down and placed a magazine in front of her so loudly it sounded like it had slapped the table. 'Look at this.'

'Hi, Bev.' Holly looked at her and then along the street. 'I think someone has just gone into the shop.'

'Oh, honestly,' Bev sighed, and stood up. 'Customers. Always at the wrong time.' She nodded at the magazine. 'See what you think of that.'

Holly picked it up.

THE LIGHTS — THE BAND THAT DISAPPEARED

The discovery that the last venue the iconic eighties band performed in has been virtually held in a time capsule — on the outside, at least — when so many others of its ilk have been knocked down or redeveloped has shone a light — pardon the pun — on the question that periodically passes the lips of every single music enthusiast on the planet: what on earth happened to the Lights?

Okay, so we know what happened to them — they split up, like so many bands do. The death of Lawrence Mandrel came a few months after that heady August night when what turned out to be their last performance disintegrated into a brawl. That's the stuff of rock and roll legend.

But, unlike many other bands, none of the members have continued in the industry. They don't have to — their music should have made them multi-millionaires by now: re-released, used in film soundtracks, loved by cover bands the world over. But don't musicians love making music? One would expect at least one or two of them to have remained knocking around the scene in some way. We sadly lost drummer Charlie Thomas in 2018, and only then discovered he had embarked on an entirely new career: farming. But what of the others?

206

The question is — were the rumours about their collective broken heart at the death of their bandmate true? Could they really not carry on making music without Lawrence? And if so, where on earth have they all gone?

Journalists have been trying for years to track them down and all they have found is a metaphorical wall.

So, what do you think the missing band members made of the scenes outside the Bollington recently, where the genuine love for the music they created was apparent for all to see? "Summer in Your Eyes" has reappeared on almost every radio station's playlist over the past two weeks. It feels like we are back in the eighties at a mate's party, but the main guests haven't turned up.

Will you please come back, guys? Just to say hello.

Holly looked over at the Bollington just as Caleb walked out of his shop, being dragged enthusiastically by Mabel.

'Did I hear a door shut? Is that him? It is, isn't it?' squeaked Claudette, who grabbed the magazine from Holly and pretended to read it.

Holly waved at him. He paused for a moment, noticed Claudette, began to walk towards them, hesitated, looked the other way, and turned and walked off in the opposite direction. Claudette didn't notice any of it.

'Appears he was in a bit of a hurry,' Holly said kindly, then instinctively stood up and walked over to the Bollington. She touched the wall, somehow sensing the sadness seeping out from under the door, and if she could have put her arm around the building and told it everything would be all right, she would have done.

'Claudette's stuck, Jack's stuck and whoever owns you is clearly stuck. And it's all because of love, isn't it?' she whispered. Then she took her phone out of her rucksack and called Keith.

'Holly. On this one occasion, I'm very glad you called.' His voice sounded weary. 'I think it's time to do something, don't you?'

CHAPTER EIGHTEEN

As I walk along the lane to Farthing Street, I am walking in the footsteps of thousands upon thousands of souls that have done the same before me — even before Farthing Street was built, or Primrose Hill, or Camden, or, indeed, London itself. When I sit at the café that takes pride of place under the canopy of trees that line the road, I can sense the energy of all of those individuals who have been a part of this tiny part of the city for millennia — they are in the walls, carried in the air, in the branches of the purple wisteria that climb above the doorway of the hardware shop. They built each dwelling, they dug the road, they sold curtains and clothes and shoes and groceries. They laughed, they loved and they lived.

And somehow, they are still here.

Someone said to me when I first accidentally discovered the street — and was then unable to find it again for a while — that it was like the Brigadoon of Primrose Hill. And maybe what they meant was that, if we just stood for a few moments and let it all wash over us, we could catch a glimpse of those that went before us going about their business, as we are, somehow still existing in another alternate universe, or perhaps just in our memories. Because, even if it is just that, they are still alive in their own way.

As for Farthing Street, every single building has a unique history — whether it be quiet, unassuming, dramatic, exuberant or infamous.

And then there is the Bollington . . .

Holly read the rest of the article through and attached it in an email to Keith. Then attached another document for social media posts.

SUBJECT: Article about Farthing Street and the Bollington
Hi Keith,

I've written the article as requested, plus the shorter version for social media, and I've copied in Jack Fambridge.

Hope you like it and that it fits the brief — although the brief was a bit vague as I don't know exactly what it's for!

Holly Merriweather
Researcher, writer

A blast from the past. She was smiling at her signature and the link to her old website that was below it. *Maybe I'll add the first piece I wrote about the Bollington. Although, maybe not.*

She pressed send and closed her laptop, then scooped Isabella up and walked out into the garden.

'I have no idea why Keith and our anonymous owner want Jack to read it,' she remarked to the cat. The sound of his name sent an unwanted, pleasurable flutter through her body, so she breathed in slowly to try to get rid of it. The cat squirmed in her arms then jumped on to the floor just as the sound of a strumming guitar floated through the air. Holly looked up, still unable to work out where it was coming from. So, she simply sat down, closed her eyes and allowed herself to enjoy it before she had to leave to help Melissa at a publicity event near Tower Bridge, for another extracurricular freelance gig.

* * *

'Are you sure you're not overdoing it?' Melissa handed Holly a lanyard and a clipboard with a list of names on it.

'A bit.' Holly yawned. 'But it's all part of my work-money-future-et-cetera strategy.'

'That sounds very complicated.' Melissa took a bright-yellow highlighter from her bag. 'Use this for the list to mark who's arrived.'

Holly scanned the paperwork without really reading it properly. 'I got so stressed when Ed mucked the money up that I decided I needed to start putting some cash away, so this is helping build up my reserves. The phone calls from the debt collectors have stopped at least.'

'Still. Don't forget to enjoy yourself,' Melissa pulled her into a hug. 'Talking of which, my Justin has suggested a day out for you in Surbiton. It's about time you met him.'

'Oh, fabulous. That would be great. I'll see him in 3D rather than just photographs.'

Melissa laughed. '3D is much better. Talking of 3D — have you put yourself on a dating app or two yet?'

'Oh no!' Holly almost shivered. 'I need to organize my thoughts before I do — I mean, developing an embarrassing crush on my colleague was not a good idea. It made me lose focus and behave like an idiot. I need a bit of space from even thinking about a relationship so I can at least approach it normally when I'm ready.'

'So, no more crush on the man at work?' Melissa raised her eyebrows. 'Really?'

'Absolutely. I've gone cold turkey. I need this job. I've got to be professional.'

'No feelings whatsoever then?' Melissa was smiling.

'Of course not,' Holly snorted. 'Completely gone.'

'Good. Because he's walking towards us.'

Holly spun around and watched as he strode along the embankment, a slightly anxious smile on his face. Butterflies surged into her stomach as if they'd been waiting in the wings, ready for their moment to dance again, just as Melissa turned and walked away. Her shoulders appeared to be shaking with laughter.

'Holly!' He waved, then tripped up a step and grabbed the railing. He hung on to it, somehow managing not to fall over, then continued to walk towards her. 'Oh dear.' He appeared slightly embarrassed. 'I honestly have been navigating London perfectly well without falling down holes for the past few weeks.'

'Oh, well, there's lots of old stuff here, so probably a lot more holes.' Holly plastered a smile on her face and tried not to blush. 'That sounded odd — I meant it's in need of repair, and . . .' She trailed off. 'It appears that today you can't walk properly, and I can't string a coherent sentence together.'

'I'm really sorry. I'm an idiot and I was very rude to you. I know you were only trying to help, but I'm out of my comfort zone, and just . . . well . . .' Jack stopped talking suddenly. 'I can't talk either, can I? That didn't come out exactly as I'd planned.'

A brass band started to play "In the Summertime" from a stage next to the greensward outside the Bridge Theatre at the same time as a tap-dancing troupe began to perform on the pavement by the river.

Holly glanced over briefly. 'That's quite a mash-up.'

'I read your article and it's wonderful.' Jack touched her hand. 'It's so clever — about the past and the present and, well, ghosts, I suppose.' His smile expanded to the crinkles around his eyes, and Holly found herself gazing into them.

'Excuse me,' a female voice suddenly whispered into her ear. 'Excuse me — I need to get in and you are at the door.'

'Oh . . . goodness.' Holly blushed. 'I was just thinking about this list.' She turned to the woman, who was holding the hand of a little girl with long, red pigtails. 'Now. Let's get you in, shall we? Can I have your name, madam?'

The little girl looked up at her mother, who nodded at her and smiled. 'I'm Daisy Buchanan,' she said very quietly.

'Right then.' Holly took her yellow marker pen and ran it down the page. 'Here you are — Daisy Buchanan. I'm just going to highlight your name, and then you and your mum can go in. Is that Lillian Buchanan?'

'Yes,' said the little girl, slightly more confidently now.

'Thank you!' Her mum gave Holly a kind smile as she stepped back and let them through.

Jack stared at her for a moment. Holly stared back, then suddenly realized what he might be thinking. 'This is just extra work to earn some cash — that is all right, isn't it? The contract didn't say anything about not doing it — I just had a bit of an issue with my ex and . . .'

'Oh, no, no! That's absolutely — yes. I'm doing a bit of freelance kayak instruction at the weekend to keep my hand in myself.'

The butterflies fell with a thud to the bottom of her stomach. 'Everything is all right with the company, isn't it? I mean, if you're doing extra work?'

'All is fine.' Jack put his hands up in front of him defensively. 'Once an outdoor pursuits instructor, always an outdoor pursuits instructor.'

A group of people walked towards them. 'I think I'd better get back to work.' She sighed, finding herself wanting Jack to stay for a while longer. *Although only because he's good company*, she told herself sternly.

'Of course. I was just walking from the office down to the Southbank Centre when I noticed you here. We're missing you at the office — well, my mum and me, and the plumber who's constantly there fixing the leaks.' He laughed. 'I'm meeting Barney — you remember him? The bookshop owner?'

'Ah yes. Say hello from me.' She glanced at the guest list as the group approached. 'I'm doing lots of research. That's why I'm not in much.'

He nodded but wasn't smiling when he did it. 'Right.' He turned to go. 'See you in the office rather than on Zoom very soon.'

She watched him as he walked away. *Don't go*, she thought, then rolled her eyes at herself. 'Stop it,' she muttered.

'Did you say something?' The man at the head of the group looked confused.

'I just like reading all the names on the list out loud to make sure I get the pronunciation right,' she said brightly.

'Oh.'

'Yes.' Holly brandished her marker pen. 'Let's get you all in, shall we? Mr Smith?'

CHAPTER NINETEEN

'"The First of August"—' Holly's dad was in her garden standing next to her lawnmower — 'is one of the most beautiful songs I have ever heard. I've always said that, haven't I, Julie?'

'Very regularly.' Holly's mother handed him a bottle of lager. 'And every single August on the first. Usually at around 8 a.m. But he starts talking about it at the end of July, so here we are . . .'

Gary took a long swig of his drink. 'I was talking to Caleb about it, what with all this recent interest in the Lights. I put a playlist together for him of some of their best songs — including a lot of album tracks that aren't so well known. He seemed pleased. Difficult to tell under that beard and with his hat and glasses, though.'

Holly's mum sat down. 'He looks like someone who should be in a band, to be honest.' She poured herself a glass of lemonade from a jug. 'Lovely this, Holly. I love home-made lemonade.'

Holly was lying in the grass wiggling her toes while Isabella chewed on a dandelion. 'It's just been so hot the last few days, it was all I could think about.'

'I was telling him about the eighties weekenders in Bognor. Said he should come along to the next one in September.' Gary put the bottle down on the table. 'Didn't say no, to be fair. I said I could introduce him to one or two of the organizers — you know, Phil Breams, Linius DuBret, Joan Jones, that lot.'

'What about Steve Mohair-Whittaker?' Julie sipped her drink delicately.

'He's gone niche now — he specializes in 1987, so he only does evening events rather than the whole weekend. Not enough artists around to fill more than four hours at a time, apparently. Still, he's passionate about it. I'll give him that.'

'It's funny, though, about the Lights, when you think about it.' Holly's mum closed her eyes. 'Like that article said, where have they all gone? I think it's sad, I really do. A lot of people are saying the same thing on our Weekender WhatsApp group. Josie and Pauline were big fans at the time and were devastated when Lawrence Mandrel passed away. They were thinking of coming down to the Bollington to leave some flowers, but I put them off. Not everyone's happy with the attention.' She nodded in the direction of Caleb's garden and mouthed, 'You know who.'

'Has it all calmed down in Farthing Street now after that flurry of activity last month?' Gary nudged his daughter with his foot. 'I'm about to power up the lawnmower, my dear, and I'd rather not leave a Holly-shaped dent in the grass by mowing around you.'

Holly sat up. 'It's still busier, which is nice.' *And something's happening with the Bollington but I don't know what.* She managed to keep the thought to herself.

'Caleb was a bit fed up when I got there, to be honest.' Holly's father sneezed loudly, then took out a handkerchief from his pocket and wiped his nose. 'I was after lemons for our gin and tonics, but the convenience store was closed today. Which is the opposite of twenty-four-hour convenience, isn't it?' He put his handkerchief away and leaned on the mower. 'I was joking with Caleb about it. He said the guy who runs it had told him about a month ago it's closing down soon. Said something about being a good friend of the previous owner. Also muttered something else about his dog.'

'Oh no. Not another place.' Holly started to feel agitated again, then reminded herself that Keith was working behind the scenes somehow and began to feel calmer. *Maybe it won't have to close, after all*, she thought.

'And how's the job going?' Julie waved the jug at her. 'Fancy a top-up?'

'It's going well,' Holly lied. It was going well because she was still keeping away from the office. The butterflies coursing around her body when she and Jack had bumped into each other near Tower Bridge had proved to her she still needed to go cold turkey as far as he was concerned — until the butterflies got the message, at least.

'You need to stand up, my dear.' Gary dragged the lawn-mower over.

'It's so nice sitting with the grass tickling my toes, though.' Holly grudgingly got up and grabbed Isabella. 'Don't want a cat-sized shape either, do you?'

'Done any more articles for your own blog?' He put his sunglasses on.

'No — haven't had time.' Holly sat next to her mum on the patio. *Or the confidence*, she thought. *Wonder what Jack really thought of the piece I wrote for Keith. And whoever Keith works for. And why did I have to send it to Jack, actually?*

'Well, I'm sure you'll do more when you get the right inspiration.' Julie tickled Isabella behind the ear and took another sip of her drink.

'Mmm,' she mumbled as her dad put some headphones on.

'Right, ladies. I'm about to make this garden look phenomenal.' He switched on the lawnmower and began to sing "Karma Chameleon" over the thrum of the mower.

'I think he's toying with the idea of going as Boy George to our next weekender,' sighed Julie. 'He's going to have to get his own make-up if he does — he's not using mine again.'

Holly giggled and leaned back in the chair. The sky was a chalky blue, and the trails of planes high above them drew the outlines of what looked like waves across it. *London*, Holly said to herself, *is really the place to be*.

* * *

'I know you've been busy doing research, but we need you to come into the office tomorrow.' Claudette's voice was kind and warm, but firm. 'We're having a catch-up about how far we've got with everything and what everyone is doing, and we need you to help us put it on a spreadsheet or wallchart, or something useful.'

'That sounds very positive.' Holly had surprised herself by sounding fairly bright and not at all defensive. 'I'll be there by nine.'

'I'll see you then.' Claudette went silent for a moment. 'Have you seen much of Caleb at all?' she almost whispered.

'No. I haven't,' Holly lied. Every time she'd seen him the past few days, he'd looked at the floor, muttered hello and hurried off, dragging an increasingly irritable Mabel behind him.

Dressed in a somewhat sedate, sky-blue sundress, she had left the house for the office, looking forward to seeing Claudette and not in the least bit concerned about encountering Jack. 'Not at all,' she'd said to herself. 'All is under control. Well, I'm under control.'

Getting off the Tube at Tower Hill, she walked over the bridge, just as she had done in the spring on her first day at work, and weaved through the crowds again, happily drinking in the bustle and life around her.

An Uber boat glided eastwards along the river past a brightly coloured sailing barge floating elegantly towards Westminster. A busker was singing an acoustic version of "Happiness" by McFly, and Holly felt lighter and more optimistic than she had for a few weeks now that Ed had begun to deal with their debtors.

The phone calls and letters had stopped, and panic had slowly subsided. Today, Holly felt she was getting on top of things again and was looking forward to spending a day doing the job she had grown to love.

She picked up a coffee from a truck round the corner from the office, then took out her key fob and let herself into the building. She climbed the stairs, smiling at the familiar portraits lining the walls as she did.

'Hi!' she almost sang, pushing the door open. 'Here I am. Ready to work very, very hard.'

Claudette looked up from her computer. 'Hello, stranger.' She beamed. 'It's lovely to see you in person again.'

Holly sat down at her workstation. 'I've got lots of research done, though, so it's been time well spent.'

'There's another leak.' Jack poked his head round the kitchen door. 'Hi, Holly. Welcome back.'

'Hi!' Holly ignored the pleasurable loop-the-loop in her stomach. 'Can I do anything to help?'

'I think we need the plumber again.' He walked into the office, drying his hands with a cloth. He was wearing a pair of long, blue, linen shorts, which showed off his very toned legs. Holly stared hard at her screen and switched on the computer.

'It's coming from inside that kind of anteroom, Mum. Honestly, I know your friends own the building but I think it's becoming a bit of a hazard. I may bring my kayak in tomorrow so I can paddle through the water instead of wading.'

'I've just sent them an email so hopefully they'll send someone soon.' She shook her head. 'And it's not that bad.'

'So.' Holly looked at them both, eager to get on. 'I'm looking forward to collating everyone's progress so far.'

'Oh yes. There are a few spreadsheets on the shared drive — one overview one, and one for each of the areas we're covering.'

'Excellent.' Holly clicked on the files.

'I've also printed all the emails out.' Jack put a pile on a desk next to Holly. 'To make it easier to track — we can each take a few, then add them to the sheets as we go. I'm sure there are more technologically sound ways of doing it.'

'Probably, but I like paper.' Holly took a bag with the letters from the debt collectors out of her rucksack and put it in front of her. She'd decided to copy them and then send the originals on to Ed. 'Is it okay if I make some copies of these? I'll pay.'

'Of course you can.' Claudette stood up. 'And you don't have to pay. I'm going to make a cup of tea before we start.'

Holly pushed the bag to one side, then took out a jiffy bag she'd bought on the way to work to put the original letters in. She planned on filing the copies somewhere so far at the back of her wardrobe she wouldn't have to look at them again — unless Ed didn't do what he was supposed to, of course. She sighed at the thought. Reliable, clever Ed had feet of clay, after all.

'Right!' Jack clapped his hands enthusiastically. 'Let's get on with this. I've been speaking to Barney and he's just given me a bit of guidance on how to manage the projects a bit better.' He took a few of the emails. 'Looks like I've got Holborn, Southwark, Pimlico and Westminster.'

'It's a bit like a lucky dip, isn't it?' Holly moved a few sheets on to her desk. 'And I have Camden, Dalston and Angel. So far.'

'No milk.' Claudette picked up her handbag. 'I'm just nipping out to get some. I'll only be a few minutes.' She closed the door behind her.

Holly put her headphones on and got to work, inputting the exact locations that had already been covered on the grid and listening to the soundtrack to *La La Land* as she did.

Halfway through "City of Stars", she felt a gentle tap on her shoulder.

'Um.' Jack had a strange look on his face. 'Can you help?'

'What is it?' Holly took her headphones off and followed his gaze. A stream of water was flowing from the ante-room. 'Oh dear!' She got up. 'That's escalated rather quickly.'

'I've phoned the maintenance team but they can't get anyone on site for an hour, so they've asked me to turn off the stopcock.' Jack walked back towards the room. 'Thing is,

I need someone to hold the cupboard door open while I do it and also hold a torch so I can see. I've been trying for the past fifteen minutes on my own with no luck.'

'That's been going on for fifteen minutes?' Holly followed him over.

'You were really focusing on your work and singing. Sort of.' He grinned and handed her a torch that was propped up on the kitchen sink.

'Oh.' Holly grimaced. 'Sort of singing. I am so very sorry.'

'It was interesting and quite . . . well, interesting.' He opened the door of the anteroom. 'It may be a good idea to take your sandals off. It's not only wet but a little bit unpleasant.'

'Yes, I see.' Holly stepped back into the office, put her sandals next to her rucksack and stood behind Jack. She switched on the torch. 'I'm ready.'

He crouched down next to the cupboard, opened the door and picked up a spanner. 'Thank God they keep a tool bag under the sink,' he muttered. 'Now, can you shine the torch in here?' He pointed at the pipes in front of him.

Holly kneeled down. Jack was leaning forward and trying to put the spanner around one of the pipes. His black hair curled at his neck, just above his T-shirt. She tried not to get too close, but was drawn in by the patchouli-and-cinnamon scent of his aftershave as she held on to the cupboard door with one hand. 'Is this okay?' she asked, shining the torch in the direction he'd asked.

'A bit closer.' He kneeled a bit further forward. 'There.' Holly watched as he managed to hook the spanner on to the right place and turned the lever.

'Can I move now?' Holly's knees were beginning to hurt.

'Oh, yes! Thanks for that.' He turned around just as Holly was moving and somehow fell over on to his back, taking her with him.

'Oh!' she screamed. Then she opened her eyes. She was lying on top of Jack. For some reason, she couldn't move. Their eyes locked as they held each other's gaze for just a moment too long. His breathing was slow and shallow, and small pricks of electricity began to trickle along her body. Suddenly, his mouth was on hers and they were kissing, long and languorous, and then more urgently. Jack put his arms around her back and began to run his fingers along her spine as Holly cupped his face in her hands.

'Hello?' Claudette's voice punctured the silence from the office.

'Oh God!' Holly stared at Jack. His eyes widened in panic as she rolled off him and on to the tiles. They glanced at each other as they lay on their backs on the wet floor and began to shake silently with laughter, then they crawled on to their knees and stood up.

'Where is everybody?' Claudette's voice began to grow closer.

'In here,' Jack shouted, looking down at his sodden T-shirt. 'We've been doing some DIY.'

Holly felt the back of her dress. It was soaking, as were her legs and feet and the backs of her arms. And her hair. Her hair was very, very wet.

'Have you been for a swim?' Claudette looked confused as she opened the door and saw them standing in the anteroom.

'The leak got worse?' Jack's voice went up at the end as if he was asking a question.

'I had to help with a torch.' Holly touched her hair. 'I slipped over in the water.'

'Me too,' added Jack. 'I had to deal with the stopcock. And Holly helped.'

'Did you now?' Holly thought that Claudette's mouth curled into a smile briefly before she changed her expression to serious again.

'Well, I best go and use the dryer in the loo to make myself less . . . um . . . like this,' muttered Holly, walking past Claudette and avoiding her gaze completely.

She then spent the following fifteen minutes photocopying the letters from the debt collectors, repeating to herself as she did, 'This is what happens when you mix work with relationships. *This* is what happens when you mix work with relationships. *This* is what happens when you mix work with relationships.'

* * *

Jack, Claudette and Holly spent the rest of the morning working quietly. Every time Jack stood up, Holly stared intently at her screen. Every time Holly moved, Jack checked his phone.

At quarter past two, Holly's phone illuminated with a message.

> *I'm so very sorry. That was completely inappropriate. Kind Regards, Jack*

> *It's okay. I'm very sorry, too. It was totally inappropriate. Yours sincerely, Holly*

> *I hope it won't affect our working relationship. It will not happen again. I take my responsibilities very seriously. Kind Regards, Jack*

> *It won't affect our working relationship, and it was as much my fault as yours. Let's pretend it never happened. Yours sincerely, Holly*

> *Thank you. Kind Regards, Jack*

Except Holly couldn't forget it had happened. She had been thrown back in time to long days in Yorkshire, when she and Ed had mixed business and pleasure quite a lot.

In fact, when she woke up at 2.05 a.m. the following morning, the first thing she remembered was her limbs entwined with Jack's on the office floor.

Pouring herself a glass of water, she opened her laptop and began to look for new job opportunities, sent an email to Claudette and Jack telling them she'd be "working out in the field" for the next few days, and dozed off at around 3 a.m. for a hot and restless sleep.

CHAPTER TWENTY

Sitting opposite Melissa, Holly sipped a pina colada disconsolately. 'Stop laughing.' She pointed her straw at her friend.

'I'm not laughing.' Melissa bit her lip. 'But it is funny. On the floor at work. By accident — you say that, anyway.'

'It wasn't supposed to happen.' Holly took a bite of a pineapple chunk. 'And I'm keeping away from the office. And I'm applying for new jobs.'

'Oh, but you love Fambridge Books!'

'I do. But I can't keep avoiding Jack. I mean, only three of us work there full-time. I've never met the friends and the other members of the family who are also part of the research team.'

'Fair point.' Melissa pulled another glass towards her. 'These three-for-the-price-of-two deals are really not ideal,' she announced before taking a long gulp.

'I've sent out ten applications in the last two days,' Holly sighed. 'My heart's not in it, though.' She looked up. 'Maybe I should just take off and go travelling again.'

'No!' Melissa spluttered and put her drink down. 'You can't just take off because things are difficult. And you've only just got back. And you have Isabella now.'

'No, of course I can't leave Isabella. And *she* won't like travelling. She's a cat, after all. I have to stay. What was I thinking?'

'How awful for you to have to stay in a cheap mews house close to Primrose Hill.' Melissa raised her eyebrows. 'Have you written any more for your own blog? That would get people's attention again.'

'No. I've got lots of ideas, but I haven't been able to get on top of anything.' Holly wanted to tell her about the article for Keith's mystery friend but took another sip of her drink instead.

'I can introduce you to someone else from work?' Melissa took her phone out. 'I can show you photos.'

'That's very kind, but I'm still not sure. And they'll be connected to your work, so it could still be awkward.'

'You and this work thing seems very unhealthy. But if you're sticking to your guns, I'm going to ask you yet again — what about internet dating?'

'I'm not ready for that.'

'My God! You and Ed have not actually been together for over a year, even if you were living in the same place. You need to take a risk, jump, be frivolous!'

'I was. Yesterday.' Holly sat back in her seat and watched Melissa laugh so much she had to pat her on the back to help her stop.

'Right,' Melissa said after regaining her composure. 'I'm taking you in hand. I have some friends at a PR company that I don't work for. Is that distant enough? Emilio is absolutely gorgeous, very easygoing and great company.'

'No.' Holly thought she sounded firm.

'You're seeing him Friday evening at 7 p.m. here. In a group. I'll be here for an hour. So, it's like dipping your toe in the dating pond. Next week it can be your foot, and then the world's your oyster.'

She suddenly glanced over her shoulder. 'He's over there, by the way. I sent him a message earlier.' Melissa waved at a tall, dark man with twinkly eyes and wavy hair.

'Oh!' Holly looked over in his direction. 'He looks nice. But what if he says no?'

'He can see you so said yes immediately. Now, we'd better go somewhere else. Don't want to spoil your sort-of date. Slight air of mystery and all that.'

They stood up and walked out, waving at Emilio as they did.

'See, you can do it. No strings. Learn to date. Get out there and just, you know, be a young woman and all that.' Melissa almost tripped up and grabbed Holly. 'Oh dear. Can you guide me to the Tube please?'

Holly went to Chalk Farm station with her friend and kissed her on the cheek before she hurried through the ticket barriers. Then she began to walk home, trying to summon up some excitement about her sort-of date, but really just felt slightly anxious.

* * *

She popped to Farthing Street the following morning for a cup of coffee before leaving to do her day's research. Bev was buying a croissant to take back to the shop when Holly sat down.

'It's all gone a bit quiet now,' she said. 'I had a couple of people in yesterday asking questions, but they didn't buy anything. As usual.'

'I suppose it was nice while it lasted.' Holly looked over at Paulo, who waved at her from inside the café.

'I quite like it quiet. If I get too many customers, I can't get on with my crosswords. And my Wordle. Anyway, best open up. No rest for the wicked.' Bev headed to her shop and Paulo put a latte on the table.

'For our Holly!' His face was serious. 'I don't suppose you have any other ideas to get people along to look at the Bollington? It really helped our trade for a few weeks, but now it's dropping off again.'

'Maybe there'll be another surge?' Holly thought about the new article and wondered whether to send Keith a message to find out what was going to happen to it.

'I hope so. Marialena's boss was here yesterday, and when he left, she was in tears. We think he may really be thinking of closing the dry-cleaner's down. But she won't talk about it, so we don't ask. And there are rumours about the convenience store, too.'

Holly took her phone out of her rucksack and found Keith's number as Paulo went over to serve some other customers. While she was thinking about how to phrase the question, she checked her emails. 'Oh!'

Dear Holly,

Thank you for your application for the role of copywriter.

Unfortunately, we are unable to offer you this position, but we are familiar with your work as a travel blogger.

A new position has become available that we think may be a better fit, and we would like to set up an informal interview with you at the earliest opportunity.

Can you let me know if you are interested and send over some times and dates that you are available?

Kind regards,

Verity Lewis

Editor

Holly grinned. *As one doorhandle gets a bit difficult to hold on to, another door opens*, she thought to herself as she began to type her reply.

* * *

Holly stared at herself in the mirror, wondering whether she was wearing the long, blue-and-white silk dress, or whether it was wearing her. It had taken her an hour to get ready for the sort-of date with Emilio, as she'd nervously tried on various dresses, skirts, tops and trousers, all of them patterned, very bright and now discarded on the floor.

She had also pinned her hair up, and put on her favourite pair of silver hooped earrings and three blue, jewelled bangles on each wrist.

'Too much?' she asked Isabella, who was sitting on a pile of clothes. 'I feel like I'm going for a weird job interview. Fancy being my age and never actually having gone out on a first date.'

Her mind wandered back to Ed walking towards her at the school disco, shy and uncertain, with "Believe" by Cher blasting out of the speakers. He'd held his hand out to her. 'Dance?' he'd shouted.

'Yes!' she'd shouted back, following him to the dance floor on to which the drama department lighting team had thrown everything they had, with lasers and fluorescent lights pumping in time to the music, pausing for occasional dramatic moments when they switched them off altogether and then back on again.

Then the music had segued into "Truly Madly Deeply" by Savage Garden, and they'd had to make a decision to go their separate ways or stay on the dance floor. And that was that.

'Could that be regarded as a first date?' she asked her reflection, fighting the urge to tell Alexa to play a school disco playlist.

No, she said to herself. *And none of the dates you went out on after that could be classed as first dates as you were already together. And you didn't actually go out on a date for two years after that night, anyway. Every other occasion was regarded as "hanging out".*

She turned to Isabella. 'So, this is a big deal. No wonder I'm nervous.'

Her doorbell rang, and she took a deep breath before hurrying down the hall to answer it.

'Well, hello you!' Melissa was standing outside with three other people, one of whom was Emilio. 'We thought we'd pop in to collect you on our way. And—' she whispered — 'in case you decided to make a run for it and not turn up.'

'I'm ready,' Holly said firmly. 'I am definitely looking forward to it.' She smiled at Emilio. 'I'll just get my things.' She rushed into her bedroom, picked up Isabella and gave her a squeeze. 'Wish me luck,' she murmured, before grabbing her bag and dashing back to the door.

As they all began to head to the main road, Emilio fell into step beside her. 'I'm Emilio,' he said, holding his hand out. Holly shook it in what she hoped was a firm yet friendly manner. 'Hello. I'm Holly. It's very nice to meet you.'

'You too,' he said. 'And that dress is beautiful. What a lovely colour. Melissa tells me you have travelled the world. We must compare notes — I've just come back from three months in Vietnam.'

'I love Vietnam! Where did you go?' They all stood at the crossing, waiting for the signal so they could walk over the road.

'I'll show you the photos when we get to the bar.' He waved his phone at her. 'All my travelling life is on here.'

'I'll look forward to it.' Holly caught Melissa's eye. She thought she saw her wink.

CHAPTER TWENTY-ONE

The message arrived at 7.05 a.m. on 5 August

We need you at the Bollington at 12.05 a.m. on 8 August, please. You need to come in via the back door, which can be reached by following the service road behind the café, which then leads to a small path. Don't tell anyone else. Keith

Holly picked up her phone and read through the text sleepily, then grinned.

Shouldn't you put "Your mission if you choose to accept it" at the beginning? Ha ha! she replied.

Climbing out of bed, she opened the blinds and allowed the shafts of sunlight to flood the room, then watched Isabella as she jumped between the shade and the light like they were steps.

I have no idea what you mean. Keith

Holly rubbed her eyes, still not quite awake. *Mission: Impossible — you know?!*

Oh yes. Now I get it. But it isn't a mission. It's an appointment. Keith

Isabella walked out into the hall, then turned around and meowed.

'Yes. Breakfast. Okay.' Holly followed her, spooned her food into a bowl and put the kettle on while watching the birds flit between the trees and bushes outside.

Then she checked her messages again, her brow furrowing in confusion. *Just checking— 12.05 a.m. is just after midnight. Do you mean just after midday?*

The answer buzzed through almost immediately. *No. Just after midnight. Keith*

She poured the boiling water on to a teabag, then walked into the garden and sat on the patio.

This is all very cloak-and-dagger, she messaged as she took a sip of her drink.

That, Holly, has been my life for many years. And remember — the added layer of cloak-and-dagger — don't tell anyone. Keith

Holly read the words again, and then again, trying to imagine what she was about to find out and who was behind it all. She glanced over at the red-brick walls of the Bollington and wondered if, when this was all done, it would look different somehow, maybe lighter, as if it could breathe again. 'If that is actually possible for a building,' she said to Isabella, who was now staring at a leaf that had floated to the ground from the cherry tree.

Could the mystery owner be Keith? she wondered. *Maybe he's just been pretending he's looking after it for someone else. Or... he mentioned a brother when I met him the first time. I'd forgotten about that!*

The first few chords of "Summer in Your Eyes" drifted into the air and she stood up, looking for clues as usual, still trying to work out where it was coming from. 'I'm going to find out soon, I reckon,' she muttered, picking up her drink and going back inside.

It could be Caleb, though, she said to herself. *Or Bev or Marialena's boyfriend or... absolutely anyone.*

Opening her laptop, she reread the message Jack had sent to the work group so they all had their instructions on where to visit over the next month and the deadlines for each submission.

An unexpected surge of electricity flew through her body at the sight of his name, the sudden memory of their encounter at the office sending a pleasant shiver down her spine. She almost slammed the laptop shut and stepped back. 'No!' she shouted.

Isabella jumped on to the table next to the front door and dislodged the jiffy bag of letters from the debt collectors, which Holly hadn't found time to take to the post office yet.

'Maybe I'll just leave it there as a permanent reminder.' She sat down and opened the laptop again, checking the group work calendar. She needed to gather some information on the hard drive before setting off on her research travels again, and that was only accessible at the office. From the calendar, she'd worked out Jack wasn't going to be in tomorrow. She sighed, relieved, and walked to the bathroom to turn the shower on.

Don't pretend you're not slightly disappointed, too. Because you are.

'I am,' she said out loud. 'But I can't do my job and constantly worry I'm going to bump into him. And, anyway—' she turned to Isabella, who was sitting on the bathroom mat watching her — 'I'm meeting Emilio for coffee after work. On our own.'

* * *

Holly sat down at a table near the window of the café where Emilio had arranged to meet her, next to the canal at Coal Drops Yard. She watched other people amble past against the backdrop of the pretty blue, green and yellow barges moored along the towpath. Putting on her headphones, she searched for some music on her phone so she wouldn't just sit staring at the door waiting for him to arrive.

This is just coffee. Her inner voice sounded almost kind. *He's a nice, attractive man but you already know there were no sparks, so just enjoy it for what it is.*

Deciding to spend her time listening to a Harry Styles playlist, she started playing "Daylight" and continued to gaze at the scene outside as if it were an accompanying music video.

'Hi!' Emilio tapped her on the shoulder halfway through another song. 'Fancy another drink?' He pointed at her cup.

Holly took her headphones off and stood up. 'Hi,' she said, as he kissed her on both cheeks. 'Another jasmine tea, please.'

Emilio touched her hand and nodded, his face lighting up as he did. 'For sure. I'll be back as quickly as I can.'

He went to queue at the counter, and Holly turned her attention back to the people wandering past outside, conjuring up sentences in her mind that she could turn into a blog post to send to Verity, the editor of the magazine who she was to talk with the following day. She was trying to feel excited about the chat but she couldn't quite muster any real enthusiasm at all.

The ever-changing tableau of humanity is a beautiful thing to observe, and it doesn't take any particular skills or a special viewpoint. All you have to do is sit down somewhere. Like I am now, on a warm August day in London, gazing at Regent's Canal from inside a café at Coal Drops Yard . . .

She stopped, feeling strangely guilty, like she was betraying Claudette and Jack — and somehow even Seth Fambridge.

Emilio sat down opposite and passed her the cup of tea. 'It's lovely to see you.'

'It's lovely to see you, too. And this is a nice café — I've never been here before.' Holly picked up the cup.

'I've forgotten to get sugar. Just a moment.' Emilio stood up and walked back to the counter, just as Jack strode past on the opposite bank. He was deep in conversation with a petite woman with black hair. Holly's stomach lurched unexpectedly, just as Jack glanced over. He seemed to stare for a moment and she looked away, hoping he hadn't actually seen her.

'Here we are!' Emilio sat down again. 'I'm trying to wean myself off sweets and cakes, but tea with sugar is a definite addiction of mine. I'm off to Thailand for work in a few days, so I'll have to be careful — there's sugar in everything.' He stirred his drink and looked at her seriously. 'I'm actually away for a couple of months, but when I'm back — if you're interested and still available, of course — perhaps we could meet up again?'

Holly forced herself to look at him and smile. He really was very attractive and extremely good company. And, more importantly, he was nothing to do with work. 'That would be very nice, thank you. Now, tell me more about your visit to Vietnam.'

* * *

The sixth of August was as hot and sunny as the previous few days. Holly got up, fed the cat and went to the café before hopping on the Tube to continue her research around Angel in Islington. But it didn't feel like the days before at all.

Verity Lewis had arranged the interview for 11.30 a.m., then at 2.30 p.m. Holly had to meet Claudette and Jack at a café on the South Bank as they had *something exciting they wanted to show her*, according to a text she'd received the previous evening.

And then on 8 August, at midnight, the secret of the Bollington would be revealed.

Everything was changing. Suddenly. Because it had to.

'And that's a good thing,' she said to her reflection in the bathroom mirror of the coffee shop she had chosen to do her interview call at. 'I need to earn more money. I need a higher profile. And . . .' She pushed her hair out of her face and leaned closer to the mirror. 'I have to stop thinking of Jack. I can't get attached to anyone. Not yet. Not at work. Not at all. Not yet.'

Taking her phone out of her rucksack, she walked back to her seat and waited for Verity's call, her heart beating with a strange sense of dread.

* * *

Taking a seat at her second coffee shop of the day, Holly ordered a pot of jasmine tea and opened her emails.

Thank you for our chat today, Holly, and for sending in a
sample article about Primrose Hill. We would like to invite
you into our offices for an interview on 8 August at 10 a.m.
Please let me know if this date and time works for you.
Kind regards,
Verity

She waited for a flurry of excitement to arrive with the anticipation of a possible new adventure, and a surge of pride at the recognition of her skills and abilities. There would be more places to visit, different perspectives to be had and another life beckoning — the one she'd been working towards the day Ed had announced he was leaving.

Taking her notebook out of her bag, she found the page where she'd written her goals when she had first arrived in London.

1. *Start Dream Job with Fambridge Books.*
2. *Start writing my travel blog again, with more social media posts, possibly a podcast, but this time about London — do alongside full-time job.*
3. *Approach publications who used to commission my work to see if I can do anything for them again — also do alongside full-time job.*
4. *Get back on track with money and writing to replenish my lost savings.*
5. *Proper job with well-known publication equals better CV, equals more opportunities, equals, in twelve months' time, the world being your oyster, Holly Merriweather.*
6. *Move on. I always move on. When I stayed in one place for four years, look what happened!*

Reading through them, she began to tick down the list of what she'd achieved since May. 'It's only August,' she said to herself. 'Don't forget the years when, just before one trip ended, you'd start planning the next one. This is the same. It's the same. This is who you are.'

Then she read the last point again.

6. *Move on. I always move on. When I stayed in one place for four years, look what happened!*

Just then, Claudette and Jack pushed the door open, smiling and waving at her as they did. Holly felt herself grin at the sight of them.

'We wanted to show you our first mock-up pages!' Jack immediately unpacked his laptop and put it on the table. 'What would you like? Another tea? Mum?'

'Just a sparkling water, please.' Claudette sat down.

'Nothing for me.' Holly realized that something had lifted from both of them — they seemed lighter somehow.

Jack hurried back with the drinks and put them on the table. 'We've taken our very first steps on our own. Barney has been helping us a bit here and there. He's got a small independent publishing company himself, and to keep us motivated suggested that we put together a few pages so we can see how it's going to look.'

'Oh, Holly. It's so wonderful.' Claudette beamed excitedly. 'As soon as I saw them, it was as if I were taking a step out of that room I mentioned — do you remember?'

'Is your foot completely out of the door yet?' Holly touched her hand.

'I have a toe on the patio!' Claudette giggled. 'But it's a start.'

'You haven't got a patio, Mum — you've got decking.' Jack was looking at them both with a very confused expression on his face. 'I have no idea what you're talking about.' Then he took a deep breath. 'Are you ready, Holly?' He opened his laptop, shaking his head. 'I can understand how Dad felt when this happened now. You know — you have an idea, you make it work, put it together and create something amazing.'

He clicked on a file in his Dropbox folder. The contents page of *London: How I See It Then and Now* appeared, with a list

235

of places and subjects. On the next page was a space with the heading *Foreword* and underneath — *to be written by Claudette*.

Next was a list of contributors, which included Holly.

North London was written on the following page, along with a list of the areas the section would cover and some post-card-like photographs of different locations dotted around the sides. 'We're getting better photos done.' Jack looked up at her, still smiling, then scrolled to the next section.

Primrose Hill.

There was the introduction Holly had written and some of the copy she had put together, along with a selection of her photos. Her heart leaped into her mouth.

'Are you all right?' Claudette looked at her anxiously. 'We thought you'd be thrilled.'

'I am.' Tears began to pour down Holly's cheeks. 'I really am.'

Jack stared at her, speechless.

'I . . . I . . .' She pulled a tissue out of her purse and blew her nose. 'Sorry. It's just that this is a childhood dream — to be part of Fambridge Books. And now I've seen my name and some of the things I've written . . . I'm overwhelmed.'

Claudette put her arms around her. 'Oh, Holly. So was I. It's such an emotional thing for all of us.'

Holly opened her own laptop and found her folder of photographs. 'Here.' She moved it so Claudette and Jack could see it. 'There's me aged eighteen at Gatwick Airport about to go off on my own for the very first time for my gap year and—' she enlarged the image — 'can you see that book? It went with me everywhere.'

The grinning young Holly was clutching a copy of *Europe: How I See It — Adventures in Many Places by an Ordinary Man with Ants in His Pants* by Seth Fambridge.

'I dabbled in writing then because he motivated me. I didn't publish anything, but Seth made me feel it was possible.'

The others both stared at the photograph, then looked away. Jack stood up and mumbled something about going to the loo, and Claudette took a deep breath and walked to the counter to ask for a cup of tea. Holly watched them and felt her heart fill with pride and happiness.

But you're moving on. It's what you do. It's who you are, whispered her inner voice. *Isn't it?*

Her phone rang just as Jack sat back down next to her and she watched the number cross the screen. It was the debt collectors. She felt sick, stared at it for a moment longer, and decided to answer it rather than wait for the voicemail.

'Excuse me, I've just got to take this.' She hurried outside. 'Holly Merriweather,' she said in a voice as efficient-sounding as she could manage.

'Hello, Miss Merriweather. I am calling concerning some unpaid debts.'

'I don't understand.' Holly turned to face the road. 'My ex-partner, Ed Purcell, has taken over dealing with this, I believe.'

'Right. Just wait a moment while I check our records. It could possibly be because they haven't updated on the system yet.' The voice on the end of the phone sounded a lot more professional than some of the others that had rung her.

Holly began to pace, trying not to panic at the thought of the calls starting again because Ed hadn't done what he'd said he would.

'Hello.' The debt collector clicked back on the line. 'I've refreshed the system, and it appears that the work-connected debt Mr Purcell had incurred is being settled and your name has been taken off the records. I apologize for the mistake.'

'So, I won't hear from you anymore?' Holly felt tears begin to prick behind her eyes again.

'No. Have a good day. Goodbye.' The line went dead and she took a few deep breaths to calm herself down.

'Never again will I mix work with pleasure,' she told a car speeding past. 'Because I thought I was going to be physically ill during that call.'

Opening the door, she went and sat down next to Jack.

'Is everything all right?' he asked, pushing a cup of coffee towards her. 'I bought you this.'

'Yes. Just echoes of the past.' Holly picked up her drink. 'Thank you,' she murmured and took a gulp.

'I thought I'd resolved things with my ex, but she's started messaging again about just that — the past.' He closed his computer. 'I have to say that getting these mock-ups together has been a real boost. But I'll never mix business with pleasure again.'

'Absolutely 100 per cent agree.' Holly nodded but managed not to make eye contact with him.

But I might be leaving, anyway, she thought. And then she felt sick again.

CHAPTER TWENTY-TWO

The seventh of August was hot and humid, slowing everyone down under the heavy, grey sky.

'Storm clouds are gathering,' Holly said to Isabella when she got out of bed. 'And maybe they are — because just after midnight, the mystery of the Bollington is revealed.'

She had settled down to work at home, listless and anxious — half excited, half worried and completely unable to concentrate on anything.

The rain started at 11 p.m., and Holly watched as the trees and bushes seemed to sigh with relief. 'That's what I'd write if I could start my blog,' she murmured, pouring herself a glass of water and glancing at her laptop. Switching on the television, the news flickered across the screen. Just images and noise in the background as she tried to work out what was going to happen that night. Because everything was about to change. She just didn't know how.

At 11.55 p.m., Holly took her umbrella from the stand, picked up her rucksack and blew Isabella a kiss. 'Won't be long,' she said. 'I hope.' Then stepped out into the rain, just as the first clap of thunder sounded in the distance.

'Oh, great,' she muttered, hurrying to the main road and along to Farthing Street.

Not sure I'm entirely happy about walking up an unlit path in the middle of the night, Keith.

Sending the text, she took a deep breath, trying to push away the sense of unease that had started to creep up on her as she left the house, and was now almost a full-blown fear as she walked around the back of the café towards the Bollington.

This is the only way I could persuade the people concerned to do anything. You'll be fine. There are security cameras set up all around the building so we can see everything. It's like a James Bond film, this! Keith

She read the message and felt the corners of her mouth curl into a smile, wondering if Keith was getting a bit excited about the whole thing, given the very slight hint of humour in the text. Then she cautiously pushed the side door of the building open and walked slowly along a narrow corridor past the back of the stage. The moon, visible through a gap in the clouds, threw narrow shafts of light on to the black floor.

Reaching the main door to the auditorium, Holly heard voices and paused for a moment, trying to work out who they belonged to, then she walked through and moved to the front, confused, just as a bolt of lightning illuminated the room.

'Dad . . . ?' she muttered. 'Mum? Mum! What are you doing here?' Her parents were sitting at a table in the middle of the room.

Thunder roared ominously.

'Hello, Holly.' Her father stood up. 'Have you got any idea what's going on?'

'Um, not really. Sort of something. But . . .' She looked at the other people who were sitting at the other tables dotted around the room. Claudette and Jack were at one, Viktor and Paulo at another, while Marialena and Bev were at a third with Caleb, and Mabel dozing at his feet. Holly's mother was sitting with her arms folded looking disgruntled.

The blackout blinds had been opened, making the room look grander than it had felt when Holly had rescued Isabella.

'What have you got us involved with, Holly?' her mother asked. 'I mean, I had to cancel a Pilates lesson for this.'

'I haven't got you involved in anything.' Holly looked around at all of them. 'In fact, I didn't know any of you would be here.'

'We all got messages the day before yesterday asking us to be here and not tell anyone else.' Marialena spoke quietly, as if she were divulging a secret. 'This is marvellous, though. Don't you think?'

'Are you going to sit down, Holly?' Keith walked in from the lobby. 'Hello, everyone. I'm Keith. I do apologize for all this — but I'm sure you'll understand why we're doing things this way.'

Holly sat down at a table. 'Is this going to be a bit emotional?'

'Yes. Yes, it is. But, as you said to me, Holly, some people here are a bit stuck. And in order to move on, sometimes things get uncomfortable for a bit. Now — I'm going to turn the lights down and we're going to watch a short video. Does anyone need to use the toilet before we start because I don't want anyone leaving the room once we get going?'

Everyone murmured that they didn't.

'Right.' Keith walked out into the lobby and they heard what sounded like him hurrying up some stairs.

A black-and-white film of five teenagers performing joyfully on a stage at a school flickered silently into life.

'Wait a minute. Is that the Lights?' Gary murmured, then turned around. 'That's the Lights, Julie — they were all at school together. I saw a documentary years ago about it. Was this their first gig?'

A selection of old photographs swept across the screen, the members of the band becoming gradually older until the video froze on a close-up of them as young adults, posing for a publicity photograph. And then the music began, the sound of the band's music filling the room, until it paused

241

again on a badly shot video of them standing on a stage, waiting to play.

At the top of the screen, a headline appeared: *The Bollington, 7 August 1981. The Lights' breakout gig.*

It morphed into a mish-mash of photographs and films — the Lights on stage, the Lights arriving in New York, the Lights at the Hollywood Bowl, the Lights performing at Wembley, out partying in Tokyo, on an *ashram* in India, and then it slowed down to show photographs of them individually.

Don C. Peterson
B.B. Jones
Charlie Thomas
Francis De Paul
Lawrence Mandrel

Then it stopped on a photograph of them on stage at the Bollington with the headline *15 August 1988*. Then "Summer in Your Eyes" began to play, and the film stopped.

Holly looked around. She wanted to cry, but she didn't know why.

Keith walked back in and sat down next to her. 'Someone here has something to say,' he announced.

'That *was* emotional.' It was Bev. Gasps filled the room, as everyone stared at her expectantly.

'No. Not her!' Keith sounded exasperated. 'Let's try again, shall we?'

'Lawrence Mandrel was my best friend,' a male voice said quietly, out of the darkness. 'He was almost my brother. My brother from another mother.' Caleb stood up. 'I never thought that, after that stupid fight over absolutely bloody nothing of any importance, he would walk out of my life, and I would never see him again.'

'Were you in the Lights?' Gary stood up again, then sat down, shaking his head. 'Wait a minute . . . C . . . ?'

'Oh, my goodness, Caleb!' Claudette hurried over and touched his hand.

'Are you Don C. Peterson?' Gary almost leaped back on to his feet.

'Yes, yes I am.'

'So, you're the owner of the Bollington?' Viktor shook his head. 'Why have you kept it like this?'

Caleb took a breath and began to talk again. 'It was the best part of my life. I bought the place just after he died. I'd heard there were thoughts about knocking it down and I couldn't let it happen. And then the shop became vacant and I took over the lease, bought a house close by.' He looked at the floor. 'One day, I decided to set it up like it was when we did our first gig here. Never thought I'd leave it like that for so many years.' He walked over to the stage and sat on it, looking at all of them, his voice becoming stronger as he did.

'I wanted it to be all in front of us again. All the hope and the excitement and the fun — the bloody great, wonderful, fantastic, life-affirming, party-till-we-dropped fun. I didn't want all of what happened as we got older to be what I held close, with all the arguments and the politics and us getting caught up with our own egos — which is what always happens.' He shrugged. 'It's life, isn't it? So, every time I came in, I'd remember how we all felt on that first night here. And then, if I ever thought of moving anything, I felt a physically sick kind of guilt. Like he'd disappear again. And I'd feel how I did just after he died. That gaping, dark hole. That absolute knowing that he'd never come back. And then when Charlie died only a few years ago — I started to come over here virtually every night.'

'It's so difficult.' Claudette went and sat next to him. 'I felt like that. I was ready to move on, and then I found those proofs and I couldn't.' She touched his hand again. 'I wanted to tell you that as I had a sense you might understand, but I couldn't quite summon up the courage.'

Caleb glanced up at the ceiling, then looked back at Claudette. 'This is all your fault. And hers.' He pointed at Holly.

'I'm confused. I don't know what you mean.' Claudette shook her head, looking slightly upset.

243

'When I met you, I couldn't tell you anything about myself. I'd hidden away — we all had, hadn't we, Keith?'

Keith nodded sadly. 'I was their roadie. None of us wanted to be in music without him. None of us wanted to talk about it, or think about it, or deal with it. So, we built several layers of protection for ourselves, with managers, music executives and solicitors dealing with everything on our behalf.'

'Then one day, Holly Merriweather, Miss Bright and Breezy and Optimistic moves in next door with her cat, who's basically now my dog's best friend. And I only got that bloody dog by accident.'

'I didn't realize I was Miss Bright and Breezy,' mumbled Holly.

'Oh, you are, my lovely girl,' her mother beamed. 'You're just a little ray of sunshine.'

Holly managed to stop herself from complaining that it made her sound like she was two years old.

'I've realized that something's pushing me. Her cat manages to find her way in here somehow.' Caleb shrugged his shoulders, amused. 'Quite an achievement with all the alarms.'

'And you had to trust Holly then, didn't you?' Keith went and sat on the stage, too.

'Then you wrote that article and really almost literally put the cat among the pigeons.' Caleb stood up and walked to the back of the stage, where he picked up a guitar. 'And if that wasn't bad enough, you introduced me to Claudette.'

'Oh dear.' Claudette made to get up.

'He means it nicely.' Keith nodded reassuringly at her, and she sat down again.

'As soon as I saw you, I knew I couldn't stay like this. It was like a half-life — trying to pretend I wasn't who I really was, that I hadn't done all the things I'd done, that I'd got myself stuck because it was easier.'

'What was it like?' Jack moved over to sit next to his mother and looked at Caleb. 'Dealing with all of that attention about the Lights over the past few weeks?'

Holly watched him, her butterflies skittering out of control again. She tried putting her hand on her stomach, but they ignored her and continued to dance.

'Extremely uncomfortable.' He shook his head. 'And I felt guilty — but, funnily enough, not about moving on but about ignoring the problems my neighbours in Farthing Street were having because I wanted to keep this a little museum all to myself. Seeing Marialena cry that time, and then finding out the convenience store might go. If it wasn't for my old mate Sven, who ran that place for years — God rest his soul — forcing me to look after her when he went into hospital, Mabel wouldn't have been in my life and . . .' his voice grew quieter, 'neither would any of you.' At the sound of her name, Mabel ran over and licked his hand. Caleb tickled her ears absentmindedly.

'So, in light of that,' Keith said, standing up, 'are you going to play something with that guitar?'

Caleb laughed. 'Not yet. I started trying to write a new song on my keyboard — not a jingle — about you, Claudette.'

'Goodness.' Claudette suddenly looked like a blushing teenage girl.

'But I got stuck with that, too. I'm just more comfortable with a guitar in my hand.'

'You may wonder,' Keith said formally, 'why we've asked you all here, now that you're over the shock of finding out who Caleb actually is.'

'Well, I'm quite confused,' Holly's dad said. 'About me and Julie — I can see why the rest of you were invited.' He shook his head. 'I can't believe I didn't recognize you, even with your beard and your glasses and your hat.'

'And you offered to introduce him to all those eighties events promoters.' Julie put her head in her hands. 'And,' she began to laugh, 'you did a playlist for him of the Lights' music. Oh, Gary!'

'I did know Steve Mohair-Whittaker, as it happens.' Caleb shook his head, smiling.

'He's a right old rascal.' Keith chuckled.

'I just need to do something.' Julie picked up her phone and brought up some photographs, then climbed up next to Caleb and studied his face. 'I can't believe this was you. I mean, I can see it now you've said it, but have we all really changed that much?' She waved the phone around. 'Look! We are all *so* old!'

'Let's have a look.' Gary joined her and nudged Caleb. 'It's the cheekbones. They give it away. The cheekbones that all the teen mags used to go on and on about.'

Caleb smiled more widely than Holly had ever seen him smile before, his entire face lighting up, and somewhere, under the beard and the glasses and the hat, she saw the young man he was before everything froze in time.

'Look,' he said. 'I don't want to change the way I live as "Caleb who runs a shop". I'm happy to be that person. I don't want any publicity about me. However, I will ride out the attention that is about to come our way because,' he looked around the room, 'this old place deserves a new life. So, I want it to become a musical community hub. I want children to learn about music here, I want bands to practise here, I want it to come alive again. And I want it to become a place where people come to find out about the Lights.'

'That is wonderful!' Paulo jumped up.

'Well, if you look at the first article on the newly relaunched Fambridge Books website, you will see that, as Holly here kindly wrote without knowing what it was for . . .' Keith handed Caleb an iPad to read from. 'Thanks, mate. Is this the social media introduction with the link to the full article?'

Keith nodded.

'Right, here we go.' Caleb cleared his throat and began to read the words out loud. 'Someone said to me when I first accidentally discovered Farthing Street — and was then unable to find it again for a while — that it was like the Brigadoon of Primrose Hill. And maybe what they meant was that, if we just stood for a few moments and let it all wash over us, we could catch a glimpse of those that went before us, going about their business, as we are — the musicians playing in the Bollington, the shopkeepers talking to their customers — somehow still existing in another alternate universe, or perhaps just in our memories. Because, even if it is just that, they are still alive in their own way.'

'Did you know about this, Jack?' Claudette looked sternly at her son.

'I got this email from Caleb with Holly's article attached, asking me to put it up, telling me that the Lights had been at the same school as Dad. And I thought — as you would say, Mum — that it was a sign.'

'I didn't know that.' Claudette looked up as if she were searching for someone. 'It *is* a sign, isn't it?'

'He was a few years above us, but head boy, destined for great things. We were scruffy idiots who thought we were cool.' Caleb strummed a chord on his guitar.

'So, the mystery musician I can hear every day from my house is you?' Holly couldn't contain her excitement. 'I thought it might be. But then I thought it could be Bev as she's got a guitar . . . or, it could have been anyone, couldn't it? So many houses, so many open windows this summer.' *He looks so at home holding the guitar*, she thought, *like it's an extension of him.*

'I practise the guitar with the window open.' Bev stood up. 'So, it could have been me. I'm rather good, too.' She dabbed her eyes with a handkerchief. 'I'm very affected by all this. I can only apologize.' She sat down again and blew her nose.

'My boyfriend also plays his guitar for me,' Marialena smiled wistfully. 'So, you could have heard him.'

Holly looked around the room. 'So, there was no mystery — everyone here is a budding rock star!'

'Well, that's good news,' Caleb grinned. 'More musicians to help with the project.'

An alarm rang on Keith's phone. 'Right, it's one o'clock everyone.'

'I think maybe, given we have work in the morning, we all need to go home?' Marialena giggled. 'I don't think I'll sleep, though. This is so wonderful.'

'Yes, of course.' Caleb held his hands up to stop them leaving immediately. 'But before you do, don't forget there's work to be done. Gary and Julie — when we're ready, will you help us get the word out to your eighties festival contacts about what we're trying to do? It was you talking about the guy at that old venue that helps children learn to play that gave me the idea to do it here.'

'I'll get the word out to the music nerds, absolutely.' Gary beamed and Julie squeezed his arm.

'All of you, my friends from Farthing Street — you are part of this. Will you help me?'

Viktor stood up and climbed on to the stage, grabbing Caleb and pulling him into a hug. 'Yes, yes. Of course. I am so moved by this.'

Keith looked at Bev. 'What about you?'

She blew her nose again. 'Yes, sorry. I've been crying ever since the film started. I'm a mess.'

Paulo took Holly's hand. 'You are very special,' he said, then kissed her on the cheek.

'The first thing we want to do is get everyone from Farthing Street here for a bit of a party in a week or so to make us all feel part of it. You know, like in those old films Holly loves — those Judy Garland ones?' Caleb grinned at her. 'Sometimes you leave your patio door open and I can hear every word.'

'Sorry.' Holly grimaced.

'Not at all — *Babes in Arms* is a very good film.' Caleb pointed at Viktor and Paulo. I was hoping you could take charge of that. It's a tight deadline — the fifteenth of August.'

Viktor looked like he was about to jump up and down, clapping his hands excitedly. 'Oh, yes! Yes!'

'And Claudette, Jack and Holly — we'd love for the Bollington and what we're doing here to be the lead, exclusive story for when you launch properly. Is that all right?'

'Our absolute pleasure,' Jack smiled, then turned to Holly. She moved towards him, unable to stop herself, as he caught her eye.

'There's a lot of work to do!' Keith warned.

They both stared at each other as soon as the word "work" left his mouth, then looked away.

'Yes. Work. Lots of it,' mumbled Holly. 'Well, I must go. This has been amazing. And . . . I'll see everyone in the morning.'

She hurried out the way she'd come in and then almost ran home, again feeling very guilty about the interview with Verity she had arranged for later that day, as if she were betraying Jack and Claudette — and even Seth himself.

CHAPTER TWENTY-THREE

Holly hovered next to one of the many entrances to Tottenham Court Road Tube station, trying to work out which way to walk. She'd clearly misread the signs underground, and had therefore arrived at ground level in the wrong place. She spun around slowly a few times, then decided to join the hordes of people walking over the road. She paused at the crossing, checked her phone, crossed the road and finally turned left into a side street in the general direction of where she thought she needed to be.

Even the sight of the British Film Institute Stephen Street building to her right, and the names of film production companies on various office blocks as she hurried past, didn't calm the anxious churning in her stomach. She was going for an interview with a company that could change her life, but the worry she was feeling wasn't just pre-interview nerves. She just didn't want to admit that she felt she was going behind the backs of the people at Fambridge Books. 'This is the right thing to do. This is the right thing to do,' she kept repeating to herself as she walked. 'This *is* the right thing to do.'

The company's headquarters was in a glossy new build-ing just off Goodge Street, with two receptionists at the desk in the foyer, comfortable chairs to sit on and expensive-looking cold and hot drink dispensers on a marble table in the corner.

'Hello. I'm here for an interview — Holly Merriweather.'

One of the receptionists checked her name on a list, gave her an identity bracelet and pointed her towards the lift. 'It's on the tenth floor,' he said. 'Someone will be up there to meet you.'

Holly got in and breathed slowly to calm her nerves. Then she pressed the button for the tenth floor and tried to channel Meryl Streep from *The Devil Wears Prada*, so she could walk into the office exuding authority and confidence. But then she had an argument with herself, as that wasn't quite the vibe she wanted for a job interview, so when the lift doors eventually opened, she knew she probably just looked confused.

'Hi.' A very tall woman with long, dark-brown hair was waiting for her outside the lift. 'I'm Verity. It's lovely to meet you.' She shook Holly's hand. 'We're in a meeting room over there.' She pointed at a door in the far corner of the room. Holly followed her gaze across desks populated with people tapping on keyboards industriously, and a small group of more smart-looking people around a table, deep in an animated discussion in front of a whiteboard with *Where shall we go?* and *Budget versus Five Star* written in blue marker pen across the top.

Holly instinctively glanced up. There were no gaps where ceiling tiles should be and no buckets collecting water dripping from pipes. *The dream*, she thought. There was also no Claudette working her way through a packet of chocolate digestives. And certainly no Jack Fambridge staring intently at his computer screen, drumming his fingers, absentmindedly scratching the stubble on his face. Holly bit her lip and pushed the image away.

'I love your writing,' Verity was saying as they weaved around the desks. 'I also thought your social media presence was very imaginative. You and your partner really knew how to use it well. The posts were a kind of masterclass in how to do it when they first started. You and . . . ?' Verity turned. 'Sorry, I've got a memory like a sieve.'

'Ed,' Holly said evenly.' We're not together anymore.'

'Oh, I'm sorry to hear that.' Verity opened a door and pointed at a chair. 'Take a seat. But what we are really interested in, Holly, is you, and how you see the world.'

'How I see the world?'

'It's unique and insightful, so yes.' Verity picked up a plate of biscuits. 'Help yourself. There are ginger-and-pomegranate oatmeal digestives, Belgian chocolate cream twirls and a selection of salted caramel Rich Teas. Also, the water is infused with grapes, lemon and sage. Would you like a glass?'

'Yes, please.' Holly took a biscuit and began to gather her thoughts, ready for the interview to begin in earnest.

'Right.' Verity leaned forward. 'So, let's start at the beginning. Can you tell me what it was that inspired you to write?'

'Seth Fambridge. It was reading *London: How I See It* when I was a child.'

'Absolute icon of travelogues and guidebooks.' Verity nodded encouragingly. 'But what was it specifically that made you put pen to paper yourself?'

Holly smiled, took a breath and began to talk.

* * *

The next few days raced along, with Holly, Claudette and Jack working with a new focus on their research for Fambridge Books, and Paulo and Viktor talking about the Bollington party every time Holly stopped off at the café.

Farthing Street seemed to acquire a new feel too, as if it knew that something good were happening.

Holly had written that on the first draft for her first proper article for the London part of her blog. But that little niggling voice was laughing. *Anthropomorphizing roads and buildings now rather than just cats and dogs?*

I couldn't agree more, she said to herself, *but I'm going to write it anyway.*

Holly had been asked back for a second interview with Verity and her two bosses, and was waiting for them to let her know if she'd been successful or not. But her emotions were in turmoil, jumping from excitement at the thought of new adventures and career advancement, and confusion about why it was mixed with a strange kind of sadness. It was all happening so quickly.

'It's because you don't want to leave Fambridge Books!' Melissa was lying down in Holly's lounge with her feet draped over the arm of the sofa.

'But that's not the plan. Fambridge Books was for a year only. I'm just exiting a few months early. Well, more than a few months early . . .'

'But you don't want to.'

'They may not want to extend my contract anyway.'

Melissa snorted. 'Don't be stupid. You're amazing. And one of the reasons you approached the other company was because you thought Fambridge were going out of business, and now they obviously are not.'

Isabella trotted up to Holly and nipped her toe, then ran away behind a chair and stared at her.

'She's started hunting me again,' Holly sighed.

'I don't really know what you think you're doing, anyway. Wouldn't this other job take you off for months at a time? And now you're mother to Isabella. Who is a cat, I know. But you love her — you really do.' Melissa stretched and took a tall glass of lemonade from the coffee table.

Isabella bounced into the kitchen before skittering back into the lounge again.

'So far, it seems that the job would mean me mostly strategizing and writing, and also commissioning other travel writers. Some travel for me, but I would be based here mostly.' The cat meowed loudly. 'She has been my constant companion since we found her in Yorkshire. Been with me through thick and thin. It was love at first sight.' Holly closed her eyes. 'Why am I so all over the place?'

'Do you know what I think?' Melissa drew her knees up and looked knowingly over at Holly.

'No, I don't.'

'You want to run away from Jack Fambridge.'

'No, I don't!' Holly was indignant. 'Well, it's not helpful with him being there, but I'm managing.'

'Ha ha. But if you go, then maybe something could happen?'

'No. It won't.'

'Why not?' Melissa stood up and walked over to Holly. 'I know why not.'

Holly rolled over and tried not to look at her. 'I don't want to get stuck again. Like I did with Ed. All that love just disappeared.'

'And now there's room for more.'

'Well, it's not part of my plan. I wrote my plan down. So, it's official.' As she said it, Isabella ran around the room, jumped over the sofa and landed on Holly's head.

Melissa sat on the floor and began to laugh. 'Now, that's entertainment. Talking of which, I'm looking forward to the select party at the Bollington. The invitation came through last night.'

'It's going to be amazing.' Holly wondered if she could tell her who Caleb actually was now.

'It's fantastic that Caleb was the lead singer of the Lights, though,' Melissa chuckled. 'Don't look at me like that — it was on the invitation. It said I was privileged to be told it and had to keep quiet about it. In fact, I even had to sign some kind of contract.'

'Oh, thank goodness you know.' Holly prised Isabella off her head. 'I would have found it very difficult to not tell you. You have a way about you.'

'I do. I'm thinking of going into investigative journalism.'

'I thought you were thinking of events, or teaching?' Holly stood up and walked to the kitchen.

'I'm weighing up all my options.' Melissa followed her. 'When do you find out about this job?'

'Tomorrow, apparently.'

'Ah, tomorrow.'

Holly got a bottle of wine out of the fridge. 'Yes, tomorrow.'

'Tomorrow is—' Melissa started.

'Another day!' cut in Holly. Shall we watch that Sandra Bullock film? You know the one where she's an author who wears a purple-sequinned jumpsuit for most of the time?'

'*The Lost City*?'

'*The Lost City*.' Holly handed Melissa a glass. 'Let's do it.'

'You know what I think?' Melissa sat down in front of the television. '*You're* the one who's stuck. You've somehow got everyone else unstuck — but you — you are stuck in running away and moving on, instead of standing still and seeing what happens.'

'That's the opposite of stuck — running away.' Holly looked at her glass.

'Don't be pedantic.'

'I'm not.'

'You are! Where's the remote? Let's just watch the film and be quiet.'

Holly decided to check her phone for emails so she wouldn't be tempted to do it during the film. Scrolling through, she opened a new one from Verity.

'Melissa!' she shouted. 'I've been offered the job!'

* * *

Crossing the road to Farthing Street, Holly heard a joyfully pounding bass beat accompanied by ripples of laughter drifting towards her. She giggled, imagining the notes dancing out from the Bollington and into the road, leaping from tree to tree, with birds hitching a ride as they soared through the sky.

Making a mental note to jot that down for her blog, Holly walked slowly towards the entrance, savouring the obvious happiness seeping from the building's walls.

She paused at the bottom of the steps, smoothed down her dress, touched her hair nervously and walked inside.

'Holly Merriweather, you are late.' Caleb was sitting behind the ticket desk with his legs on the counter, strumming random notes on his guitar.

'Sorry — I had some work to attend to.' As soon as she said it, Holly felt flat.

'Welcome!' he sang. 'Come inside, Holly, for you are the last to arrive.'

He guided her into the auditorium, where some of the Farthing Street shopkeepers were already clustered, nibbling on treats being carried around on platters by Paulo. Viktor was standing behind the bar serving the drinks.

Her parents were talking to Claudette, and Keith was dancing with a tiny, blonde lady, who Holly assumed was Rosita. Bev was laughing at Marialena, who was trying and failing to encourage Mabel to twirl in exchange for a biscuit. The owner of the dry-cleaner's was standing next to them looking confused but happy.

Melissa was on the stage with Geraint, who was moving animatedly between all the instruments shouting, 'Cool! Amazing! Wow! I just can't believe this,' on rotation.

Jack walked out from behind the curtain with the woman Holly had seen him with on the day she'd had coffee with Emilio.

'Oh.' She surprised herself. *Is that a drop of jealousy I am picking up?* her inner voice whispered.

No, it isn't. I'm just surprised, Holly argued back. She took a flute of champagne from the tray of drinks Paulo was serving. *And a bit disappointed, I suppose*, she finally admitted to herself.

She joined Claudette and her parents.

'Oh, isn't this lovely?' Claudette squeezed her hand. 'I've seen Caleb virtually every day since "the big reveal".' She made exuberant air quotes with her fingers. 'And I am now completely outside, standing on that patio. In fact, I'm dancing and singing and just . . .' She trailed off. 'Isn't it exciting?

Frightening but absolutely thrilling. And,' she beamed, 'he's a famous rock star. I'm dating a rock star. I'm a rock chick now!'

'What patio?' Holly's mum asked.

'It's a bit of a metaphor, to be honest.' Claudette leaned forward. 'All about love and loss and getting unstuck. I'll explain later after I've had a few more glasses of champers.'

'I cannot believe I am at a party at the express invitation of Don C. Peterson.' Her father was almost levitating with excitement. 'But, I said this to your mother earlier, didn't I Julie? — at the express invitation of our friend, Caleb, which is what the "C" stands for, of course!'

'You've been saying that at half-hourly intervals since seven o'clock this morning, Gary.' Julie kissed him on the cheek. 'Which is why I love you.'

Holly sighed happily. She didn't want to say anything. The room was speaking for itself, as if the sadness had been unlocked and was now screaming with relief, ready to party like the old days.

Like the old days, the building seemed to whisper. *Just as it was . . .*

'You're very quiet.' Her mother put her hand out and moved her fringe. 'You really need to get this cut again.'

'I'm just enjoying the fact that everyone seems to be so happy.' Holly picked up her drink. 'Cheers.'

Caleb climbed on to the stage and stood behind the microphone with his guitar. 'Hello, everyone — to all my neighbours and friends in Farthing Street.' He played a chord and beamed. 'Welcome to my party. It's both the end of something and the beginning of something.' He looked at Keith. 'It's the fifteenth of August. Which, to me, is a significant date. Isn't it, mate?' Keith gave him the thumbs up as he began to play the first few bars of "Summer in Your Eyes". 'Because it's the date the Lights played their last gig here at the Bollington. And a day I have always dreaded for many years. However, I now pledge that today is the day I look forward instead of back.' He blew Claudette a kiss.

'And before we begin the long job of bringing this beautiful building up to scratch so we can make music in it again, I decided we should all have a celebration.'

He began to sing the first verse of "Summer in Your Eyes", the sound of the guitar filling the room, his words clear and beautiful and mesmerizing. When he got to the chorus, Caleb put his hands in the air and started to clap. 'Come on, everybody!' he shouted. 'Sing along with me. This is our song. Our song now.'

And gradually each of them began to sing, quietly at first, until they built to a crescendo and were almost shouting.

> *Summer*
> *Summer*
> *Summer*
> *Summer*
> *In*
> *Your*
> *Eyes*

Then two other people joined him on the stage and began to play — a woman and a man. The woman had a bass guitar, and the man sat down at the keyboard near the wings.

'Come on, Keith, mate,' shouted Caleb. 'Play the drums for us.'

Keith jumped on the stage to a resounding cheer.

'Oh my God, Julie!' Holly's father was practically screaming. 'It's the Lights. It's the other ones — the surviving ones! B.B. Jones and Francis De Paul! I can't believe it!'

A loud and excited roar echoed around the room from the audience. Geraint looked like he was crying and Claudette stood open-mouthed by the stage as Jack put his arm around her shoulder so they were both moving in time to the music.

The band played the next verse and Caleb started to jump around, so that by the time they began the chorus the second time, everyone was singing, dancing and laughing.

For verse three, the whole room just shouted the words and, at that moment, Holly knew what pure joy felt like. She looked around. The sadness had completely gone.

'Holly Merriweather.' Jack was suddenly next to her, touching her arm. 'This is partly your doing, you know?'

'Oh, I'm not so sure.' Holly wanted to reach her hand out and touch his face. 'I just wanted to help.'

'Well, it worked.' He smiled at her almost shyly. 'There's something I need to talk to you about.' It was now that the woman who he'd arrived with walked over and stood next to him. 'Oh, yes. This is Melody.'

'Hello.' Holly shook her hand. She couldn't work out why she was feeling so wounded. He was her colleague, and the attraction was just physical, wasn't it? That was all. Physical. There were no actual emotions involved. Were there?

Melissa ambled over. 'Hi, Holly. You look beautiful. As always.' She grabbed her friend and pulled her into a hug. 'Have you told them about the new job yet?' she whispered a little too loudly.

'New job?' Jack looked confused. 'But, that's . . .'

Holly grimaced. 'I. No. Um, Melissa.' She turned to her friend and raised her eyebrows.

'Oh God. I've done it again, haven't I?'

'And now, for my next song.' Caleb laughed. 'Only kidding. I haven't performed anything new in years. We'll have a bit of music, and then I'll tell you all what we're planning to do here.'

Holly stepped back and weaved through the tables, then rushed out of the door. She didn't want to be there anymore, but couldn't work out why.

* * *

The sound of music continued to drift from the Bollington, with the noise of people laughing and chattering hanging in the air. Holly glanced over and couldn't help beaming with pleasure despite the other emotions she was feeling. The building seemed to be glowing with new life.

Mabel barked somewhere in the distance and Isabella jumped on to the fence, staring around as if she were searching for her friend.

Kicking off her sandals, Holly put her bare feet on the warm grass and breathed in. The honeysuckle and jasmine climbing the walls between the houses were in full bloom, and the early-evening air was filled with their delicate, intoxicating scent.

'Of all the places I have been in the world, Isabella,' she said to the cat, 'I would not want to be anywhere else. Not today. But why am I so sad?'

She sat down and opened the message from Verity, reading it again.

As I said, we'd love you to be our travel editor. It would involve some travel, as well as commissioning other contributors to write pieces, too.

Isabella jumped back into the garden and ambled over to Holly, then sat at her feet and gazed up at her.

'Dream job.' Holly looked down at the cat. 'But how would that actually fit around you, do you think?'

The cat pounced, nibbled Holly's left foot for a moment, and then skipped off to investigate a rose petal that had fallen on to the grass.

'Why do I feel so flat when I've just been offered my dream job, Isabella?'

Caleb began to play "Summer in Your Eyes" again to a resounding cheer from the partygoers. At that point, Holly decided to get herself a glass of wine, so walked into the kitchen and took a bottle out of the fridge just as someone began knocking on the door.

'Holly? Holly!' It was Jack. His voice sounded strange. 'I need to speak to you!'

Her heart lurched. An image of him standing up on Tower Bridge in slow motion all those months ago flew into her mind, and then she realized — it wasn't just physical at all, was it? It never had been.

'Oh no,' she muttered under her breath as she opened the door.

He stared at her. 'Can I come in?'

'Yes,' she said quietly, standing to one side.

Jack moved forward and tripped over the step, landing on his knees in front of her. 'Oh God, not again!'

Holly watched him stand up. He was moving in slow motion. *Oh God, not again!* she thought.

'Um,' he said. 'You can't leave.'

'Would you like a glass of wine?' Holly walked into the kitchen, unable to think clearly. Random words were flying through her mind. They mainly said things like, *You love him. You've fallen in love with him. You bloody idiot, you've accidentally fallen in love with him.*

'Yes. Okay.' He followed her and leaned against a countertop as Holly poured him a glass and handed it to him. 'I'm leaving,' he said. 'But you can't.'

'Where are you going? Abroad? Costa Rica?

'A lake south of the Thames, actually.' He took a gulp of the drink and put the glass down.

'I don't understand.' Holly tried not to meet his gaze, remembering the pretty woman he was at the party with.

'I'm leaving Fambridge Books. Barney is taking over, and my mother will take a consultancy role.'

'And the lake?'

'I'm setting up an outdoor pursuits company with Marco. Which is what I should have done in the first place.' He picked up the glass and took another large gulp. 'I'm not a publisher. I was frightened of ruining my father's legacy. That's why I was so slow at everything. I was completely out of my depth.'

'Right. I see. I understand.' Holly remained at the opposite end of the kitchen from him, too frightened to move any closer in case she gave her feelings away.

261

'And when I began to ask Barney for advice, it was clear he would be much better at this than me. And, weirdly, once we put those mock-ups together, I felt I'd proved myself, that my dad would be proud, that I could finally go.' He looked at her. 'Does that sound weird?'

'No. Not weird at all.'

'So, you can't go.'

'I don't understand.'

'This is a bit embarrassing.' He finished his drink. 'Bear with me, okay?' He cleared his throat. 'Do you remember that day I had a bit of a turn when we got stuck at Elephant and Castle? I told you my father had shown me some articles by people he thought were good writers. One in particular.' He took a step forward. 'Well, I have very recently discovered that it was you. The writer was you.'

'Me?' Along with the random words flying through her mind, Holly was beginning to experience several emotions all at once. She held on to the countertop with one hand.

'When you applied for the job, we didn't interview anyone else. To put it in the words of my mother, I felt it was a sign.'

'A sign?' Holly was unable to say any more than that.

'I was too all over the place to tell you — I wanted to — but every time I tried to, the words got sort of stuck.'

'Ah, stuck.' Isabella ambled into the kitchen and sat down on the floor between them. 'But I'm confused about the sign?'

'As soon as we heard your voice on that call, we knew you belonged with us. Again, does that sound strange?'

Holly couldn't take her eyes off his face. *Run over to him and . . . just . . . you know?* She felt herself lean forward slightly.

He took a breath and began to talk quickly. 'I found some of the old articles my father had kept when I was helping my mother sort things out. I think I told you they were virtually shreds of paper with no names on. Well, I was over there yesterday and I found the proper copies, with the authors' names on them. So, when you—' he paused, seemingly to search for the right word — 'rescued me at Elephant and Castle, I now know it was a sign. You do believe in signs, don't you?'

'Well, um . . .' Holly gave in to the butterflies, which were having a riotous party all over her body now.

Jack took a folded-up piece of paper out of his pocket and handed it to her.

Holly read the title out loud. *'Riding Round Lake Como on a Motorbike — Holly Merriweather.'* She glanced up at him then carried on reading. 'I was told I was to be driven around the lake by Annamaria's fiancé, Roberto, as everyone else was going to be too busy transforming the tomato crop into sauce and passata for the winter. Disappointed not to be included in this late August ritual, I followed Roberto outside, leaving all the excited chatter and hubbub behind, and climbed on to the back of his motorbike. Only a few minutes later I realized that what I had been given was a gift . . .' It was here she paused before continuing to read. 'Have you ever been to Lake Como? You need to go. It's green and pink and red and blue and bright and beautiful, and it gleams and glows with luscious opulence. Glamorous and gorgeous, and like a film set — so perfect, no one would believe it was real.' She sucked in a deep breath. 'That was one of the first things I ever posted.' Holly turned the piece of paper over. 'No photos — it was before phones on cameras were any good, and I didn't even have access to a good digital camera at that point.'

'The words had to speak for themselves then, didn't they.' Jack edged forward slightly.

Holly looked up at him. 'Your father liked this? Seth Fambridge, who inspired me to write, actually liked this?'

'Yes. Which means you're supposed to be at Fambridge Books and I'm not. So, please don't go. Please?'

'But you'd still be involved?' Holly could feel herself pulling back, trying to find excuses not to stay, but that was all she really wanted to do. She knew it was fear. Blind fright. She was scared of staying still and scared of moving forward. *Stuck.*

'Part of me knew it was you. That first day I saw you walking over Tower Bridge. You made me fall over. You always make me fall over. It's your fault. Your expression kept changing — like you were composing words in your head.'

'You saw me first?'

'Yes.'

'Oh.'

'And the day we first met in the office, and I realized I'd been right, I tripped over again.'

'You're very smooth.' Holly felt her heart flutter.

'I'm known for it.' He shook his head. 'But we work together, and I was sort of almost your boss, so anything between us would have been inappropriate, and it would have also just been bad. Given my past. Given your past.'

'Absolutely.' Holly let go of the countertop and took a step towards Jack.

'Would it frighten you if I told you I loved you? I mean, I've confessed you made me fall over. I've got nothing to lose.'

'But what about Melody?' Holly asked uncertainly.

'My cousin? She's helping out with the research.'

'Oh . . . I see.'

'It's weird.' Jack held his hand out. 'You seem like you're moving in slow motion. Like we're in a film or something.'

'I love you, too.' Holly almost shouted the words. 'But I don't want to, because I've only just come out of a long-term relationship . . . and it's too quick . . . and I'm scared.'

'Exactly. Me too.' Jack edged closer until she could feel his breath.

'I've been finding excuses.'

'Again, the same.'

She touched his face, he pulled her to him, and then they were kissing again. Urgent, passionate kisses that brought them crashing against the door, their arms tangling together as they sank to the floor.

'Holly Merriweather and Jack Fambridge.' A voice boomed from somewhere in the distance.

'Did you hear that?' Holly paused and looked up. 'It sounded like someone was shouting our names through a megaphone.

'Come back and join the party.'

'That *is* a megaphone,' whispered Jack.

They clambered to their feet and hurried into the garden.

'This is Caleb. We know where you are. You have to come back. We've all got to do something. We're all starting again. We await your presence.'

'My God, it's like one of those sci-fi films.' Jack began to laugh, then took Holly's hand. 'Looks like the mothership has summoned us. We can get there in two minutes.' He lowered his voice. 'I know a shortcut. But don't tell anyone.'

They ran through the house, but not before Holly picked up Isabella and quickly put her in the cat carrier. 'I think she needs to come, too. Because the whole Bollington thing is her fault for climbing in through an open window. Naughty cat.'

They hurried along the lane and into Farthing Street, rushing up the steps and back into the venue.

'Welcome!' Caleb was standing on the stage, still talking through the megaphone, but now Keith climbed up next to him and pulled it away. 'It's not a toy,' he muttered.

'Where have you been and what have you been doing?' Melissa kissed Holly on the cheek. 'We all know. Ha ha!'

Holly put Isabella's carrier on the table. 'Here we are, sweetie — look what you've done,' she whispered.

'Right. Now we're all back here—' Caleb was using the microphone again — 'the first song the Lights ever played publicly, and the first song of our first ever set here, was a cover version of something very special.'

He picked up his guitar. 'Lawrence and I used to jump around to this in my parents' garage, plotting our first moves up the music ladder. Every time I hear it, I feel exactly as I did then. Full of life, of anger, of hope. Full of music.' Caleb turned to B.B. and Francis. 'Ready?' He played a chord. 'So, any time things are getting you down, or you're sad, or you can't see a way through, listen to this. Think of us all here.

Think of us at our new beginning. For this old place. For Farthing Street. Here's to not being stuck.'

'What is it then?' Keith shouted.

'You know what it is, Keith, my old mate,' Caleb laughed. 'Eddie and the Hot Rods. "Do Anything You Wanna Do". Because we can and we will.'

He began to play, and then to sing, and the old building was filled yet again with love and laughter — *and*, thought Holly, while jumping up and down joyfully in time to the music, *endless, endless possibilities*.

She imagined a camera sweeping backwards, out through the door and along Farthing Street, sailing upwards over the rooftops of London, with the Bollington still glowing in the darkness, its music flowing out across the city, rising higher and higher into the stars, until the notes danced into the words.

This is just the beginning
And the credits rolled
Summer in Your Eyes
Cast
Holly Merriweather — Holly Merriweather
Jack Fambridge — Jack Fambridge
Claudette Fambridge — Claudette Fambridge
Holly's mum — Julie Merriweather
Holly's dad — Gary Merriweather
Melissa — Melissa Draper
Special guest stars
Caleb — Donald C. Peterson
Keith — Keith
And featuring
Isabella the cat
Mabel the dog
The residents of Farthing Street

'I know what you're doing.' Melissa had grabbed her hand, laughing. 'And I bet I'm not in the credits of the film that's going on in your head, am I?'

'You are!' But not sure if halfway down is good enough.' Holly put her arms around her. 'I'm thinking that you should be the important name at the end — as in *and* Melissa Draper.'

'I like that.' Melissa pointed at Jack. 'So, is this handsome gent the leading man?'

Holly smiled as Jack took his mother's hand and began to dance with her. 'He is. He most certainly is.' Their conversation was interrupted when she heard her name being called from the stage.

'Holly Merriweather — get on that table,' shouted Caleb. 'Go on, climb up!'

Holly looked at him, confused. He pointed at the table again. 'Okay?' she murmured, clambering on to a chair and then the table, before looking around as everyone in the room stopped talking and waited.

Caleb cleared his throat. 'I'd like you all to look at this lady.' His voice was quiet. 'When they decide to make the film of the book — which she will inevitably write — you must ensure she forces the producers to use this song at the end. It's a perfect love letter to London. For a while, Lawrence and I just wanted to be the Kinks.' He turned around to the other members of the band, 'But we became the Lights, didn't we? Still love the Kinks, though. Now, take it away, lads! and lady — sorry, B.B.'

The band played the first few chords of "Waterloo Sunset".

'Promise me, Holly,' he called over to her. 'Promise me!'

'I promise! Now just play the song, Don C. Peterson!'

'I'm an old rocker.' Caleb held his guitar above his head. 'And there's always an encore.' He jumped again, turned around and then yelled, 'Take it away, the Bollington.'

The room erupted with noise as they finally began to play.

Jack climbed up next to Holly, pulled her to him and kissed her, and she forgot where she was, or who she was, or what words she would use to describe the moment in her next article.

She was just a girl, kissing the man she loved on a table in an old music venue with one of the greatest bands of all time playing in the background.

THE END

THANK YOU

Dear reader,

Thank you for choosing *Summer in Your Eyes*. I hope you enjoyed it.

It's set in London, a city I love and which I spend hours ambling around aimlessly, or as I sometimes call it, "doing research".

While I was writing the book, I realized that I am a frustrated travel writer, just waiting for an opportunity to paint pictures with words of some of the places I've seen. So, all of Holly's blogs are based on my experiences — and I've been carrying some of them around in my mind for years!

If you have enjoyed *Summer in Your Eyes*, please leave a review on the website of the retailer from where you bought it.

If you want to find out more about me, I am on Facebook and Twitter — the details of those are at the bottom of the About the Author page.

THE CHOC LIT STORY

Established in 2009, Choc Lit is an independent, award-winning publisher dedicated to creating a delicious selection of quality women's fiction.

We have won 18 awards, including Publisher of the Year and the Romantic Novel of the Year, and have been shortlisted for countless others.

All our novels are selected by genuine readers. We are proud to publish talented first-time authors, as well as established writers whose books we love introducing to a new generation of readers.

In 2023, we became a Joffe Books company. Best known for publishing a wide range of commercial fiction, Joffe Books has its roots in women's fiction. Today it is one of the largest independent publishers in the UK.

We love to hear from you, so please email us about absolutely anything bookish at choc-lit@joffebooks.com

If you want to hear about all our bargain new releases, join our mailing list: www.choc-lit.com